BEAUTIFULLY BROKEN

BAILEY B

Fantasy Novels

<u>The Lost Darling</u>

<u>Second Star to the Right</u>

<u>The Island of the Lost</u>

The Cerise

ROMANCE NOVELS UNDER THE NAME BAILEY B

<u>Broken Love Series</u>

<u>1. Beautifully Broken</u>

<u>1.5 Paper Hearts</u>

<u>2. I Hate You, I Love You Part 1</u>

<u>3. I Love You, I Hate You Part 2</u>

<u>Stand Alones:</u>

<u>Unexpected</u>

<u>Falling for You</u>

<u>In Too Deep</u>

Thirty seconds.

That's how long it's been since I took my last breath. Since my eyes found the worry on the face in front of me. Thirty seconds was all it took for me to realize I was in love with Rex.

Thirty. Seconds.

Such a small amount of time for such a monumental revelation. The funny thing about time, sometimes it passes soul-crushingly slow. Other times it goes in the blink of an eye. There's no rhyme or reason. Time, like Life and Death, does what she wants.

Thinking back to the last eight weeks, she flew by faster than hummingbird wings beating over a hollyhock. Faster than she's moved my whole life, and now, in this moment, Time has slowed to a crawl.

People say that, before events of extreme trauma and almost death, your life flashes before your eyes. I think that's what's happening, only I don't see my whole life. Except for a few key moments, it's been shit and not worth remembering. Instead, I see the last eight weeks.

I. See. Rex.

He made these last two months memorable. His persistence and damn near electric touch made me feel things I didn't know I was capable of. He brought the light when I was consumed in darkness. He saved me in every sense of the word.

It's my turn to save him.

Just one second after my life-altering revelation, a bullet no bigger than my thumbnail will shoot out of a slate black barrel. And if I let it, that tiny piece of metal will snuff out Rex's light. Darkness will consume him, devour me, and I'll be left with nothing but a broken heart and shattered will to live. I can live with dying inside, but I can't let the darkness take him.

The arm keeping me from Rex loosens as a fat finger moves to pull the trigger. My spine no longer presses against a stomach, round from too much whiskey and gas station food. A chill slides through me. Sweat on the small of my back icing over as the cold lobby air blows our way.

This is my chance.

I can't hesitate. I lunge myself forward milliseconds before the boom of the pistol echoes in the lobby. I'm sure the hotel's guests hear it, I can't see how they didn't, but to my knowledge no one is downstairs with us. The concierge lady ran away ages ago. The kitchen staff is probably hiding and anyone who might have been making their way to an early breakfast has likely taken cover. None of this matters. Whoever they are, they don't matter.

The only person I'm worried about is Rex.

Pain pierces my shoulder, rippling throughout my chest. My hands find Rex's shirtless body, touching his silky skin for what probably will be the last time. I shove him out of the way and fall to the ground, the wind is knocked from my lungs.

Please let me have reached him in time.

I roll onto my back and struggle to fill the empty spaces inside with air. Each breath tangles with fire that seeps into every crevice of my being. My lungs fill, air pressing down on me with the force of an elephant. I exhale, bubbles rumbling beneath my chest, and attempt to take another breath.

"Stupid bitch." Our assailant says, barely a foot away. His voice is lost, muffled as if it's on the other end of a tunnel.

I should see more, feel more, but the world's hazy. A blur of swirling colors and lights. A dark shadow towers over me. I want to see the face, but it's a pit of darkness. This is the moment I realize that I'm about to get what I wanted. Well, used to want. Death has finally come to take me away.

Only I'm not ready to go anymore. I need to know that Rex is okay. That I saved him. My life has meant nothing. I've done nothing purposeful, but to die in place of someone I love would make my miserable existence worth something. I turn my head, searching where I think he should be, but I can't see anything.

Icy fingers curl around my wrist. I shiver, mentally willing death to leave me be, begging her to give me five more minutes. A chill slithers through my veins like venom from a snake, paralyzing me from head to toe.

The shadowy figure above me leans closer, "Piper."

I'm the school slut. It's a title I wear—not proudly—but because it's what's expected of me. Everyone at St. A's High School knows my bio-mom, Monica, is a whore. A real screw-you-for-money whore, that slept with the physics teacher last week.

Thank you, Facebook, for tagging me in that humiliating article.

Not.

They also know that Monica was arrested for all of two seconds before making bail, thanks to her pimp, and the John she got caught with. He just so happens to be my first-period teacher this year. So, on top of the daily whispers spread about me, that mess is going around, too.

It's fine.

I'm used to my name being in everyone's mouth. It's been that way since the third grade. Back then, people talked about my dirty nails, how skinny I was, and how my best friend was a boy. In high school, the daily gossip changed to where I moved to, what alleged drugs I'm on, and eventually, who I've spread my legs for. When last year's rumor started—the one about me giving a killer blowjob for fifty bucks—no one doubted it. Why would they? I'm the girl with a whore for a mom. The girl from the wrong side of the tracks.

Literally.

There's the rich side of town where my classmates live, the good side of the tracks, and then there's *that* side. It's like the shadowy place in *The Lion King* Mufasa warned Simba to stay away from. Yeah…Monica lives there.

Anyway, not long after that rumor about me started, I figured, what the hell. They say when life gives you lemons, make lemonade. I was given stupid, horny boys. So, I made money.

For the record, I've never actually touched anybody. At first, I turned down anyone who approached me; but there have been a select few I've said yes to. The most selfish, arrogant, disrespectful guys in our school get special treatment.

Underneath the shadows of the stadium bleachers, they dropped their pants, exposed their less-than-exciting junk to me, and then I kicked in the balls. Those jerks fell to their knees, cursing my name while I took all the cash from their wallets.

It is the perfect hustle.

Anyway, all of this is why Tad Parker is staring me down. Captain of the baseball team, running back on the football team, and a total tool. Bloodshot eyes narrow on my face, expecting a different answer to this morning's question.

"It's still a hard no, Tad."

I stop walking and cross my arms. While I'd love to take the pretty boy for all he's got, I'm trying to turn a new leaf and make the most of what's left of my senior year. I don't expect to fix my reputation, but I'm trying to change how I see myself. Which means no more pretend illicit acts for money.

Tad rolls his red-rimmed eyes and pulls a brown leather wallet from his back pocket. He thumbs through his cash, offering more twenties than I've held at one time in my entire life. "Come on, Piper. I'll make it worth your while. Five hundred dollars, right now, for five minutes in the bathroom."

Tad's a good-looking guy if you're into that classic blond-haired, blue-eyed, prince-charming wannabe with the attitude of Gaston. He has no shortage of self-entitled princesses throwing themselves at him. I don't understand why he's chasing me.

I shake my head and push his arm back. My checking account may be teetering on the edge of zero, but I'm not this desperate. "Why not hit up one of the JV cheerleaders? They'd jump at the chance to get tangled up with you. For free."

"Because they aren't Piper-fucking-Lovelace. Now come on." Tad's hand curls around my arm. He squeezes, pulling me toward the stadium bathrooms, and it sets off a chain reaction within me.

One Mississippi.

My airway constricts. Bats swarm in my stomach, threatening to bring up the vending machine cinnamon roll I had after fourth period. I detest being touched; it sets off a catalyst of reactions that steadily get worse. My one and only thought at this point is to make Tad let go.

I dig my heels into the ground and yank my arm back, but my efforts go unnoticed. I try to pry his fingers off me, punch him, kick him in the leg, but nothing I do makes a difference. Tad's too strong. Even with my best attempt at a struggle, he almost effortlessly drags me clear across the parking lot.

Two Mississippi.

My hands tremble, sending vibrations up my arms and throughout my body. I need help. I hate asking for help almost as much as I hate being touched, but I don't have much choice. I look to my left and then to my right, but there's no one in sight. No one to hear my screams. I try anyway, opening my mouth to yell, but nothing comes out. *This can't be happening.* I swallow the tiny bit of saliva in my bone-dry throat and try again.

Nothing but air.

Beads of sweat drip down my neck as the feeling of impending doom lingers. The memory of a crooked grin I'll never forget flashes before my eyes, amping the intensity of my breakdown.

I spent a good part of this year in counseling to learn how to manage my panic attacks and finding ways to keep everyone from noticing my freak-outs, all for those skills to fail me when I need them most. Tad makes me feel like I'm trapped, watching from the outside, as I lose all control.

Three Mississippi.

Logically, I know it's been more than three seconds. It has to have been, but I'm stuck in a time warp. Everything happens at a snail-slow pace yet lightning fast at the same time.

Tad pushes me against a wall near the girl's bathroom at the stadium. He lets go of my arm and presses his hands on either side of me, caging me in. I realize this situation probably isn't going to end well, but my anxiety begins to subside. As close as Tad is, he's not touching me anymore.

I can think again.

Feel again.

Pain surges through my arm like a lightning bolt. It was probably there the whole time, but I didn't notice it before. I'm going to have five little bruises in the shape of his fingers, but I don't move to soothe the throbbing. I hold my ground, fists balled at my sides, and stare up at him.

"I'm not above dragging you into the bathroom, but I don't want to do that. I just need you to go in there with me, Piper." Tad rests his forehead against the wall, his breaths loud and shaky beside my ear.

"A thousand dollars," he says suddenly, turning his head, begging me with his eyes to concede. "Walk in there with me. Please. That's all you have to do."

If my heart wasn't already racing, it would be. That's a lot of money, enough for a ticket out of town and a few nights at a cheap motel. It's not nearly enough to pay Monica's debts, but it would put a dent in them, and maybe even keep everyone off my back a little longer.

I don't know, though. Whatever rumor is bound to start about me would be gone in eight short weeks, but this situation doesn't feel right. Something's off. "I need that money. More than you can imagine, but no."

Tad beats his fist on the bricks beside me. I flinch, but he's so lost in himself that he doesn't notice. "What the fuck, Piper? I've offered you ten times more than your worth. If you don't go in there, I'm gonna be..." He shakes his head.

"I don't want—"

Tad turns to me again, this time crashing his lips onto mine. He tastes like cigarettes and tuna fish, two things I hate. His hands push into my hair, tangling and pulling my roots and bile creeps up my throat.

I don't want this.

I don't want him.

No! I bite down on the tongue invading my mouth and press my palms to Tad's chest, pushing as hard as I can. He stumbles back a step and stares at me, wide-eyed, shocked that I rejected him.

"You bitch!" He raises his hand and slaps me across the face. "You don't want to do this the easy way, fine. We can do it—!"

"Hey!" A deep voice booms from my right. A wide, tall body comes out of nowhere, physically shielding me with its massive frame while a hand shoves Tad's shoulder.

Tad loses his balance and stumbles a step to the right. "What the fuck do you want, Montgomery?"

Rex Montgomery—the owner of said voice—reaches behind him and puts a protective hand on my hip. With everything happening, my brain doesn't seem to register the touch. It can't; it's too stunned that he, of all people, came to my rescue.

I mean, the man is a living work of art. At six-foot-four, Rex towers over almost everyone at St. A's. Teachers included. It's a known fact that he played ice hockey at his last school, and rumor has it he's already been drafted to go semi-pro next season.

Every inch of him is carved from gold. Not really, but I hear his muscles are drool-worthy. Add to that near-perfect body a strong jawline and an angled nose. Yeah, girls swoon just from hearing his name. I'll admit, I might be one of them too, sometimes, but never in public.

"Leave her alone," he growls.

Tad snorts. "That's cute. You sticking up for the trash. This bitch doesn't belong here, Rex. All girls like her are good for is a quick lay."

"Fuck you!" I yell.

Rex squeezes my hip, probably trying to be reassuring. Oddly enough, it works. A calm settles over me, releasing an unexpected smile. *What the heck is happening right now?*

"Tell you what, you can take her into the boys' bathroom first. When you're done, I'll do my thing with her in the girls'. My treat, man."

Rex swings, catching Tad off guard with a right hook to the eye. He moves like a shark. Agile. Quick. And with precision. He swings again, hitting with enough force to knock Tad back a step.

I stand there, mouth open, eyes gaping as if this is the first time I've witnessed two boys throw down. I've seen fights before. Hell, my tattoo artist runs a backyard fight club once a month that, once upon a time, I used to go to.

But this is different.

The rage in Rex's eyes is unlike anything I've ever seen. It's terrifying and unbelievably hot at the same time. I couldn't tear my gaze away even if I tried.

Tad grunts and lunges forward, hitting Rex in the stomach with his shoulder, but he barely moves. Rex punches him in the side, once, twice, then slams Tad's face onto his knee.

Tad falls to the ground, panting, blood seeping from his nose and a cut on his brow. He took a hell of a beating, and I have no clue how he's still conscious. Must be all that practice getting his ass handed to him on the football field. Defeated, Tad holds a hand up in surrender.

All of this is going on and I'm over here less than three feet from the action, fighting the urge to jump up and down like a freaking cheerleader. Something has to be wrong with me today. I've never been the preppy ra-ra type. I'm more of a glare-at-you-from-a-distance kind of girl, but watching Rex kick Tad's ass has me feeling some kind of way.

"Since you were too stupid to listen the first time, I'll tell you again. Piper is closed for business," Rex growls. "You will not stop her in the hallway or corner her when she's alone. Your days of talking to or thinking about Piper are done. If I find you in the same room as her outside of class, I'll kick your ass three ways from Sunday. Got it?"

All the bubbly feelings I had watching Rex kick Tad's ass disappear. Reality smacks me in the face with a horde of questions.

What does Rex mean by the first time?

Is he the reason everyone has left me alone the last few weeks?

What the hell is going on!?

Tad spits blood onto the ground and nods. "Got it."

"Good," Rex says, rising to his feet. "Now get the hell out of here before I beat the living shit out of you again."

I watch Rex while he watches Tad walk away, guarding me until that low-life is out of sight.

Rex turns. His dark brown hair, short on the sides but long enough to run your fingers through on top, blows in the rare Florida breeze like he's in a shampoo commercial. Under normal circumstances, I'd make fun of him for it, but I'm too stunned to speak. My mind's still tripping over the fact that *he* saved me, that he touched me, and that my pulse is racing faster than a greyhound from the way he is *still* looking at me.

"Are you okay?" Rex takes my chin between his thumb and forefinger to examine my face.

My breath catches. Not because I'm anxious, but because the feeling of impending doom isn't there. There is no tightness in my chest or nervous shakes. No needles shooting down my spine or fuzziness in my head. Instead, there's an electric current pulsating between us that I've never felt before, similar to my anxiety needles, yet different.

"I'm fine." I'm not fine. My skin is on fire, the space between my legs aches, and I'm a confused mess.

Rex is the first person to touch me this year who doesn't send my body into shock. His skin on mine should ignite a catalyst of crippling reactions. Instead, heat spreads from my cheeks down to my core. Awakening parts of me I thought died long ago.

Rex drops his hand. Deep blues study me, combing over every feature. My insecurities bubble up: the bags under my eyes, the scars on my arms, some hidden beneath a colorful tattoo, others still visible to all who look beyond the dozen rubber bracelets.

"Wanna get out of here?" He asks with zero traces of hidden innuendo.

Another first. The only time guys—who aren't the Harris twins—talk to me is to ask for a favor. An unfortunate hazard of my reputation.

Please don't let Rex ask a favor.

"Piper?"

Shit. I must have zoned out. *No, I don't want to leave with you because I don't know what's going on with me!* I shake my head, hoping I didn't actually say those words aloud.

Rex smiles, revealing two deep, beautiful dimples.

The overwhelming need to have his hands on my body consumes me. Tears prick the back of my eyes again because, for the first time in a year, I want to be held. What's worse, I want to be comforted by him— the hot almost-stranger who saved me.

I hate it.

I like it.

I don't know how to take it. I've gone so long learning how to cope with the anxiety of unwanted touch that I forgot how to react when it's desired.

I look up at Rex unsure of what to do next. Should I say thank you? Is that enough? I mean, what he just did, saving me, is huge!

"Can I walk you inside? I'm sure Cooper wouldn't want you by yourself after that bullshit. And I..." he rubs at the back of his neck. "I don't want to leave you alone. You know, in case Tad comes back."

"Okay." My voice cracks, sounding nothing like its usual calm, collected self. Rex steps closer and tucks me under his arm. There's a bubble in my chest, but I can still breathe—still function.

I think I'm nervous.

Go figure. The hottest guy in school that I'll *never* have a chance with is ushering me inside and *now* my brain starts to act like a teenage girl. If I can't get this under control, I'm screwed.

Rex angles his body to shield me from eyes that might be watching as we cross the parking lot. The smell of musk and clean linen swirls in my head. It's delicious. I sniff again, committing the scent to memory because the likelihood that I'll be this close to him again is slim to none. Even if Rex can touch me without causing a debilitating panic attack, handsome, popular guys don't actually like girls like me.

They just like the way we make them feel.

Can you believe it? Poor Tad.
Did you see his face? I heard Piper's pimp jumped him for money.
I heard Piper went psycho and started beating on Tad because he said she was nasty.
Well, I heard she's knocked up and Tad found out who the baby daddy is.

I keep my head up, gaze focused, ignoring the daily gossip. Nine times out of ten, it's about me. I used to stick up for myself, but fighting would only fuel the fire. Now, I just don't care... much. I'm used to it, but that doesn't mean the talk doesn't bother me.

I keep walking, ignoring more whispers from people who think I can't hear them because they're two steps behind me. These parents pay a fortune for their kids to be here. No one said anything about making them smart.

I heard...

The sound of a body being pushed into a locker slows my stride. I glance over my shoulder, searching for where it came from. A small circle forms behind me. Two guys are at the center of it, the tops of their heads barely visible through the crowd.

"Fix this," one voice growls. The deep rumble is an undeniable mix of northern twang and country sass. *Rex.*

I duck around the corner and hide in a doorway. Close enough to hear what's happening but far enough that no one notices me. The last thing I need is a rumor about me liking Rex because I stopped to watch the fight. Yes, people are that petty. I can't even stop and enjoy someone else's drama without it somehow biting me in the ass.

The body slams against the smooth metal again. The blonde boy, the one pinned against the lockers, chuckles. "I don't know what you're talking about."

Tiny hairs on the back of my neck stand on end. I shudder thinking about what could have happened yesterday if Rex had been a minute later. Tad's voice will forever be etched in my mind. The events of yesterday added to the loop of trauma my photographic memory won't let me forget.

Tad's back slams against the locker again.

"One day," Rex warns. "You've got one day to put a stop to the rumors, or I promise everyone will know exactly how much of a piece of shit you really are."

"You can't prove anything."

"One word, asshole. Cameras."

Out of nowhere, Cooper Harris—illegitimate foster brother number one—crosses my path. He raises his eyebrows, then tilts his head towards the North stairwell. I follow, five paces behind. Once we're hidden behind closed doors, he pulls me into a hug.

I should have expected it. Even though Cooper and I share a room, I've barely seen him the past two days. He's been out with some mystery girl until the wee hours of the night, and I pretend to be sleeping when he crawls into bed.

Yes, we share a bed because he and Mamma T agreed I shouldn't be left alone after what happened this summer.

Both arms wrap around me, squeezing me against his rock-hard body. Cooper is the *only* person allowed to hug me, and it takes all the willpower I have not to shove him away when he does. I squeeze my eyes shut and hold my breath, anxious for him to let go.

One Mississippi.

Pressure in my chest builds, increasing at a devastatingly quick speed. The best way I can describe my anxiety is that I'm on an uphill climb of a rollercoaster. Only the fall from the top isn't exhilarating, it's damn near crippling.

I force my fingertips to touch Cooper's back. He needs the reassurance that I'm alright. That it's okay to hold me. It's not. I don't think it ever will be, but I'll never tell him that.

Two Mississippi.

My featherlight touch seems to have done the trick. Cooper's hold on me loosens, but it's too slow. My throat constricts, and the air can barely find my lungs. I open my mouth to speak, but the words are lost somewhere deep inside me again.

Three Mississippi.

Cooper's arms finally fall to his sides. I open my eyes and take a step back, my anxiety disappearing the moment there's space between us. I wish I could enjoy our embrace. Years ago, when we were kids, I did.

"Heard you got reamed for having a new tattoo."

I flash an exaggerated grin and hold my wrist out to him. I've got a fresh three-inch black phoenix drawn from a pattern of twisting lines with a red and yellow watercolor backsplash. Rebirth among the ashes. It's beyond beautiful. My favorite tattoo so far.

My other wrist has a cherry blossom branch that stretches halfway up my forearm. I love cherry blossoms but their beauty, while spectacular, is short-lived—much like everything good in my life.

"When did you get this done?" Cooper drawls, running his thumb across my flesh. Across the scars that went the wrong way.

A lump builds in my throat. With slow, controlled movements, I pull my hand back and let it fall at my side. I want to clutch it to my chest and curl up inside myself, but that would only make Cooper worry. He worries enough for the both of us as it is, and that's my fault, too. "Last night."

I don't have to say where I went. He knows Bane is the person I go to for ink. This is my sixth tattoo, and Bane has done them all. I got my first when I was sixteen. A cartoon sketch of a T-rex on my hip and I've been semi-addicted ever since.

"You know I hate you going over there."

I roll my eyes. I don't need or want a lecture about my only friend on that side of the tracks. I'm careful, only visiting when I know it's safe. "What's up, Coop?"

"Heard you slurped Tad's gherkin."

I shake my head and laugh. How is it that a man who is so smart, 3.9 GPA smart, can sound so stupid? Who in the hell says gherkin? It sounds like a medieval weapon or an STD. Both of which I don't, and never have, had.

"Where in the world did you hear that?"

Cooper gives me a knowing look. "Everyone's talking about how you're open for business again, Pipes. I thought you were done with all that."

I figured it wouldn't take long for Tad's story to find its way back to Cooper. This is high school, rumors spread like herpes, but he knows the truth behind the lies. I think that's why his disappointed expression hurts so much. He's looking at me like he believes them this time. I shake my head. "No, Doofus. And gherkin?"

Cooper chuckles and runs a hand through his sandy blond hair, pushing the long strands out of his eyes only for them to fall back in place a second later. He gives me a lopsided smile. "Online slang dictionary. They have some hoopla words on there."

He's beyond ridiculous. I bite back a grin and punch him in the shoulder. "Quit, or UF's spies will think you're an idiot and take back their scholarship."

Cooper's face pales. I can practically see the gears in his head turning. While the Harris's have more money than I'll ever see in my lifetime, Mamma T isn't rolling in dough anymore. When she and Mr. H divorced, he took all his money bags and ran away with the maid he was having an affair with.

Sure, Mamma T has her restaurant and gets a sizable check for alimony and child support, but it's not enough to put two boys through an Ivy League college. Logan, my other illegitimate foster brother, still talks to the man from time to time and will likely have Daddy Dearest pay his tuition, but Cooper can't stand their dad and refuses to take a penny of his money.

"They have those?"

I roll my eyes. He's so cute. So gullible. "No, dipshit. They don't."

"Oh, thank God. I about shit myself. Seriously though, what's up with you blowing that dickbag yesterday?"

And we're back to this. "I didn't."

Cooper crosses his arms and arches his brows. "That's not what's going around. Did you do something with Rex, too? Y'all looked pretty cozy after school."

He's such a jerk. If I didn't love him like a brother, I'd nutcheck him. "Bite me."

Cooper flips me the bird, showcasing his only tattoo, and no, Bane didn't do it for him. It's a single letter on his ring finger—P.

I swat his hand away, my fingers touching the soft skin of his wrist. There's no balloon in my chest with this touch. No feeling of being strangled by demons I can't see because I initiated the contact. Not the other way around.

My anxiety is weird. I don't try to understand it, just survive it.

Cooper smiles, pleased that I've made physical contact. He is one of the few people who know about my anxiety issues. He thinks our hugs help, that he's healing me. They don't. "Why'd Mom say you're off tonight?"

"I'm supposed to do dinner with Monica because it's her birthday or some shit."

He cocks a brow, fully aware of my disdain for the woman who birthed me. "And you're going?"

"Hell no!"

The bell sounds, echoing in the confined stairwell. We have two minutes to get to our next class. Cooper puts his arm around my shoulders and pulls me in for a sideways hug.

One Mississippi.

EVER SINCE REX TRANSFERRED TO ST. A'S BACK IN JANUARY, HE'S MADE it clear he's a lone wolf. He doesn't do commitment or second dates, only one-night fun fucks. Lunch and free periods are spent in the gym working out, and while he throws the best parties since the Harris's New Year's Bash, don't expect to be acknowledged beyond the white vinyl fence surrounding his yard.

All of this I know because of the three girls who insist on sitting with me at lunch this semester. They ramble, nonstop, about mindless crap no one gives two shits about. If it wasn't for the five-star cuisine that puts half of the restaurants in town to shame, I wouldn't even come to the cafeteria. Besides, it's not like any of them are my friends.

These girls, and a revolving door of others over the years, sit at my pity-party-for-one table because, at some point during lunch, one, if not both, of the Harris twins will join me.

"You'll never guess who I went home with last night." Melody, head cheerleader and world-class bitch, boasts, setting her tray down across from me. Her clones, Sarah and Rachel—bleached hair, too much makeup, and scraps of fabric that violate the dress code—sit down with her.

I stab a plastic fork at the truffle macaroni on my styrofoam tray. My Dollar Store earbuds are hidden beneath my hair, a dark purple cord attached to my phone, the only indicator they're in, but today there is no music because my wannabe smartphone's battery is almost dead and I forgot my charger.

"Please don't tell me you let Logan do you in his car again," Sarah whines. "You deserve so much better."

Melody wrinkles her nose. "Ew. No. That was a one-time lapse in judgment." She pauses. "Okay, twice." Sarah arches her brows in that knowing way moms do. Melody sighs. "Okay, fine, it was three times, but that's it. I swear."

I bite back a laugh. Everyone knows Melody is not so secretly in love with Logan. Has been ever since freshman year, back when she had braces and the coordination of a toddler learning to walk. This year, she came back to school as a new woman. New boobs. New nose. No braces. And a whole new attitude.

"Something funny, slut?" Melody asks, narrowing her eyes at me.

I pull my earbuds out and wrap them around my phone. It's not like I could listen to anything even if I wanted to. Might as well give up the ruse. "Besides your face? I mean, really, Melody! All that money, and the doctors couldn't do better than *that*?"

Over-plucked, penciled in, eyebrows arch, nearly jumping off her forehead. "Excuse me?"

I tuck my phone into my bag and lean on the table, giving Melody a "sorry dear" smile. The doctors actually did a good job on her face. She's beautiful in that California clone kind of way, but no matter how pretty she is on the outside, her cold, black heart and rotten soul will always shine through.

If Logan took Melody to bed, which I highly doubt, I'm sure he's kicking himself for it. "If anyone had a lapse in judgment that night, it was Logan. Try all you want; you'll never replace Danika."

Melody grips her plastic fork. Shit brown eyes betray her, spilling her pathetic plan to stab me somewhere boring. Like my hand or arm, maybe. I'm not worried. Melody doesn't have it in her to hurt a fly.

Raised by a couple of doctors without borders parents and a pot-smoking hippie for a nanny, she's about as tough as a marshmallow. Sarah, on the other hand, looks generally concerned—for Melody, not me— and she rests her hand on Melody's arm, easing her off the ledge. "Let it go, Mel."

Melody glares, her beady brown eyes trying to intimidate me. It's comical., and then, like magic, her attitude shifts. Red lips pumped with filler curl at the corners. She sits up straighter, puffing her chest and batting her glued-on lashes. "Hey, Logan."

Logan Harris, foster brother number two, ignores Melody and sits on my side of the table, facing me. His tattered black skinny jeans and unbuttoned shirt violate the dress code but at this point in the year, our teachers are picking their battles. He steals Rachel's untouched fork off her tray and swipes my last bite of Mac and Cheese. "You good?"

I force a smile and nod. Logan and I have a strange relationship. I moved in with the Harris family the summer of my eighth birthday. Cooper and I clicked instantly, but Logan was standoffish. It took a full six weeks for him to talk to me. I think it was a mix of nerves and embarrassment. He used to stutter. Still does, sometimes, when he's nervous.

Flash forward to the middle of our freshman year when the Department of Children and Families pulled me out of the Harris's home and forced me to live with Monica again, which by the way, sucked. Logan pulled away. The fragile relationship we'd formed over the years seemed to dissolve the minute we were no longer family. If things hadn't gone down the way they did this summer, and I hadn't moved back in with them, he'd probably still treat me like a stranger.

"Have you thought about prom?" Melody asks, sticking a straw in her coke. She eyes Logan seductively as her lips curl around the plastic. "I vote we get a limo."

Rachel gasps, "Really? I've never been in a limo."

Rachel's here on a cheerleading scholarship. While our sports teams are shit, our cheerleaders are nationally ranked. Everyone who was on St. A's team in the last five years went on to cheer at Ivy League schools, and many furthered their careers into the NFL.

How do I know?

Principal White has their headshots plastered on the sports trophy walls with details of their life accomplishments. It's supposed to motivate our team to do their best. I think Principal White just likes to fluff his own feathers. I'm rambling. The point is that even though Rachel is here on a scholarship, like me, she's accepted because she has a purpose.

I'm considered a waste of space.

Melody flashes a bless-your-heart smile and turns her attention back to Logan. "Should we add your address to the pickup list?"

Logan pulls a pack of Reds from his shirt pocket and sticks a cigarette between his lips, knowing we're a tobacco-free campus. With the flick of a contraband Zippo, it's lit, adding more tar to his lungs. He takes a drag and then exhales, blowing a tuft of white smoke in Melody's face. "Hard pass."

Melody waves her hand, pushing the cloud away, and glares at me again. "You got something to say?"

I didn't do anything. I didn't smirk, or giggle, or make any indication that I had an opinion. Her feelings are hurt and she's taking it out on me. "Nothing you want to hear."

"No one ever wants to hear you." Melody and her friends snicker. She acts like her rebuttal is some huge insult but it's weak, especially considering this is the girl who stuck Kool-Aid-soaked pads to my locker a few weeks ago.

Logan blows another cloud of smoke in their faces, his silent way of sticking up for me. His attempt is appreciated, but not helpful.

I chew on the tip of my plastic fork, feigning indifference, but inside, my skin is crawling. I hate confrontation. In a fight-or-flight situation, my initial instinct is flight; but high school is a war zone. If you don't fight, you die—metaphorically speaking—and I'll be damned if this bitch is what kills me. "Seems like we have something in common."

Melody's nose wrinkles, which is surprising considering how much work she's had done. "I have nothing in common with you."

I cross my arms and lean on the table. Melody scoots back. She's nervous, which makes me oddly happy. I don't think of myself as intimidating, but it's nice to know that I can be if needed.

"I hear it all, Melody. You love to whisper about me. About how I'm on drugs and laugh about who I've done this and that with, but what you don't realize is that people whisper about you, too. Your friends..." I look at Sarah and Rachel, innocent bystanders in this conversation. "Not these two," My gaze finds Melody again, "but your other *friends* talk about you almost as much as you talk about me. The only difference between us is I get paid to spread my legs. Last I heard, your last hookup gave you chlamydia."

Logan snickers, exhaling another cloud of smoke in their direction. Melody stands. She grabs the styrofoam cup on Sarah's tray and tosses the orange liquid on my face.

"Hey!" Sarah yells.

Melody ignores her friend and smirks.

I wipe my eyes with the hem of my shirt, seemingly unfazed. I have a spare shirt in my shoulder bag. I'm not worried about it. Just a little irritated. Actually, I should thank Melody. I have a calculus exam next period. She just got me out of it.

Logan, however, is pissed. He stands and shoves the tip of his cigarette in the middle of Melody's overpriced veggie burger. He raises his hand, pointing a finger in her face. "Back the fuck off."

Melody puts her hands on her hips. "What the hell, Logan? Is she that good in bed?"

"Fuck you!" I spit, reaching for a few napkins. I dab at my shirt, but it's useless. It's a huge orange shit-stain and my bra's peeking through the wetness.

"I can end you, Melody." Logan flips what's left of her tray off the table. It flies a foot in the air and then falls into a heaping mess beside us. A few heads turn, curious but not willing to intervene where Logan's concerned.

"What, like you ended Piper?" She scoffs and then turns her attention to me. "You know he's the one who told everyone you gave a killer blowjob for fifty bucks."

"Shit," Logan runs a hand through his dark hair.

My heart squeezes. Logan and I may not have been friends last year, but I didn't think we were enemies. As betrayed as I feel, I won't give Melody the satisfaction of seeing me wounded.

"That's because he knows firsthand." Internally, I'm gagging at the thought of Logan and me together, but to them, I'm smiling. Happy to brag about another conquest. "Face it, bitch, you got my sloppy seconds."

Knock. Knock. Knock.

"Piper?" Logan asks, quietly opening our bedroom door.

I press my hands against the gray comforter, push myself into a sitting position, and then cross my legs. My phone rests beside me, the Kindle app still open. I read a lot of romance novels. Our school counselor said I needed a reminder that not all men are the same. Reading is supposed to be a safe way for me to overcome some of my issues. The problem with my counselor's theory is that real life isn't a storybook. Some hot guy with abs of steel and a giant dick isn't going to rescue me and make everything better.

"You're up late," I say, getting comfortable. This time of night, it should be Cooper coming in. Instead, I'm met with the other Harris brother.

Logan crosses the room. His strides, while long, are slow. Even though baseball and football season are over, he still wakes up at the crack of dawn to work out, making today longer than normal for him. The end of my California King bed dips as he sits, one leg under him, the other off the bed.

"Can't shut my mind off enough to sleep." There's a vulnerability to Logan tonight that I don't often see. It reminds me of the quiet eight-year-old boy I used to know.

Logan's the resident troubled guy girls can't get enough of. It doesn't matter that he treats them like they're disposable. That pretty face of his keeps them coming back, which only feeds his ever-growing ego. His shoulders hunch forward, eyes looking at my stomach, not my face. "Can we talk?"

"Isn't that what we're doing?"

"I owe you an apology."

I'm owed more than an apology. Logan ruined the second half of my junior year. Crushed what little self-respect I had left and forced me to find a creative way to handle the mess he'd made for me. Some random tool twisting my life down this path... that's fine, I can understand.

Maybe.

But someone I thought was family?

I just can't...

"Why'd you do it?"

Logan picks at invisible lint specks on the comforter. Even as a kid, when he was in trouble, he wouldn't look at you. It used to piss Mr. Harris off. Eventually, Logan learned to look people in the eye, but it took years. I think it was a nervous tick, like his stuttering. "I was always jealous of you and Cooper. Did you know that?"

I shake my head but quickly realize he can't see the movement. "No."

"Growing up, Cooper was the golden boy. Dad loved that he looked like Mom and bragged to anyone who would listen about his natural athletic ability. All anyone noticed about me was my speech issues. Mom tried to make me feel special, but there was always that gleam in her eye when someone brought up Cooper. And then you moved in and I became obsolete. Mom doted on you. Cooper took you under his wing. Even Dad was nice to you. I didn't matter anymore."

My heart breaks for little Logan. I remember how timid and quiet he was. I always thought it was his way of being rebellious. You know, perfect life and all. I never imagined those antisocial traits were because of his insecurities. "That's not true, Logan. Everyone loved you."

"Yeah, right." He pauses for a slow, shaky breath, then continues. "I thought you and I would be close. We were both rejects in our families— no offense—but then you fell under the Cooper spell, too."

"You wouldn't talk to me," I say sheepishly. Those first few weeks, I tried to be his friend. I'd sit next to Logan, a big smile on my face, and say *hey*. Logan would then stare at me, eyes wide, mouth slack. After that, he'd either run to his room and lock himself inside or ignore me altogether. Eventually, he started waving or giving timid smiles when I was in the room.

It took years, but I eventually got sentences out of him.

"I couldn't talk to you, Piper. Physically, I couldn't, and then Cooper had to go and be your savior the first night when you had that nightmare. Any chance I had at you noticing me was gone the moment I saw you blinded by all that is Cooper."

"You were there for that?" I ask, trying my hardest to remember that night. My nightmares back then were simple: locked out of the house, trapped in a closet, forgotten for days without food. They were nothing compared to what I've got now.

"Yeah, Piper. I watched from the doorway as everyone rushed in to save you."

"I...I didn't know."

"Everything was always about you and Cooper." He shakes his head, years of disappointment written on his face. "You know, I scored the winning touchdown at our freshman homecoming game, but all Mom cared about was you. How you were going to handle moving back in with your *real* mother. She didn't even tell me I did a good job at the game. It's like she wasn't even there, but I know she was because I saw her in the stands. That's the moment I started to hate you."

Logan exhales and looks up at me. "People talked about you all the time. Everything they said fizzled out in a day or two. So, when Tad asked why Cooper was always up your ass, I made something up. I didn't know *that* rumor would take off like it did. It snowballed out of control, and it's all my fault, and then with everything that happened this year..." He sucks his bottom lip between his teeth, shakes his head, and reaches for my hand, fingers curling around my palm.

One Mississippi.

The balloon in my chest inflates. Tiny needles spread from my hand up my arm, similar to the feeling of when your foot falls asleep but ten times worse. My head is foggy, and I hear his words, but they aren't fully processing in my mind.

"I wish I had been a better brother to you. I was stupid and selfish and, in reality, jealous. Maybe you would have come to me instead of leaving the party that night if we were closer. If we had a better relationship, maybe that asshole wouldn't have...and you wouldn't have..."

I pull my hand from underneath Logan's and rest it on his shoulder. The pressure in my chest deflates, needles disappearing almost as quickly as they came. Logan's honey eyes, red-rimmed and puffy, meet my grays. "Nothing you could have done would have changed what happened. You can't blame yourself for the way that night went down."

Logan gives a half chuckle. "You'd make a good therapist."

"I've seen our counselor more times than I'll admit this year. I'd be disappointed if I couldn't offer some advice at this point."

A BLUE BALLPOINT PEN RAPS AGAINST THE LINED PAPER IN MY INCH-thick file. The pages inside are riddled with notes about my mom, how I've adjusted this year, and the days we've sat in silence.

Mamma T forced me to see Mrs. Cherrybroom when I was released from the psych ward last September. I was only there for three days, the mandatory minimum when Baker Acted, but believe me when I say three days in there is three too many. I left with a prescription for anti-depressants that I refuse to take and a referral for a therapist. My weekly turned monthly visits with the school counselor were our compromise.

Tap. Tap. Tap.

"We're down to three sessions, Piper." Mrs. Cherrybroom's a big lady. Not fat, just big. Like an Amazonian. The large oak desk that fills most of the room looks small under her. Conversely, the leather seat I'm in, purchased as a matching set, practically swallows me.

Tap. Tap. Tap.

"I wish you'd consider Post-Secondary School. You're too smart to waste your life in a dead-end job. I've got connections at the Community College here. We can work something out and get you an academic scholarship. There's no reason why our valedictorian can't go to school."

Same song, different tune. Mrs. Cherrybroom is convinced my attempt at taking my life was a fluke. She doesn't know the reason behind it or about the two other failed attempts. She did, however, teach me how to manage my anxiety attacks better: breathe through them, control the situation, picture myself in a happy place, etc.

Now that I'm all better—in her eyes— she's convinced I'm ready for the real world, which includes parties, college, and things she can't legally talk about...whatever that means.

"I'm moving the day after graduation."

Mrs. Cherrybroom's eyes light up. "I'm so glad to hear that. Where did you enroll?"

"I didn't." And I won't. Every day I stay in this tiny town, I play with fire. Monica's drug dealer, Gerald, is owed a debt. I refused to pay with the currency she offered and pissed him off in the process. At the very least, he's going to want payback.

For the moment, I'm safe. He is locked up on a violation of probation charge for three more months, giving me time to graduate and get out of dodge. I don't know where I'm going yet, but leaving is my *only* option.

Mrs. Cherrybroom sags back into her seat and drops her pen. It rolls off the desk, landing near my feet. "I worry about you, Piper. We've made such great progress this year." Her long, manicured nail taps the leather armrest of her chair. She's plotting, choosing her next words carefully because she knows our time's running out.

Tap. Tap. Tap.

My phone vibrates at my side, signaling my alarm. I slip the strap of my bag onto my shoulder and stand. "Time's up."

"Piper, I know our session is over, but please don't leave yet."

"Same time next month?"

P.E. can kiss my ass. I hate running almost as much as I hate being touched, and for some God-forsaken reason, Coach Riley has decided to end the year with endurance sprints.

I extend the time on my counseling excuse pass and skip the rest of first period, physics, and my next class, P.E. Settling under the largest oak tree behind the football stadium, I pull out my phone and open the Kindle app.

The air is a crisp seventy-eight degrees. It's hot by anyone else's standards, but comfortable to me since Florida frequently hovers in the high nineties before humidity. I sit on a few fallen leaves and lean against the tree trunk.

"Shouldn't you be in class?" Rex asks, walking up the hill to join me.

Good Lord, that accent is sexy. No wonder Melody and her friends all but stalk Rex.

I set my phone in my lap and fight the smile forming. I don't want to feel the fluttering in my stomach or the racing of my heart. I want to make it through the next seven and a half weeks without hiccups. All boys—specifically this one— are a hiccup. But what I want and what my body wants are two different things.

Stupid hormones.

"Shouldn't you?" It's a lame rebuttal, but it's all I've got. The banter I'm used to entails slinging insults and usually begins with a derogatory comment. Rex is different from the guys who talk to me, meaning I should probably play nice.

There's a small grunt, followed by a faint chuckle. A few moments of soft shuffling later, Rex is next to me. Heat bounces off his skin, setting mine on fire— that's how close we are. I turn my head to look up at him because, yes, even sitting down, he's a head taller than me.

Rex runs his fingers through the grass—always green because winter only vacations in Florida. He pulls, separating a few blades from their roots, then lets them fall back to the ground. "I like your tattoo."

"Thanks," I say, pulling the sleeve of my sweater down. Even though I'm proud of the artwork, I'm ashamed of what's underneath it. Hiding my ink means Rex can't ask to look at the cherry blossoms, which means he can't ask about my scars.

Instead, he asks, "Want to have lunch with me today?"

Do I what? You don't eat lunch! You disappear, hiding your gorgeous face from all of us fangirls trying to sneak a peek at it. I mean, have you looked in a mirror lately?

Rex chuckles.

Oh gosh, I didn't say that out loud. Did I? Maybe he's laughing at something else, like the beyond embarrassed look on my face. Or maybe he has a weird tick where he laughs before a sneeze or something. Yeah, that's it. Any second now, he will sneeze.

Please sneeze.

"It won't kill you to hang out with me, Piper."

I bring my legs in, crossing them, then push my skirt down so he can't see my underwear. I need to calm down. Rex is just a boy. A ridiculously hot boy who asked me out on my first date. No big deal.

Yeah, right.

"It might. You know, kill me." It won't. Death is a bitch, just like Life. I swear they're best friends and have made a pact never to give me what I want. Two strikes, three if you count the time I cut the wrong way. I should have been out, but no. I'm still here. Mocked by Death and laughed at by Life. The story of my life, ladies and gentlemen.

Rex has a smile that's almost as irritating as it is cute. "If it does, I'll just have to give you CPR and bring you back to me."

My cheeks heat at the thought of Rex's mouth on mine. I bet he's a good kisser. *Yeah, because he's had lots of practice.*

I push those thoughts away and roll my eyes, feigning indifference. I don't know how it's possible, but his grin grows, stretching ear to ear. The dude's got a big mouth, like Chord Overstreet from *Glee*. It's not unattractive, just different.

"If you're worried I want to do something sexual, I don't."

I want to believe him, but experience has made me weary. "Sure you don't."

Rex looks me dead in the eye, bright blues meeting my grays. "You don't trust me?"

"Hell, no," I say a little too quickly. Rex's lips press into a tight line. He nods and turns his gaze to the parking lot.

Shit. I think I hurt his feelings. I reach out and set my hand on his arm. A zing of electricity passes between us, but I do my best to ignore it because he's made no indication that he feels it, too. Hell, for all I know, this crazy attraction is one-sided. Truthfully, that would be the best-case scenario. "It's nothing personal, I don't trust anyone."

Rex cocks a brow. "Not even Cooper?"

Damn him for calling my bluff. Cooper is an anomaly, and so is Bane, but for argument's sake, I say, "I trust him as far as I can throw him."

Rex smirks, reaches out, and tucks the errant hair that has fallen between us behind my ear. A classic movie-boyfriend move. All that's missing now is the big kiss. I lean closer until our shoulders touch. The fire of his skin on mine burns through the sleeve of both my shirt and sweater. Rex's head tilts, angling down and to the side. I feel my heart everywhere—my stomach, eyes, even my toes.

This is a bad idea.

Bbbbrrrriiiinnnggg! The bell screams, and I don't know if I'm more relieved or disappointed that it interrupts our almost kiss. Rex grunts and leans back against the tree, eyes closed. He stands a moment later, smiling down at me like nothing happened, and extends his hand. I take it, letting him help me to my feet even though I have no plans of leaving.

Rex dips his head again. His baby blues lock onto my grays once more, sucking me in. I lick my lips, unintentionally, and his gaze falls to my mouth. Our eyes meet again a split second later. He leans closer, his breath tickling my ear. I breathe him in. He smells of clean laundry, aftershave, and mint. Much better than last time.

"Offer stands. Breakfast, lunch, or dinner." Rex pulls me against his chest. I wrap my arms around his waist, enjoying what it feels like to be held for the second time in almost a year, and listen to his racing heart.

All of this happens in less than a minute. A minute that lasts forever yet flies by too fast at the same time. I want to feel Rex's body against mine a little longer. There's no pressure or needles or any of the usual discomfort my anxiety creates.

There's just Rex.

I walk onto the back patio for the second time tonight and shut the double-paned doors behind me. Bodies are everywhere. Dancing. Drinking. Laughing. People making out on my mother's olive-green lounge chairs and hooking up in the shell-shaped pool. There's enough semen floating in it to make another football team of self-entitled pricks. The girls swimming in there are practically asking to get pregnant. Thank God for chlorine.

Mother spared no expense in this house moving me—not us, me—here. She never does. Instead of transporting all our possessions from one place to the next, like a normal person, she stocks the house with shiny new things. Insisting that each home be perfect in the unlikely event we decide to visit one on a whim, which has never happened.

But come on, who needs eight houses spread across the country, fully furnished and stocked with enough clothes to fill a department store? Apparently, we do.

More people, whose names I don't care to learn because in a little less than seven weeks they will be obsolete, gather around a plastic table procured from the pool house. A pool house my guests felt comfortable enough to go in without asking. That's what happens when you throw three parties a week every week since January.

Why? Because a house full of strangers is still better than an empty one. Besides, who's gonna stop me?

For almost everyone here, I'm the story they'll tell their college buddies. They've been to country singer Kip Montgomery's house. Were best friends with his son. Hung out with him every weekend.

Blah. Blah. Blah.

No one gives two shits about me. It's all about my dad.

Even my mother doesn't care about me. When I was four, she left me at an airport. I don't know if she did it on purpose, but somehow, in the midst of grabbing her purse— which I don't actually remember since she always has a bag comparable to *Mary Poppins,* only a thousand times more expensive— she got up and left without me.

Mother of the Year right there.

I remember falling asleep because it was nap time and waking up by myself. I wasn't scared. That's usually what happened at home. But then I realized the faces around me were different. Four-year-old me was still pretty chill because I was a cool motherfucker even back then, but a kid can only be calm for so long.

I walked for what felt like forever, the bubble of tears in my throat building until I couldn't take it anymore. I collapsed on the floor in a fit of liquid distress. Eventually, some lady stopped and asked the questions you're supposed to ask when you find a young kid all alone.

What's your name?

Where are your parents?

Are you okay?

I didn't answer any of them. I may have been freaked the fuck out, but I still remembered the golden rule—don't talk to strangers. Eventually, an officer came and took me to a secret room, the staff lounge. It was sheer luck someone had a magazine on the table open to an article about my dad. An article that just so happened to have a picture of me in it.

Airport security reached out and got ahold of my dad's PR person. Hours passed before anyone came to get me. The shit thing, the person who showed up wasn't my mom. It wasn't even anyone I'd ever seen before. My parents sent a strange woman with tired eyes and a sad smile to claim me like I was lost luggage. A woman I later found out would be my nanny for the next fourteen years, Gretchen.

The moral of my story, my own parents don't give a damn about me. I sure as shit don't expect the strangers who fill my house to, either.

"Hey, Rex." Thin arms wrap around my waist as someone's chest presses against my back.

I recognize the voice and turn to find Sarah Archer, one of the few names I do know, smiling up at me. Sarah's a nice girl. The doodle my last name on her notebook type, but still nice. We have statistics together. She flirts shamelessly in class, but I'm not interested.

My mind's been on one raven-haired girl since moving to this fiery pit of hell four months ago. I'm not saying that I haven't hooked up since moving here, but that's all those girls were. An easy way to pass the time, and Sarah's too sweet to fuck and forget. She links her fingers with mine, pulling me closer. I take a step forward, entertaining her desires, if only for a moment.

"Come swim with me."

I could peel my shirt off and swim in my shorts, but I don't want to lead her on. Contrary to how the tabloids portray me, I'm not a bad guy. I don't make sport of breaking hearts. Everyone I've slept with, here or elsewhere, knew long before I fucked them that there would be no dates. No future. No us. "Can't. Not dressed for it."

Sarah stops pulling but doesn't let go. She chews on her cherry red lip then flashes a come-and-get-me grin. "Neither am I, but who says we need clothes?"

"Ahhh." I shake my hand free from her death grip and tuck my thumbs into the band of my pants "Sarah, you're a great girl, but I'm not feeling it. Not tonight. Sorry."

Sarah's cheeks flush. Unlike most of the girls who approach me, she doesn't strike me as the one-night-stand kind of girl. Outside of her poor choice of friends, she's cool. She forces a smile. "No biggie, Rex. See you around."

Sarah practically runs to the beer pong table and disappears into the crowd of people watching the game. She'll be alright. A little alcohol and attention from some of the guys over there will soothe her bruised ego.

I look around and sigh. My house is full of people, but the one I want is nowhere to be seen.

Why did I come outside again?

Better yet, why did I throw this party tonight?

Because you're lonely with no family and no real friends.

I grab a red Solo cup from beside the keg and fill it. *Bottoms up.* I down its contents in one big swallow, not feeling any better about myself than I did a minute ago. As I'm refilling it, Logan Harris catches my eye. Another name I know simply because he's at every party I throw. He jumps out of my pool and runs towards the back gate, catching a dark-haired girl in his arms and swinging her around until his twin brother, Cooper, shoves him in the shoulder.

Piper.

Piper Lovelace is like a comet—fascinating to look at but disastrous. Nearly every caution sign that my dad's publicist warned me about over the years is there. Still, I'm drawn to her. She's by far the most beautiful girl I've ever seen, and she doesn't even know it. Raven hair. Skin as fair as moonlight. Cold gray eyes that harbor a pain I don't understand but can relate to. Full lips begging to be kissed.

The need to know her is all-consuming, but the thought of actually speaking to her is terrifying. She makes me nervous, and I have no clue why. I'm the son of a major country singer. I can score girls by sneezing. But Piper's shown no interest in my dad or me. It's almost as insulting as it is intriguing.

As horrible as it sounds, I'm glad I caught Tad trying to do whatever it was he was gonna do to Piper the other day. It gave me a chance to talk to her without the assumption that I wanted sex. That's the only time anyone talks to Piper is when they want a favor.

I spent the next few days trying to figure out how to break the ice between us again, and then it hit me: her monthly meetings with the school counselor. Piper almost never shows up to first period after her session. So, I sat behind her favorite oak tree, the one she was probably going to when Tad dragged her to the bathrooms. Anyway, I sat there waiting.

And waiting.

And waiting.

Finally, after what felt like forever, I heard feet shuffling. I peeked around the side of the tree and saw the bottom of boots—Piper's signa-ture shoe. Every day is the same: knee-high black boots, a uniform-issued black skirt, and a white button-down blouse, because that's what every-one's forced to wear, with some sort of black sweater over it. And then, my favorite part, black hair with dark purple tips. I don't think her natural color is so dark. Her eyebrows are a medium brown, but the black hair looks good paired with all her dark eyeliner.

I took a minute to calm my thoughts. I'd never asked a girl out before, and Piper would be my first. Jenny, my only friend back in New York, says it's because I'm scared to be rejected. She thinks my fears and social issues stem from my parents' lack of involvement. Whatever the case, this was a huge moment for me.

I mustered up the courage to talk to Piper. Everything was going well until I went and ruined it. She shot me down, but I'm not done yet. Gretchen says, "If it's easy, it ain't worth it." From what I can tell, Piper's worth it. She's edgy and not afraid to be herself. She's real, aside from her hair color. Best of all, she doesn't give two shits that my dad is famous.

Piper's thrown a long-sleeved Red Onion work shirt on with her school skirt tonight. Her hair is pulled into a messy ponytail with stray pieces falling around her face. I smile, taking in just how beautiful she is. Long legs. Round cheeks. Plump, red lips. Yeah...not even going to fight it, I'm screwed.

I grab another red cup and fill it to the brim with more head than beer. My heart races faster than a greyhound as I run over to her. *Slow down.* I force myself to walk, and it's hell. After the longest thirty seconds of my life, I stand beside her lawn chair, a smile that feels as lame as it probably looks, greeting her. "Hey."

Piper looks up at me, a small grin tugging at her lips. Her smiles at school are few and far between. This tiny bit of happiness I caused is gold. "Hey."

I extend my hand with the extra beer too fast, spilling the frothy yellow liquid all over her boots. *Smooth.* I bring my arm back, spilling it yet again, this time all over my flip-flop. *This is going great—not.*

"I'm not a fan," she says, looking across the pool. I can't be sure, but I think she's watching the Harris twins.

Logan and Cooper are still going at it. Cooper points in our direction, brows furrowed as he lectures his brother. I've studied them, Cooper and Piper, for the last few weeks. I don't understand their relationship. He hovers like an overprotective parent, squashing every rumor, fighting battles I'm sure Piper doesn't realize exist.

On top of his classes and football practice, he still finds the time to be alone with her at school. Stealing a few minutes at lunch, walking her to class, and sometimes even hiding out in the north stairwell. Anyone with eyes can see how enamored he is with her. And yet they live together as siblings.

It's weird as fuck, but they don't kiss or hug in public, and that one bit of knowledge is what keeps me going; gives me a sliver of hope that I've got a shot.

That and the fact that Piper's rumored to be the school slut. From what I've seen, I don't think it's true, but Cooper doesn't seem like the type of person to date an easy girl. Not saying that Piper's easy. *Fuck.* I'm glad she can't hear me right now; she'd think I'm an idiot.

"A fan of fights or drinking?" I ask.

"Both." She says, her eyes glued to her foster brothers.

I study Piper's face and find a small yellow bruise on her cheek, carefully hidden by makeup, unnoticeable to the passerby, but I know what happened. The faint discoloration under her concealer jumps out to me, especially being this close.

"Are you okay?" I ask, sitting beside her.

"I'm fine." Piper looks out of her element. It might be the party. She's pretty antisocial and probably isn't comfortable around all these people. If she's uncomfortable, she'll leave, and I'm not ready for her to go.

"Want to head inside? It's quiet. No one's allowed in, and I promise I won't touch you or ask you to do anything."

"Good, because I won't," she says flatly.

"I know that."

She snorts. "Sure you do."

Piper has no reason to trust me. A Google search of my name doesn't paint me in the best light. Not to mention, the guys at our school are total douches and by default, I've probably been lumped in with them.

So, I level with her and let her have a piece of me, hoping to earn her trust. "My dad's been the target of rumors for years. Paparazzi love to make shit up. Happy families and good decisions don't sell papers. Sometimes, they'd attack me, put it out to the world how I'm on benders and partying myself to death. What I'm trying to say is that the rumors about you and your reputation mean nothing to me. Until I catch you with your lips around some dude's cock in the bathroom and watch him hand you fifty bucks, I don't believe them."

"Were any of the tabloids true?"

I tilt my head from side to side, thinking. How do I explain that for a year or so, they were? I was young, maybe ninth grade, when my parents moved me—not us, me— across the country halfway into my freshman year.

I liked living in Anaheim. I'd wormed my way into the popular group which, at the time, felt important. I opened up to the idea of having friends because I'd been there for over a year. So, when Mother uprooted me without warning to New York and didn't bother to come too...I acted out. I drank. I fought. I fucked the wrong girl, twice, landing some not-so-great pictures in some very unreliable gossip magazines. I did everything shy of getting arrested for my parents' attention. They never showed and Gretchen was worn out.

After that year, I made a promise to myself. I wasn't going to try anymore. Gretchen wasn't my nanny or my friend. I realized she was my mother, even though she hadn't birthed me. I played with her kids and we spent the holidays together. She wasn't part of my family, but I was part of hers.

However, it didn't matter that I turned my life around. Tabloids still printed stories and made me out to be a hot-headed, drunken man-whore when in fact, I've only slept with six women. "Some of it was true, but they kept the stories running even after I got my act together. Like I said, good decisions don't sell papers."

Gray eyes, dusted with powder blue and silver slivers, finally find mine. She smiles. It's small and only lasts a fraction of a second, but I see it. "Okay."

My heart hammers in my chest. Did I hear her right? "Okay, what?"

Our gazes dance together for what feels like an eternity, and my heart beats against my ribcage with Hulk-like intensity. It wants her. It wants to hold this beautifully broken girl and show her she's worthy of love.

Not that I love her, but I like her.

A lot.

Finally, Piper says, "Let's go inside. I'm giving you a chance. Don't make me regret it."

I f someone would have told me back in August that I'd be at a party this year, I would have laughed in their face. If they'd have told me I would be at said party to chase a boy, I would have said they'd lost their mind.

And yet, here I am, doing both.

Convincing Cooper to drive me after work was too easy. I almost think he *wanted* to come, although I can't imagine why. He seemed to lose interest in high school parties around the same time I did.

We park halfway down the street behind an overpriced Lexus. It's just one of the two dozen cars lining the sidewalk to Rex's mini-mansion. Walking through the back gate, I was prepared for people. I was prepared for loud music. I wasn't prepared for Logan to hug me.

In the ten years we've known each other, Logan has *never* hugged me. He's taking this good-brother thing to the extreme. I appreciate the effort, but I don't need it. One overbearing Harris man is more than enough. Also, Logan doesn't know about my issues with being touched. Cooper does, and from my peripheral vision, he doesn't look happy.

The instant Logan's arms are around me, every bit of confidence I have walking into the party vanishes, squashed by the balloon inflating in my chest. He sets me on my feet and I dart to one of the ugliest patio chairs I've ever seen, away from the crowd of people partying, and away from the Harris boys so they wouldn't notice my trembling.

And then, just when I start to worry that I can't get my shaking under control, Rex comes over. Just his presence eases my nerves, and I don't know why.

Rex sits next to me, his pinky brushing against my leg with a whisper of a touch. I wait for the tightness in my chest, or the shakes, or sweats, or something to come back, but they never do. There's nothing but excited tingles and I'm not sure how to take it.

Rex sets both cups, which seem to have spilled everywhere, on the ground and stands. He rubs his hands down the side of his shorts, then turns and waits for me to follow. We take a winding path, twisting and turning through a sea of bodies. It looks like every senior and a good amount of our juniors are here tonight, unsurprisingly so. This is my first Montgomery party, and it exceeds the rumors.

Rex opens a set of double-paned doors and lets me into his house. I gasp as he leads me into his kitchen. It's huge, bigger than Monica's whole apartment, and this is just the kitchen! I can't begin to imagine what the rest of the house is like. There are probably servants' quarters, hidden elevators, and a recording studio somewhere.

Rex flips a switch, illuminating the room. Spotless marble counter-tops shine under the crystal chandelier, reflecting light toward the stainless steel appliances and Spanish tiles. He walks around the island in the center of the kitchen and opens one side of the fridge. "Water?"

I shake my head. Rex grabs a bottle of Zephyrhills water for himself and then closes the door. He twists the cap off and takes a sip. I watch, mesmerized, as his Adam's apple bobs with each swallow. Once satisfied, he puts the cap back on and sets the bottle on the counter. It's such a normal act, but it looks inhumanly hot when he does it. Life's not fair. I clear my throat and avert my eyes to the island, running my hands over the smooth marble.

"Come on." Rex leads me out of the kitchen and through what feels like a maze of rooms.

I take in each breathtaking feature, mesmerized by the beauty of his house. Rose-colored Spanish tiles with paw prints embedded in them. Framed oil paintings. Perfect, flawless, dustless armoires and fresh flower displays on end tables. A Victorian-style table carved from cherry wood, large enough to seat twenty, with leather high-back throne-like chairs to match. A doorway connects each room we pass to the next, all seemingly serving the same purpose: sit or stand, but let me entertain you. Let me welcome you into my home.

I stop in the hallway to look at the collage of pictures on the wall. Rex as a baby. Rex and his family in the hospital together. A few of Rex throughout the years. A handful of his parents on luxurious vacations, but only one of the three of them together. Strange. "This place is beautiful."

"It's a house," he says with zero enthusiasm. His hand settles on my lower back and, to my surprise and excitement, I'm okay. The only thing I feel is the fluttering of my heart and the spinning of my head, which is worse than all of my anxiety attacks combined.

I don't want to feel this. I don't want to like Rex, but I think I do.

He guides me deeper into the mini-mansion. "Come on. You haven't reached the best part yet."

We pass the front door and a set of stairs, then finally make it to the living room. Of all the rooms we've crossed through, this one is the simplest. A large leather sectional with, not two but six, reclining seats is the room's focal point. There are two end tables, a coffee table, and a bookshelf filled with DVDs, but no TV.

"You're gonna love that," Rex says, his gaze dancing to the couch.

He opens the drawer in the coffee table nearest the door and pulls out a remote, then pushes a button on the remote and the wood paneling wall in front of us slides open, revealing a hidden, monstrous flat-screen TV. He then switches controllers, clicks the screen on, and hands me the one controlling the TV. "Find something you'd like to watch. I'll be right back."

I walk to the furthest end of the couch and sit. The leather is soft, swallowing me in cloud-like cushions. I bring my legs up and the back of the seat reclines. *Comfy*.

I push the red Netflix button and let the default profile load. I haven't watched Netflix since I moved out of the Harris's house my freshman year. Monica couldn't afford it and I haven't felt much like watching TV lately. My jaw falls open once the profile loads. There are so many options! New movies. Old movies. Netflix Originals. TV shows. How does anyone choose?

Five minutes later, Rex enters the room with a large bowl of popcorn and two water bottles. He sets the waters on the end table and then sits at the other corner of the couch, leaving enough space to fit a family of five between us. The buttery, salty smell of popcorn makes my stomach growl. I scoot closer, noticing a cheeky grin on Rex's face. I like his smile. It's playful and sweet, with just enough of a smirk that he always looks like his mind is in the gutter. He extends his arm with the bowl so I can grab a handful of kernels, but I'm too far away. I scoot even closer, past the center of the sectional.

The sneaky bastard is tricking me into sitting next to him.

I reach into the bowl, grab a fistful of popcorn, and then retract my hand to my lap. I pick up one kernel and plop it into my mouth. I close my eyes, savoring the salty-sweetness. I can't remember the last time I had popcorn. When I open my eyes for another piece Rex is staring at me. I plop a second kernel into my mouth. "What?"

"If those are the noises you make eating popcorn, I can't imagine—" he cuts himself off, grins, and shakes his head. "Never mind."

Rex keeps all body parts to himself throughout our movie. He doesn't try to put his arm around me or hold my hand. To kiss me or cuddle close. But every now and then, I catch him unabashedly watching me instead of the TV.

"Stop," I mumble, my smile growing harder to contain. There's a playful energy building between us, one I wish he'd act on.

The corner of Rex's lips twitch as he tries to hold a straight face. "Stop what?"

"Looking at me. It's weird." My heart hammers in my chest, beating against my flesh like a caged animal desperate to be free.

I lick my lips. Why? I don't know. Apparently, my tongue has a mind of its own and wants his attention. Rex's gaze flickers down to it for a full second, then finds my eyes again. He shifts, turning his body towards me, leaning an inch closer.

I can do this. If he can touch me, he can kiss me. What's the worst that can happen? *I don't know, a debilitating panic attack where you seize up and die?* Meh, I'll risk it.

"I can't help it," Rex says, breaking eye contact to take a sip of his water. "You're beautiful."

Butterflies swarm in my stomach. I don't know how he's doing this to me. I feel alive again. Maybe this is why Death didn't take me. Maybe she knew Life had a plan and something good was coming. Rex could be that something good.

I roll my eyes, a nervous laugh escaping me. "Yeah. Okay."

Rex leans back against the arm of the couch, his brows knitting together. "Can I ask you something?"

Oh gosh, this is it. He's going to ask to kiss me like a true gentleman. *Yes! The answer is yes!* "Maybe."

He chuckles and the sound sends those annoying butterflies into overdrive. There's so much flipping and thumping inside me. I can't take the anticipation anymore. I'm ready.

"If you could do anything, no worrying about salary or location, what would you do?"

My stomach drops, and every butterfly inside dies and falls into a bottomless pit. I fake smile and say, "That's easy. I'd be a librarian."

Rex crosses his leg over his knee, hands going behind his head. "No shit? Why?"

"I don't know... because I love to read." I do. The Kindle app on my phone and Amazon's free books have been a godsend, but I'll never tell Mrs. Cherrybroom. Falling into someone else's life, where no matter what, they get their happily ever after, usually with a jaw-droppingly hot guy, is a slice of heaven I'll happily sign up for.

Rex raises his brows and gives me a pointed look. "I've never seen you with a book that wasn't school-related."

"Have you been watching me, Mr. Montgomery?"

He freezes like a kid caught with his hand in the candy jar. "No. I...uh...I'm just saying when I see you around campus, you never have a book. I mean, you always have schoolbooks, but not, like, fun books. I guess I never pegged you for the reading type."

"And what exactly does the reading type look like?"

F *oot. Meet. Mouth.* If I could facepalm myself right now I would, but then I'd look even more lame than I feel.

What does the reading type look like?

Is there even a right way to answer this? I scratch the back of my neck. "Uh... well... umm.... shit. There's nothing I could say right now that wouldn't make me sound like a total dick. Is there?"

Piper smirks. "Nope."

Netflix pauses, giving us their infamous *are you there* screen. Piper half-chuckles, apparently finding its question funny, then crosses her long legs under her. "I started reading because my bio-mom said girls like me don't need to be smart. All I needed was a pretty mouth and a thin body and guys would pay to make my life easy. Being the brat I was, I read as many books as I could, just to spite her."

Seriously? Who tells their daughter that? Little girls should be raised to believe they're princesses. They should be spoiled rotten, with impeccable manners, and taught that they are capable of anything. They should be reminded every day of their self-worth. My future daughter will be given the world one day. "Your mother sounds like a piece of work."

Piper snort-laughs, a shadow falling across her face as she looks down at her hands. "You don't know the half of it."

I nudge her shoulder with mine. "Well, I think you'd make the cutest librarian."

She smirks. Her smiles, while brief, are like opals—beautiful, rare, and worth cherishing. I don't know why, but I'm excited that I keep causing them.

"I can see you now with a messy bun surrounded by books. You'd be just like Belle, only more hardcore."

"Who?"

Piper's joking. She has to be. I can't think of I girl I know who hasn't seen *Beauty and the Beast*, especially since they made that live-action one a few summers ago. "Belle? From *Beauty and the Beast*."

Piper shakes her head. "Wait, wasn't that the movie the chick who played Hermione Granger was in a few years ago? Emma something?"

"Oh, my god. You've got to be kidding me. You've never seen it? Tell me you've seen it."

She shrugs, a smile playing on her lips.

"It's a Disney classic. Have you seen any Disney princess movies?"

"You obviously have," she teases.

Piper has no idea. I've seen everything Disney has ever made, even the black-and-white movies that weren't animated. Can't say I liked those as much, but I've still seen them. "My nanny growing up, Gretchen, was obsessed with all things Disney. Every Halloween, when she took me trick or treating, she'd dress up as one of the princesses. Pretty sure I can quote every line Aladdin says in the first movie." Probably the second one, too, but Piper doesn't need to know how much of a closet nerd I am.

"Gretchen sounds amazing."

There's a longing in her voice I can relate to. Piper's relationship with her mom sounds just as fucked up as mine. People think because my dad is famous that I have this perfect life. More money than God. Two doting parents. Vacations on yachts and exotic islands. They couldn't be more wrong.

"She is, but she wasn't my mom. For years, I hated Gretchen. I thought if I made her life a living hell that she'd quit and that mom would come home, but she never did. Gretchen was too stubborn and Mom was too busy with Dad and his career."

I made Gretchen's life unnecessarily hard growing up, but like a true mother, she stuck it out. Showed me that no matter what she would love me and be there, unlike my real mother. Even now, she still calls me once a week just to see how I'm doing. My mom texts me about once a month

—boring, stupid GIFs that are as impersonal as an emailed birthday card.

And yes, Mother has sent me those too.

Piper grows quiet and stares at the TV. She looks lost, struggling with a faraway thought deep in her mind. I rub my finger down her nose, light as a feather, earning yet another small smile. "What's going through that pretty little mind of yours?"

Piper shakes her head. "Nothing, really. I guess I was just thinking that we have something in common. Your mother was never around. She abandoned you in the literal sense of the word, whereas mine was there for a decent portion of my childhood but never gave a crap about me, and then she went to jail."

She giggles and holds a hand up. "High five for mommy issues."

Our hands slap together. I'm not sure why we're celebrating our shitty childhoods, but Piper's laughing again. She slips her bottom lip between her teeth. I watch it slide out, a thin trail of saliva glistening in the light. That's twice now. She has to be doing it on purpose. There's no way she doesn't realize it turns me on, making me want to suck on that lip and kiss her. I know I said I wouldn't touch her, but fuck it.

I lean in too quickly. Or perhaps I bobbed and she weaved. Whatever the case, our foreheads slam together in the most awkward, uncoordinated, non-kiss in the history of kissing.

"Ouch," she whispers, her hand rubbing the sore spot.

I'm beyond embarrassed. I wasn't even this lame when I was twelve. I need to get Piper to think about something other than that failed attempt at a kiss. I stand and walk to the armoire by the window.

"Where are you going?" she asks, a hint of fear in her eyes.

I open the wooden doors and search our DVD collection. We have hundreds of them, all arranged alphabetically, so finding the one I'm looking for is easy. I could load the Disney+ app, but there's something satisfying about holding a DVD. I grab it and walk over to the TV; it has a built-in disc reader. I open the case and slide the disc in. "We are going to watch the original *Beauty and the Beast* and then maybe the live-action... if you're up for it."

"Shut up," she says, her lips curving in playful irritation.

"Get ready to have your mind blown, my little librarian."

Piper reaches beside her and chucks a decorative pillow at me. I instinctively block and it falls at my feet. "You're gonna wish you had that to drown out my awful singing."

Thirty minutes into the first movie Piper has fallen asleep. She's not in my lap, but her pillow touches my leg. A small win for such a guarded girl. I get up, careful not to disturb her, and go outside to check on the party. It's dead. The music's stopped. Keg's empty. Trash is overflowing with plastic cups. Everyone's gone except for a couple of guys who have passed out on the lounge chairs.

I look at the clock on the wall of the pool house by the outdoor shower. One-thirty. It was only eleven when Piper and I went inside. *Where did the time go?*

I toss a towel over Logan, one of the guys passed out on the patio, and jump when the pool house door creeps open. I look over my shoulder to see Cooper and Sarah sneaking out. They freeze like deer in headlights when they realize they aren't alone.

Cooper rubs the back of his neck, probably embarrassed to be caught mid-walk of shame. "Sorry, man, I guess we fell asleep in there."

Sarah gives Cooper a quick kiss on the cheek and then waves goodbye. We watch as she stumbles around the sleeping drunks and out the gate. She probably shouldn't be driving, but I'm not about to invite her to stay lest it sends mixed signals.

"No problem," I tell Cooper. "You can crash here for the night if you want."

"Nah, my mom will kill me if I don't come home. I'm supposed to be the good kid," he says with a sad smile. "Have you seen Piper?"

"Yeah." I hitch my thumb behind me. "She's asleep on the couch. Want me to get her?"

Cooper's eyes widen. "No shit? Can I see?"

He follows me back into the house and to the living room. Piper's still asleep, softly snoring right where I left her. It's not a big deal, but the way Cooper's looking at her, all wide-eyed and proud, like a new dad, something's up.

"Well, I'll be damned," he mumbles. "She almost never sleeps."

"You're joking, right?"

He shakes his head. "Nah. She'll close her eyes when she thinks I'm watching, but I can always tell when she's faking it. I think I've caught Piper *really* sleeping once in the last six months. Most nights, her alarms go off every twenty minutes because she's afraid to dream."

I can't begin to imagine what insomnia must be like, even if it is by choice. I love sleeping. I'd sleep until noon every day if my body would let me, but my training schedule has me up around five, even on the days when I don't have school or practice. "How do you know all this?"

"We share a bed at home. When she doesn't sleep, I don't sleep." Cooper studies my face. Lord only knows what he sees. Confusion? Worry? Frustration? Jealousy? He raises a brow and chuckles. "We're just friends, dude."

Am I that obvious? I need to get myself in check. I like Piper, a lot, but I don't need her or anyone else thinking I'm a jealous prick. Even though I am...jealous. "Why doesn't she like to sleep?"

Cooper crosses the room, grabs a blanket out of the basket in the corner, and then lays it over Piper. "Night terrors. She used to get them when we were kids, but they've gotten worse this year."

"Any idea why?"

"Mmm..." Cooper pauses, a frown falling on his face. "That's her story to tell, not mine. Can she crash here tonight? I don't want to wake her."

"Of course."

"Thanks, man. Just give me a call in the morning whenever Piper wakes up. I'll come get her."

That won't be necessary, but I smile and nod just the same. I'm going to spend the day with Piper, show her a good time and work on breaking down her walls. The fact that she's got a troubled past draws me to her even more.

She's real.

She's broken.

She's just like me.

I WAKE WITH A START TO A HIGH-PITCHED SHRIEK. I JUMP OUT OF BED and run downstairs to see what's going on. In hindsight, I probably should have thrown a pair of shorts over my boxers, but I wasn't thinking about how Piper might react to seeing me almost naked. My only thought was to get downstairs as fast as possible and murder whoever was hurting her.

Piper tosses and turns on the living room couch. She's still asleep, screaming at someone in her dream, "No! Stop! Please!"

I run over and kneel beside her. If this is what Piper goes through every time she closes her eyes, I'd fight sleep too. I set my hand on her shoulder. She's burning up, sweat clinging to her long-sleeved shirt. "Hey. Hey, it's okay."

Piper opens her eyes. She looks around, her gaze bouncing from one thing to the next until finally settling on my face. When she doesn't say anything, I ask, "Do you want a glass of water?"

She swallows hard and nods.

I scramble to my feet and rush to the kitchen. We're out of water bottles, so I grab a glass from the cabinet, fill it with water from the fridge, and am back at her side a minute later.

"Thanks," she says, her voice hoarse.

"Are you alright?"

Piper nods again. I'm unconvinced, but if she's not ready to share what tonight was about I won't push her. One thing I've learned over the years is that you can't force someone to open up. They'll let you in when they're ready. Seeing as she's not ready yet, I stand.

Piper grabs my wrist and I look down at her. "Will you stay with me?"

E arly morning light peeks through the window, blinding me. I squeeze my eyes shut, eager to keep the sun's rays at bay and enjoy the darkness a little longer.

How is it morning already?

Better yet, how long was I asleep? My alarms didn't go off, which is odd because I always set them. I groan, too tired to get up, and search for my phone.

Something shifts behind me and the cushion dips, sliding me into a warm body. It's then I realize an arm is draped over my side, resting on my chest. My breath catches in my throat. I open my eyes and immediately recognize the brown leather cushions I've wedged myself in.

I fell asleep at Rex's house.

A shiver of fear runs through me. I look down, praying that my shirt and skirt are still on. I let out a breath of relief, but that relief is short-lived because Rex is in his boxers. Only his boxers.

Did I let Rex touch me?

Did I touch him?

Why can't I remember?

My skin crawls, panic bubbling inside me. The questions and worries about the unknown trigger phantom hands around my neck. My nightmare comes rushing back. Every painstaking moment that vividly plays out in my dreams is now in my conscious mind.

I sit up and try to catch my breath, but my airway closes, making each inhale painful and scarce. This is terrible, beyond terrible. If there is a single word for a terrible-painful-traumatizing-and-immobilizing sensation, I need to learn it because that's how this feels.

Rex stirs beside me. "Hey, what's wrong?"

"I. Can't. Breath," I manage to squeak out.

Rex jumps up and scoops me into his arms and runs through this room, to the next, and through another after that, making his way across the house.

I shake uncontrollably and try to wiggle free because the last thing I want is to be touched, but he pulls me closer. I squeeze my eyes shut and try to find a rhythm. Try to slow my heart rate and regain control of my body with slow, deep breaths.

Rex kicks open a door. Rings of a curtain scream as they slide across the rod. Water breaks free, crashing on the ground. The sound bounces off the walls, echoing in what must be a smaller room. I force my eyes open. Slate blue tile. Silver fixtures. My mind takes each detail in like broken fragments of a picture until finally it connects: we're in a bathroom.

Without waiting for the water to warm, Rex carries me in. I gasp as the cold spray jolts air into my lungs. I push my arms against his chest and try to wiggle free. He lets my legs drop, allowing me to stand, but stays by my side. After a few minutes, my heart slows, my breathing steadies, and I can think again.

Why did I not set my alarms?

I take a step back and look down at my toes. The water warms and swirls at our feet, dancing against the tile before slipping down the drain. "I'm so sorry. I didn't mean to fall asleep. I thought I would be okay, but your couch was so comfy, and I just..." I sigh. I don't want to ramble, but I feel as if I should explain, only I don't know how. Not without telling him everything.

Rex takes my chin between his thumb and forefinger, lifting my gaze from his feet to his face. An electric tingle spreads in my veins, burning me up from the inside out. I don't understand how he makes me feel this way. It's exhilarating and terrifying because when each touch ends, I crave the next.

Rex flashes a lopsided grin and shrugs. "It's cool. I needed a shower anyway."

"Did we..." I can't bring myself to finish my sentence. The thought is sickening. Not because Rex is unattractive. He's one of the most hand-some men I've ever met, but because I always thought the moment I got over my insecurities and chose to do *anything* with a man, it would be special. Not a black hole in my mind.

"Oh! God, no!" he says and the relief I thought I'd feel is masked with disappointment. I suck in a breath, grateful nothing happened last night, but the way Rex yelled no hurts. I must have made a face because his eyes widen. "Crap! No. It's not like that. I mean, I'd love to fuck you. I mean...ugh." Rex rubs at the back of his neck. "Shit."

Tears of embarrassment, confusion, and disappointment dance on my lashes. Before I can turn away, Rex reaches up and cradles my cheeks. "I'm fucking this up, Piper. I'm sorry. You make me nervous."

I nod, a single drop of liquid disquiet breaking free.

Rex pushes it away with his thumb and crouches to be at eye level. "You fell asleep around one last night and woke up later screaming. I came downstairs to check on you. When you were calm again, you asked me to stay. I laid beside you and ran my fingers through your hair until you fell asleep again. I guess I did too, and for that, I'm sorry, but believe me, Piper, when I say that as much as I would love to make you mine in every way possible, I will never do anything until you consciously ask me to."

"Thanks." I step back, freeing myself from his touch and leaving the warm water's spray. Out of everything I'm feeling right now, embarrass-ment is the reigning emotion. I made a fool out of myself last night, needing Rex to soothe me to sleep. Then I woke up in a panic, forcing him to save me yet again. On top of all this, I accused him of taking advantage of me. Can I just melt and be washed down the drain, please?

"Are you okay to get out, or do you want to stay in the shower?"

I'm at war with myself, craving Rex's touch yet wanting to push him away. I've set the tone that I'm an unstable mess, the perfect excuse to keep our distance, but for some reason, all I want to do is redeem myself. I could use a few minutes to figure out my next move. "Would this shower be alone?"

Rex chuckles. "Of course."

I step out of the bathroom wrapped in a cloud that I never want to take off, but I need clothes. As amazing as the towel feels against my skin, I don't want to be naked all day.

Walking into the hallway, I'm lost. The house is a maze of rooms, most of which connect to each other, and I wasn't paying attention to our path when Rex carried me in.

"Rex?"

"Hey, Piper," he says, rounding the corner, hands in the pockets of his gray shorts. A plain white tee hugs his chest and arms, highlighting each muscle. I don't usually pay attention to how a guy dresses, but damn he looks good. "Feeling better?"

"Yes." *Words. Stop thinking about how amazing Rex looks and find your words!* "Um...do you know where my bag is?"

"What bag?"

No. No. No! Please tell me I brought my bag in last night. I couldn't have forgotten it, wouldn't have. "It's a gray *Nirvana* shoulder bag. It's literally my life."

"You didn't have a bag last night."

Shoot. That means I left it in Cooper's car. My bag. My extra clothes. My phone. I have nothing but a drenched school skirt and work shirt. "Perfect."

Rex's eyes shine brightly at me, a hint of danger playing in his smile. "I'm guessing you don't want to hang out in a towel all day?"

I look down at my feet, my cheeks burning hotter than the sun. "Not really."

"Want to go to the beach? You can be naked there," he says, with a grin the size of Texas. "I'll even join you."

Oh, God. Rex is thinking about me naked. He can't see me naked! I'm not presentable. Wait... why am I worried about how I look? He will *never* see me naked.

I bet he looks amazing naked, nothing but pure muscle and hard all over.

My cheeks heat again. We need to talk about something else. Anything other than Rex thinking about me naked because now I'm thinking about him. My gaze drifts to his package, a large bulge clear as the day is long that shows through those thin shorts. Scarily, it doesn't look hard, just big. There's no way he can't tell I'm checking him out, and yet I can't stop.

"Like what you see?"

I look up, mortified, but ignore the question because I'm not ready to go there... yet. "What about the mess outside?"

Rex shrugs, a cocky grin glued to his face. "The maid will clean it. She comes every Saturday and Wednesday."

Why am I not surprised he has a maid? Rex doesn't strike me as the clean-up after himself type. He leans in, invading my personal space and our gazes lock, gray meeting blue. My breaths are ragged and harsh from being this close.

What is he doing?

Is he going to kiss me? Do I want Rex to kiss me? That's a stupid question. Of course, I want him to kiss me, but twice now, I've been let down. What makes this time any different?

"You smell nice." Rex steps around me and starts up the stairs. "I know of a nude beach a few hours from here. Just saying."

I roll my eyes, pretending not to be disappointed yet again, and follow him. "You're so funny, I forgot to laugh."

Even though I work minutes from the beach, I can't remember the last time I went to it. Monica might have brought me as a kid, but I doubt it, and with a pool in the Harris's backyard, there was no reason to go. If there were clothes involved... a beach day might be nice. "Mirrors break when they see me naked. Trust me, no one wants to see this."

"I do," he mumbles.

I pretend not to hear because if I acknowledge that comment there's no going back. I'm not ready to cross that bridge yet. Dance on it a little, sure, but not cross it. "You know we could just throw my clothes in the dryer."

Rex leads me through even more rooms and then motions for me to follow him up the stairs. "Where's the fun in that?"

I chew on my lip. Rex is such a tease. I'm sure he's doing this on purpose. I need to work harder at not falling for his charm. It's probably been perfected over the years to suck girls. That won't be me. I refuse to end up in the tabloids as the latest chick whose heart was crushed by this philanderer.

Rex stops at the top of the stairs and looks down at me. "You coming?"

It's now or never.

I skip up the steps two at a time. Rex waits for me, then twists a brass handle, pushing a set of white doors open. I step inside, completely in awe, looking around. The room is vast, nearly the size of the kitchen downstairs. Bright morning light shines through open windows, painting the white carpet a pale yellow.

Rex crosses in front of a king-sized four-poster bed and heads for the closet. My fingers trail across the silk comforter, making ripples along its pristine surface.

"Alright," he says, pulling two more doors open. "I think you and my mom are about the same size. Her bathing suits are there, and sundresses are here. Pick whatever. We are going to the beach. Clothing optional, of course."

I cross my arms and lean against one of the tall posts of the bed. "You're not worried about me stealing something?"

Rex steps out of the closet, stopping inches away, the warmth of his breath tickling my cheek. He smells of coffee and mint, and I'm reminded that I haven't eaten yet when my stomach rumbles.

He glances down at my hungry tummy and smirks. One hand curls around the wooden post towering over my head, and the other settles on the footboard beside my hip. "Should I be worried?"

There's no doubt in his question. He knows the answer but asks anyway, simply for curiosity's sake. We both know I'm not what people make me out to be. Not a whore and certainly not a thief.

Walk away, Piper, before someone gets hurt.

Recognizing what I should do doesn't stop the heat from claiming my body. I tilt my head towards the jewelry on display on the vanity to my left. "That watch over there would get me a pretty penny if I pawned it."

Rex's hand moves from beside me and settles on my hip. My breath hitches. I don't know what to do with myself. *Before* Piper would have seized the moment and kissed Rex. *After* Piper would shove him in the chest and run away. But *this* Piper, this new evolving version of me, is torn between the two.

Rex leans into my hair, his chest flush against mine, and whispers, "You wouldn't dare."

His lips kiss my cheeks with a whisper of a touch and chills run down my spine to my toes. I lean a fraction of an inch closer as he backs away, our eyes locking. My pulse is everywhere again. He's close enough that I could easily reach up and pull his mouth to mine. I want his lips on mine, but am I ready for what could happen next?

My heart skips another beat. This is too many feelings too soon. I need a scapegoat, so I poke him in the ribs. "You don't know me."

Rex clears his throat and steps into his mother's closet. He runs his hand across a wall of dresses, making a wave of fabric behind him. "You're so much more than what everyone thinks you are, Piper." He turns, walks past me, then closes me in his mother's room.

Alone.

I don't dwell on his words. I can't. Rex doesn't know the first thing about me. We aren't friends. We're barely acquaintances. The instant we're back at school and surrounded by everyone, I'll be forgotten. Hanging out with me is the equivalent of committing social suicide.

But I'll bask in the limelight for a day. Live my own *Cinderella* story until the magic runs out. And yes, I know who the princesses are. I'd be a poor excuse for a girl if I didn't know at least one. I just like seeing Rex flustered. It's cute when his cheeks flush.

I step into the closet and look around. There are hundreds of thousands of dollars worth of clothes and shoes inside. Dresses from stores I probably wouldn't be allowed to enter. The clerks would take one look at my tattered school uniform and faded black hair and decide I was there to steal something. I wouldn't be, but they'd still judge me nonetheless.

I take a moment and walk to the back of the closet. Long ball gowns with sequins and feathers and decadent lace fight for space. A black one with a silver lace overlay catches my eye. I take it off the rack and walk ten steps to a full-length mirror. I hold the dress in front of me, imagining what it would be like to wear such a thing of beauty. To have my hair washed and styled by a professional. The thought saddens me.

I'll never own a dress like this.

Girls like me don't get to go to the ball.

Not in real life.

Rolling waves with bright green and blue flurries rush to shore, tumbling upon themselves to kiss paper-white sand. The crashing sound as water meets land is magnificent. Calming. Countless nights this could have soothed my nerves, lulling me into a semi-lucid sense of peace. I should have come here ages ago.

I lie on a rented lounge chair, one arm under my head and the other over my eyes. My breakdown this morning runs through my mind on a loop. I'm ashamed and embarrassed. I never should have fallen asleep. I knew better, but those damn couches got me. "I feel like I owe you an explanation."

"For what?" Rex reclines in the bright blue and white lounge chair beside me, lost in the vortex that is the TikTok app. He rented our chairs from the Horizon Hotel, as well as matching beach towels and an umbrella.

Show up with nothing. Leave with nothing. The ultimate stress-free beach experience. But renting beach gear at sixty dollars an hour is a luxury only the wealthy can afford and I'm far from wealthy.

I shift onto my side, using my hand as a shade while I squint. Rex is even more gorgeous up close than he is from afar. I couldn't appreciate his near-naked body this morning, but I have no shame in fangirling from a foot away.

His arms are bigger than I realized. Tan and veiny and muscular. Absolutely mesmerizing. His chest is defined, without an ounce of hair on his perfect body except for the small trail leading from his belly button beneath the band of gray board shorts hanging low on his hips, tempting everyone's eyes to follow it down to his package.

Mine do. Again.

"For this morning. My freak out."

Rex lets his phone fall to his lap and looks at me through his dark Oakley glasses. "It's no big deal. I'm just glad I could help. I did help...didn't I?"

"You did. Thank you." I pause, carefully choosing my next words. Rex doesn't need to know everything. The truth will scare him away, but he deserves to know something.

"I get nightmares sometimes. This morning was an exceptionally bad one. I don't know why, but it was. I just...I just wanted you to know I'm not always *that* messed up."

Rex lifts his sunglasses so I can see the blue of his irises. He squints in the sun but tries his best to look me in the eyes. "I know. Cooper warned me about them last night before he left."

Ughh...Cooper knows? Could this day get any worse?

"Do you want to talk about them?"

"Not really."

Rex sits up and kicks his legs over the side of the chair. He leans his forearms onto his legs, looks out at the ocean for a moment, and then looks back at me. "We skipped breakfast. Are you hungry?"

I'm starving.

"I could eat." I reach for my phone to check the time, then remember it's still in Cooper's car. I hate not having my bag with me. I feel naked without it. "What time is it?"

Rex chuckles. It's low and hearty, sending my pulse racing a mile a minute. "Why? You got a hot date?"

"Maybe," I smirk. "Are you jealous?"

"Definitely." Rex pushes himself out of the chair and extends a hand for me.

I hesitate. What if something changed last night? What if the switch flipped back in my brain and he can't touch me anymore?

Fearful, I take his hand, letting him pull me to my feet. To both my shock and relief, I'm fine. If anything, I'm a little excited. Rex has touched me thrice, and I've been okay each time. Maybe things are finally starting to turn around.

"It's eleven-thirty. Let's grab some brunch." Rex runs up to the tiki booth and collects his keys; they hold them hostage to ensure payment.

I slip on the cotton floral dress I found in his mom's closet. It's pretty and flowy and made by some lady named Lily. I wouldn't be caught dead in it at school. It's too colorful, but for the beach, it's nice. By the time I'm dressed, Rex is back at my side. He slips his shirt on and holds his hand out for me again. "Ready?"

I suck in a breath and reach out. My fingers touch his, inch by treacherous inch, until our hands link together. I haven't held anyone's hand since I was twelve. Even then, it was in a hurry-up kind of way. This kind of hand-holding comes with an unspoken announcement that we are something. What it might be... I don't know, but we're something.

Rex's black Oakley's rise at an angle from his lopsided smile. He squeezes my hand twice and says, "Breathe, Piper. You're alright."

And just like that, I release the air trapped in my lungs. We walk the shoreline with waves nipping at our toes. I'm flying high above cloud nine, soaking up the sun and what is probably the most perfect day I've had all year... aside from this morning's panic attack.

We walk about a mile, hand in hand, to the boardwalk. Rex lets me go, following close behind as we ascend the not-quite-wide-enough-for-two stairs. Once at street level, he links his fingers with mine again and leads us down the sidewalk. The hair on the back of my neck rises when I realize where we're going.

"What's wrong?" Rex asks.

"How did you—"

He chuckles and pulls me closer, wrapping his arm around my waist. "Your brows knit together when you're worried."

I try to smooth my forehead by spreading my eyebrows as far apart as possible. A lady walks by with her kid. The girl is five years old, maybe six, and she's staring. I must look like a freak in this bright dress, making a weird face. I bite back a laugh at the realization. I'm being stupid. I should be flattered Rex notices little things about me, not trying to change who I am. "They do not."

"Yes, they do. You wear your heart on your sleeve, Piper. If anyone paid attention, they'd see everything."

No one pays attention to me. I'm not pretty enough or rich enough.

I'm a shadow in the dark, merely existing until someone brighter comes into the room, and everyone is brighter than me. "Like what?"

"Like how the tough girl act you put on at school is just that, an act. You walk with your head held high, but clutch your books tight to your chest like your life depends on them. Your muscles tense and all color washes from your face when people touch you, even accidentally. Yet, if you touch them first you're almost fine. At first, I didn't see it, but once Cooper told me about how you don't like to be touched, I saw it every time."

For the second time today, Rex takes my breath away. "You talked to Cooper about me?"

He shrugs. "From the first day we ran into each other, I knew you were different. You just didn't know who I was."

I knew.

Whispers of Rex's arrival spread through the halls weeks before he came. Everyone wanted to meet him. Girls fanned themselves, saying how Rex would take them to New York or Paris when they dated. They'd giggle and go on and on about the life they'd have as the girlfriend of a country star's son. I swear some of them even began planning their weddings in Martha's Vineyard.

"Or maybe you did know me and didn't care. Whatever the case, it put you on my radar." Rex laughs, but there's a sadness in his eyes when they reach mine again. "Having a famous father means I have to be careful. People use me to get to him or further their agendas all the time. I needed to make sure you weren't that type of person."

"And what type of person am I?"

"The kind who would rather sit alone under a tree during her free period at the end of the day than deal with the bullshit that is our school."

I tear my gaze away from Rex's gorgeous face, needing a moment to think. I look up at the same door I've walked through three days a week. I take a deep breath and let it out through my nose.

Fuck.

We're here.

An over-the-doorbell chimes when I pull the Red Onion's door open, holding it to let Piper pass through first. Our fingers untangle as she walks by me, but I quickly claim them again once we're both inside.

Logan stands behind the counter, staring, eyes bouncing from Piper to me, back and forth more times than I'm comfortable with. He takes his phone out of his pocket, snaps a picture, then sets it on the counter.

Piper pulls her hand from mine. I grit my teeth and walk toward him, my mood souring. He's probably gonna sell that photo to the tabloids for a few hundred bucks. That's the *only* reason anyone randomly snaps pictures of me or my parents. Give it a week and people across the country will be talking about my new raven-haired girlfriend.

"What can I get you?" Logan asks with a mocking grin.

I don't bother to smile but keep my tone light. "What's good?"

Logan tips his head from side to side. "I say our lobster roll, made with real lobster on a toasted bun, smothered in butter and our almost-famous dressing, but Piper will say the BLT."

Neither sound appealing. I'm a burger and fries kind of guy, but I'm not against trying something new, especially when I just found out one of my girl's favorite foods. "I'll take one of each."

"Oh, I don't need anything," Piper chimes from behind me.

Somehow she's drifted towards the back of the room, near the door. Poor thing looks more uncomfortable than a long-tailed cat in a room full of rocking chairs. We should probably take our food to go and eat in the park a few blocks over. She seems to do better when it's just her and I. "We'll take them to go. Add two Cokes to the order, too."

"Dude, Piper just said she's not hungry. I'll get you the lobster roll but not the BLT." Logan writes a ticket and then sticks it to a nail on the doorframe in the kitchen. A hand reaches out, grabs the paper, then disappears. "That'll be eighteen-seventy-five."

Piper, not fifteen minutes ago, said that she could eat, but I'm not about to explain myself. Logan's not her keeper. Or mine. I'll order what I want and get it because the customer is always right. I cross my arms. "I want both."

"I'm not stupid, Bro."

"Never said you were, but if you think you are, I won't argue." I know I'm a jock—so to speak— but high school football players have a stereotype, even more than hockey players.

Logan's brother, Cooper, lives up to this stereotype. Good looking. Dumb. And a pussy magnet, although he does well to keep that on the DL. It only makes sense that Logan is all of that with a dash of fuck-the-world.

"Logan, it's fine." Piper steps into my peripheral vision. She drops her arms to the side and stands up tall, but red marks from her nails pepper her wrist. It's obvious she has a history of self-harm; her tattoos do a shit job of hiding it. My brows furrow as a new thought crosses my mind, and I hope I'm not pushing her too far out of her comfort zone.

"No. It's not okay, Piper. Why are you here with *him?*" Logan growls, holding a hand out at me.

I take a deep breath, count to three in my head before exhaling, and try to think before I speak. All the things the counselor at my old school said to try to help me keep my cool. His methods are bullshit. "Why do you care?"

"Logan, stop." Piper's voice cracks. She's on the verge of tears again, and he doesn't seem to notice. The poor girl might be about to have a repeat of this morning and this prick won't back down.

"Because she's my brother's best friend and practically my sister. And you're a dick," Logan barks.

Just because I don't want to deal with the everyday drama of people that I don't give two shits about doesn't make me a dick. Logan, on the other hand, is practically a modern-day Edward Cullen with his dark hair, selectively social ways, and overall fuck the world attitude. "Says the biggest asshole in the room."

"At least I don't lead girls on. Fuck them and then purposely break their hearts." Logan's voice is so loud it bounces off the walls.

Everyone in the room is watching us, but I don't care. He started this war and I'm going to finish it on principle. Besides, I love a good fight. Words, fists, or feet, the messier the better. "The hell you don't! You've tagged more pussy in the past four months than Hugh Hefner did in his prime."

Logan's face pinches together. "Who the fuck is Hugh Hefner?"

All this yelling is bound to set Piper off, and I don't want to be that catalyst. I take another slow breath and give him the calmest, most placating tone I can manage. "I'm not a player, Logan. Whoever you're pissed off about knew long before she crawled into bed with me that I don't date."

"Exactly! And I don't want Piper crawling in bed with you!" Logan yells.

Fuck being calm! I'm so mad I could punch Logan in the face. He's lucky there's a counter between us and a room full of people with the possibility of too many cameras. I don't need another lecture about my temper from my dad's publicist. "Well, I don't think what Piper does is any of your business!"

"Enough!" Piper shouts.

PIPER

I should have suggested someplace different as soon as I realized where we were going. Being Saturday, I thought—no, hoped—Logan would be in the kitchen today and not at the counter. It's not often, but he'll cook and let Juan man the counter when his hangover is bad enough. I crossed my fingers and wished that he drank too much last night.

As usual, luck isn't on my side.

Logan's beady brown eyes stare at me. Judging me for my bright colors and for walking in with Rex. The little blue vein next to his right eye bulges, a tell-tale sign of a storm brewing inside him, so I wiggle my hand away from Rex and take a step back. Logan's never seen me with anyone other than Cooper. This protective big brother thing he's got going on, mixed with his temper, is a recipe for disaster.

I'm not wrong. Rex and Logan are arguing. I dig my nails into my wrist, hoping the pressure will stop the noose tightening around my neck. My scars hum, reminding me I'm weak and can't even die when things get *sticky*. Even though I'm trying to move on with my life, every time things get hard my wrists scream: *Try again. You'll get it this time.*

I cover my ears with my hands. There's too much yelling—both inside my brain and out. I can't take it anymore. It's too much. "Enough!"

Both boys stop arguing and stare at me.

Silence. *Thank God.* I lower my hands and cross my arms. My body trembles, the invisible noose so tight around my neck that I can barely swallow my saliva, but I do my best to keep it together.

"I don't want you hanging out with him, Piper." Logan crosses his arms. "The dude is trouble."

Logan has no idea what trouble is. He thinks losing a football game is the end of the world. Grow up playing in the streets with no shoes, in tattered clothes while your mamma screws someone in your bed, then talk to me about trouble. "Weren't you just at Rex's house last night?"

"Yeah, and so were you." Logan pauses. His brows knit together as recognition that I was at a party sinks in. "Wait... why were you there? You hate parties."

I flick my hand at him dismissively. "It doesn't matter, Logan. You're out of line. Rex has been amazing today. You owe him an apology."

Logan chuckles condescendingly. He takes a small step forward and rests his hands on the counter, looking me dead in the eyes. "Are you serious? What are you gonna do, Pipes? You're all bark and no bite. Everyone knows you're soft."

So much for Brother of the Year.

Even though I knew eventually Logan would show his true colors again, the cut of his rough edges still hurts. He had been so sweet and caring the last eight months I'd almost forgotten how much of a dick he could be.

This was the Logan who hated me, the one who started the rumors.

I step closer, reach across the counter, and grab Logan by the shirt collar. "Try me, Logan. I've been through enough shit to give your nightmares nightmares. Just because you're family doesn't mean I won't break you the way you tried to break me."

EIGHT DAYS LATER

*D*ing. *Ding. Ding.*

The alert of my phone breaks the silence around me, killing any chance I had at a stealthy entry into Monica's house. I should have put it on Do Not Disturb. I flip the button on the side of my phone, killing the ringer before I forget again. Stopping beside a bush, I look around, making sure I'm not being watched before reading the text.

> Unknown Number: Hey! I looked for you at lunch.
>
> Unknown Number: I actually went into the cafeteria. You should feel loved.
>
> Unknown Number: Did you ditch?
>
> Unknown Number: It's Rex btw.

A small smile graces my lips. I checked my phone way too many times last week after giving Rex my number. Considering how everything went down with Logan and our awkward goodbye, I wasn't sure I'd hear from him, but I was hopeful.

After the first day, I thought he was doing that wait-so-you-don't-seem-anxious-thing. After two days, I began to worry and almost texted him, but didn't. I refuse to come off as that girl who can't take a hint.

61

Besides, I didn't want to embarrass myself on the off chance that I was a charity case.

After three days, I gave up all hope of hearing from him. And then, a full eight days later, after I've washed all thoughts of Rex from my mind and accepted that last weekend was nothing more than a pity hang-out, he texts me.

My stomach flutters, but I kill the feeling with emotional cyanide—this is probably just a booty text. After all, I'm supposed to be the school slut. Why else would Rex wait a whole week to text? Still, I save his number and shoot back a quick reply.

> Me: Yeah. Had some stuff to do that couldn't wait.

Like sneak into my bio-mom's apartment and steal her child support check.

> Me: Where were you last week?

> Rex: It was Gretchen's birthday. I flew back to New York to celebrate.

Ah...the nanny. That was nice of him. Too bad he forgot how to use a phone in New York.

> Me: For a week?

> Rex: Go big or go home.

> Rex: Did you miss me? ;)

A little.

> Me: You wish.

Three little thought dots appear on the screen, then disappear. They do that six times before another text finally comes through.

I shove my phone back in my bag and take a deep breath. I hate coming home, not that I've ever considered this place home. It has four walls, a front door, a dirty kitchen, a bathroom, and two tiny bedrooms, but that's all. There have never been any family pictures on the walls or home-cooked meals, no goodnight kisses or how was your day hugs. These four walls are as empty of love and nurturing as my wallet is of money.

With a trembling hand, I turn the handle on our front door. I don't have a key, let alone need one, because the house is never locked. Anything of value was sold years ago to feed Monica's habits or stolen by the people she brought home.

The door creaks as it opens. I peek my head in, making sure the coast is clear before stepping inside and closing it behind me. It's been five weeks since I've been here, but nothing's changed, not that I expected it to. Flies buzz over molding pizza boxes and faded red solo cups that cover every inch of the kitchen counter. I cover my mouth, choking back a gag.

I walk around the couch to the coffee table, where mail is piled a mile high, and freeze.

Monica is passed out on the couch, one arm over her eyes. The other dangles off the side, her fingers brushing the floor. She's even thinner than the last time I saw her, practically skin and bones. Box red hair, more of a faded maroon than the desired color, is splayed across her cheeks and pillow. Her skin has transcended from a warm olive to an almost translucent yellow in this dim lighting. Track marks scar her arms and for a moment I feel bad for her.

Life is just a catalyst of decisions, spinning you high above the clouds or burying you beneath the dirt. One wrong choice and I could easily end up like her. I can't help but wonder what happened to her. What terrible experience made her feel the need to banish all thoughts, all worries, with heroin and alcohol and everything else she does?

I push these thoughts aside. It doesn't matter what happened to Monica. Nothing in her past will ever excuse what she did to me.

I crouch down and sift through dozens of envelopes filled with past-due notices and collection letters. It's a wonder how she hasn't been evicted yet. I used to pay everything— the lights, the water, most of the rent. The landlord, when we were short, which was practically a monthly occurrence, would take payment in the form of Monica's pussy. She probably still pays him that way. Finally, I find the envelope I'm looking for and tuck it into my back pocket.

"Where do you think you're going?" Monica mumbles as I rise to my feet. Her voice is like nails on a chalkboard, grating my nerves and inciting a rage I'm not proud of.

"Out."

"I have a client tonight," she hollers from the couch.

I walk to the kitchen and open the fridge. Unsurprisingly, it's empty. By the looks of things, it has been for a while. I slam it closed and half-empty bottles of liquor rattle like a deranged wind chime. "You always have a client." *Or five.*

Monica quit working Avenue D when she met Gerald last year, which was more of a curse than a blessing. Gerald brought his clients, his drugs, and his thugs into my four walls, and there was nothing I could do about it. What's worse, he was Monica's supplier, paying her with heroin more nights than not. "Don't bite the hand that feeds you."

"When exactly was the last time you fed me, Monica?"

She sits up and throws a wrinkled McDonald's bag at me. "There, I fed you."

It lands at my feet as she lies back on the couch. She clicks the TV on, watching static on the cable-less screen. I pick up the bag and unroll it open. My stomach lurches into my throat from the smell. I crumble the bag and toss it onto the mountain of filth that is her trash can.

"Yeah, because giving me rotten food counts as feeding." I roll my eyes and cross the room to the front door. I need to leave. These walls are paper-thin. Someone is bound to hear us arguing, and that someone will probably tell one of Gerald's thugs I'm back. The last thing I need is a tail.

Monica sits up again, and her lips purse together, making her hollow cheeks even more skeletal. "You're an ungrateful little bitch."

"What do I have to be grateful for?" I scoff. The piss-yellow walls from all the cigarette smoke in the house? Piles of dirty dishes in the sink that I *refuse* to wash because I don't live here? The cockroaches that scurry from one leftover fast food container to another because her so-called friends don't know how to throw shit away? Or how about the pimp who broke into my room and tried to rape me?

Monica's up and in my face before I can finish my thoughts. Bone chillingly thin hands on her scrawny hips. For a half-dead thing, she moves fast. "I keep a roof over your head. If not for me, you'd be out on the streets."

Mommy dearest is delusional. She still thinks I hide in my room at night, pretending monsters aren't real. Newsflash. They are. She let them into our house, and now they claw into my dreams. "Keep telling yourself that, *Mom*."

SMACK.

My fists ball at my sides. I clench my teeth and look back at Monica's smug expression, ignoring my throbbing cheek. She crosses her arms, proud of herself, like she just caught me sneaking out in the middle of the night. Mother of the year right here. I roll my tongue across my teeth and nod. I'm done. Done talking to her. Done being here. Just done.

She arches a drawn-on brow. "You got something to say?"

"Nope," I say and walk out the door.

Chapter 11
PIPER

"**Y**ou're fucking stupid," a familiar voice rumbles as I walk into the breezeway of Monica's apartment.

"Tell me something I don't know," I say, shutting the door behind me. I rub my cheek. Monica hit the same spot Tad did a couple of weeks ago. I'll be lucky if it doesn't bruise again.

Bane, my tattoo artist and best friend on this side of town, holds his hand out. I shake it, our usual greeting, and step in for a hug— an unusual part of our greeting. My small arms wrap around his hard frame, clad in dark blue jeans and a heavy metal T-shirt.

I ignore the pressure in my chest building with each millisecond we touch because, like Cooper, he needs to know I'm okay. He wraps one arm around me and dozens of needles spread down my spine.

"Woah, Piper." He takes a step back, puzzled. Like Cooper, he knows my issues with touch, which means he realizes how special this moment is. "What was that for?"

I blink back tears and smile, then shrug. I owe Bane everything. He kept me safe when I ran to his house covered in blood. He took me to the shower, stripped me down, and cleaned me off with no questions asked. He covered for me when the goons came knocking. Kept me hidden for a few days until it was safe to move me. Without him, I'd probably be dead... No, I'd definitely be dead.

"How are you?"

"Not too bad, actually." I lean against the wall and prop one foot up.

Even though I saw Bane when he did my tattoo a few days ago, I miss how things used to be. I miss hanging out every night and how he'd walk me home to make sure I arrived safely, practically tucking me in while threatening any *John* who looked my way. I guess I just miss him.

"I see this. You're practically glowing."

I roll my eyes. "Bite me."

"Tell me when." He grins, but that smile falls as quickly as it comes. "Bad news, love."

We take the stairs, one step at a time, enjoying each other's company even if our conversation is weighted. "There's a bounty on your head. Fifty-thousand to the person that brings you to Gerald alive when he gets out."

I stop two steps from the bottom, my heart fluttering faster than a cheetah on crack. I assumed Gerald was trying to find me, but hearing Bane's words validate my fears. I look around again. There are no eyes that I can see, but that doesn't mean someone we don't know isn't watching. "Is that why you came to Monica's, to collect me?"

I already know the answer. Bane wouldn't betray me like that. Our history goes back to before I got picked up by CPS. We lived in the same apartment building back in the day. His mamma used to feed me when mine was too busy to remember I existed.

Flash forward to when I moved back to this side of the tracks almost four years ago. Monica moved to a new building, much to my disappointment, yet somehow Bane knew I'd returned. He came to my door, hugging me the moment I opened it—before I had a chance to speak, before I could ask who he was, not that I needed to. He found me and has been my guardian on this side of the tracks ever since.

"Never, Pipes." Bane takes a step closer and smiles down at me. His shoulders round, fingers clenching and unclenching at his sides. He wants to touch me to assure me that he's got my back, but he won't. "I knew you'd come for the check. I wanted to warn you."

I relax, but only a little. My life is still on the line. Even under his protection, every second I waste in this shitty neighborhood puts me at risk of being discovered. "I'm a dead girl walking. Got it."

Bane sits on the bottom step, his broad frame filling most of the space. To me, he's a grizzly bear and about as scary as they get around here. At five-foot-eleven, the guy is stout. All muscle and covered with more tattoos than Travis Barker, but it's not his appearance that people fear. His dad is Gerald, the drug dealer Monica sold my virginity to. The most dangerous, heartless man in the tri-county area.

"May tenth," he says, and I feel the color drain from my face.

"No." I fall to the ground beside him, my dreams and plans crumbling all at once. It can't be the tenth. If I don't walk at graduation, any hope I had at a semi-decent paying job after high school goes out the window.

Once again, Life's fucked me.

"Graduation?" he asks, connecting the dots.

"Yeah, it's May fifteenth."

Bane sighs and pulls a pack of cigarettes from his pocket. He slips one slender stick between his lips and holds the pack out for me. I shake my head. I don't smoke, hardly ever drink, and damn sure don't do drugs. Covering the end with his hand, he flicks the spinner on his lighter and sucks in a breath. "Fuck," he says on an exhale. "Can you still get your diploma if you skip it?"

I shake my head. My heart's about to burst out of my chest and run across town to find out without me. I take Bane's lighter and play with the spinner because doing *something* settles my nerves. "I don't know, but I can ask."

"Do it. I've got a guy on the inside. I've heard what Gerald's got planned for you," Bane pauses and rests his hand on mine. My gaze drifts upward, meeting his. Green eyes brimmed with worry stare into mine. "He can't have you, Piper."

"I'VE WAITED A LONG TIME FOR THIS," HIS DEEP VOICE PURRS.

My eyes flutter open to the sound of a door clicking shut. The room is spinning like an amusement park ride, only it's far from enjoyable, and everything is blurry.

I shouldn't have drunk so much tonight, but a girl only turns eighteen once. I try to sit up but a hand pushes me back down.

"Shhhh," he says.

The bed dips as someone sits on top of me. Adrenaline kicks in and my brain begins to work again—my vision clears, the room stops spinning, and what's left of my drunken hangover is gone.

"What the hell do you think you're doing? Get off me!" I scream.

Gerald, my mom's drug dealer, laughs and unbuckles his belt. "I paid a pretty penny to have you, Piper. You're finally going to be a woman tonight."

I suck in a breath, frozen underneath his weight. Monica couldn't have sold my virginity. She wouldn't. But deep down, I know that was a lie.

Monica has never had a motherly bone in her body. If not for the government benefits—food stamps, housing assistance, and a monthly stipend—I would have been out on the street the week Child Services moved me back in.

"Two hundred dollars for one night with Monica's pretty little girl." Gerald runs a cold, fat finger down my cheek. "Mommy dearest wouldn't budge at first, but when I cut off her supply, she caved, desperate for it like a cat in heat."

I won't let this happen. I refuse to lose my virginity to an obese drug dealer with a god complex. Adrenaline pumps through my veins, freeing my body from its statue-like state. I beat my fists against his chest and try to wiggle and push him off me. He shifts his body, maybe because of me or maybe by his own doing; either way, the change in his weight distribution is killing my legs. "I'll pay whatever you want! Just get off me, Gerald!"

"Quit your fussing."

I lift my knees a fraction of an inch, wiggle my hips, and press my hands against the mattress to pull myself from underneath him, but he's too heavy. So, I try something else. I scream, "Help!"

A fist the size of a softball hits my cheek, silencing me. The world turns black for a moment, then comes into focus again in spotty circles. I stretch my jaw. Pain radiates up my cheek and down my neck, but I can still move it. I don't think it's broken.

I shift to wipe blood from my lip. Gerald takes hold of that hand first, then the other, holding both above my head. He wraps something around my wrists and ties me to the bed frame. I wiggle, tug, and pull again but nothing I do makes a difference.

Tears flow from me like a wide-open faucet. "Please don't do this. Think about Bane. He'll hate us both."

Gerald laughs, uninterested in what his son thinks of him. He fists the neck of my tank-top, and in one swift motion, my shirt is ripped open. A calloused hand cups my breast, squeezing so hard it feels like he's about to rip my skin off. His other hand slips beneath the band of my shorts, his fingers touching me where no man has been, nails scraping at my insides. "You're so fucking tight."

I whimper, too scared to move lest it makes the pain worse. Tampons suck, but this feels like a million razor blades making tiny cuts between my legs.

He pushes another finger inside.

The mascara I wore earlier in the night stains my cheek. I turn my head, biting my lip to keep from screaming because it hurts so bad. I can't imagine what sex feels like. If it's anything like this, I don't want to find out.

I have to do something to make him stop. I open my eyes and scan my bedside table and a glimmer of blue and silver catches my attention.

Gerald takes my chin between his thumb and forefinger, forcing me to look at him. "You will watch, you will scream, and you'll remember that I own you now, puppet."

I WAKE UP TREMBLING, DRENCHED IN SWEAT, MY SHIRT STICKING TO whatever it is I'm lying on. My breaths come in shaky bursts as I look around—dim lights, blue benches, black windows—I'm still on the bus.

I crashed on the bus.

It was only ten-thirty when I sat down after my shift at the Red Onion, but now... I pull my phone out of my shoulder bag and look at the screen, ignoring Cooper's two dozen text messages and his three voicemails. One AM. I passed out for almost four hours.

What the hell is up with me not setting my alarms?

I grab my bag, stuff my phone inside, and walk down the narrow aisle to the front bench.

Sheila, the driver, smiles at me through the large mirror above the windshield. "Morning, pumpkin."

Before moving back in with the Harris's this year, I spent many nights on this bus. Sheila would be ready with a pillow and blanket, picking me up at the start of her shift at nine and dropping me off at school at six, no questions asked. She was a godsend.

I slide into the bench nearest her. The bus is empty except for Homeless Fred, who's passed out in the middle row. "Where are we?"

"A1A. I'm fixing to be at my Casa Linda stop. It's not on my route, but I can circle down to Delaware and then take you home, if you want, unless you're back at that one house again. I can take you there too, sugar."

Rex lives in Venetian Village off of Casa Linda. I mull over my options. I don't want to go home and answer Cooper's questions. He means well but, right now, I need a friend, not a dad. And I damn sure don't want to go back to sleep. I think Rex said he was having a party. It's late, everyone should be gone. Then again, it would be my luck that everyone is still there. Whatever, I'll give it a shot. I shake my head. "Nah, I'll get off at the next stop."

We arrive at Casa Linda's community gate a few minutes later. Sheila parks the bus but doesn't immediately open the door. Her gaze rakes over me, a concerned look on her face. "You sure you're alright, pumpkin?"

I sling my bag over my shoulder and stand. "Yup, just a bad dream."

A CLOUDLESS NIGHT SMILES DOWN ON ME AS I WALK THE DESERTED road, thousands of bright stars twinkling in a moonless sky. A lifetime ago, on a night like this, I would have laid on the hood of Bane's late nineties model Lincoln, listening to him talk about the constellations. He loves astronomy. Now, they're just one more reminder of the life I'll have to give up.

I feel a mixture of unease and relief as I come up to Rex's house. Dozens of overpriced imports linger along the street like a beacon to my safe haven—Mercedes, Lexus, Ferrari, BMW— it's a carjacker's heaven. Just for the hell of it, I touch the handle of the car nearest me, a sleek black BMW that probably belongs to some rich-bitch at school who can't stand me. The handle lifts. The door opens. No alarm.

Idiot.

I slip inside, leaving the door ajar. I run my hands over the steering wheel, imagining what it would be like to have a car. Not this one. I don't need something this fancy. Just something. The only thing I have that's mine is my clothes, and I don't have much of those either.

The memory of my nightmare hangs over me like a shadow, it's why I try not to sleep. Every time I close my eyes, bits and pieces of that night come back to haunt me. Most of the time, I wake before anything real happens. Sometimes, it'll be flashbacks of the party and me stumbling into my room or the sound of the door creaking open, waking me. But tonight...I shake my head. My hands tremble, each breath a task of its own. I need to forget.

I sigh and let my head fall against the back of the plush seat. The silver cap of a bottle hiding in the passenger door catches my eye—vanilla rum. I grab it, twist the cap off the half-empty bottle, and bring the rim to my lips. It's sweet. Sickeningly sweet, but for a moment, Gerald's face is gone. My trembling hands steady, and I take the easiest breath I've taken all night. I take another swallow and get out, letting the door slam shut behind me.

I don't drink anymore because of that night. I can't help but think that if I hadn't been so fucked up, I could have woken sooner, maybe even stopped things before they went as far as they did. But if drinking makes the memories go away, then fuck it. I take another sip and the overly sweet flavor becomes more tolerable with each step, each swallow.

For the first time in a long time, I feel alright.

"Rex!" Piper squeals excitedly when I step onto the back patio.

I went inside to piss and, like a birthday wish come true, she's here. I missed her this week. As much as I wanted to call, I couldn't. I promised Gretchen a distraction-free week for her birthday. I spent too many days on my phone, paying attention to people who didn't matter instead of giving her the time of day. I took Gretchen for granted and this week was my happy-birthday-I'm-sorry-I-appreciate-you present. Which meant that from the moment she picked me up from the airport until I came home my phone was off.

Piper is practically glowing tonight, free of all the troubles she normally carries around. Her head tilts and a sexy smile graces those deep red lips. A mostly empty bottle of what looks like rum slips from her hands and falls to the floor, forgotten. She runs over to me and throws her arms around my neck.

I pull Piper tight against my chest, lifting her off her feet, relishing this moment because I know it might be a while before I get to have her like this again.

From everything I've gathered, Piper hates all human contact, but for some reason she likes me. I drink her in, her soft curves molding against my hard edges. After not nearly enough time, I set her back on her feet. I know I'm pushing my luck, but my hands settle on her hips because I'm not ready to let her go.

Glossy gray eyes look up to me. So light. So happy. They crush my soul because as much as I love seeing Piper so free, it's fake. She's drunk, and from everything I've learned, this is unusual.

Piper chews on her bottom lip, then rises onto her toes, pressing her mouth against mine. Her lips are softer than the petals of a rose. She tastes like vanilla mixed with pure desire. I thread my fingers through her hair, ruining her ponytail, deepening the kiss. Our tongues dance together, discovering more of each other and she groans into my mouth, pulling me further down the rabbit hole that is Piper. I know I shouldn't let myself fall into her lips. Nothing good can come of it.

But she kissed me first.

Piper pulls back, her lips swollen from pressing against mine. Heavy lids hide most of her eyes. "Mmm," she grins. "You're good at that." She spins in my arms, throws her hands up, and yells, "Woooo!"

Piper drifts to the center of the room and dances to a Top-40 song by herself. Her hips sway, dipping low, then coming back up again. It's a beautiful sight, even if she is clumsy and drunk. I step forward, ready to claim her as mine again when someone claps their hand on my shoulder, "My man!"

I look behind me and am met with brown hair and bloodshot eyes. Irritated at his timing, I force a grin. Every second I spend talking to this jackass is that much longer I'm away from Piper. I've already spent nine painstaking days wondering what it would be like to have her in my arms. Now that I know, I want her back in them as soon as possible. "Hey, Logan."

He is lit. Having drank a handle of Captain Morgan by himself, I don't know how he's still standing. All night, he's pretended the argument at the Red Onion last week never happened, acting like we're old buddies. I play his game, hoping Piper will see that I can be the bigger person.

Logan holds up his phone and takes a video of Piper dancing. It's irritating because somehow, I know this is going to bite Piper in the ass so I push his phone down.

Logan, seemingly unaware that I moved his arm, tucks his phone back into his pocket. "Dude, I don't know how you did it, but thanks."

Before I can reply, Tad slinks up behind Piper. I grit my teeth, pissed, because that should be me. Also, I warned him to stay away. Had I known Piper was coming tonight, I would have kicked him out the moment he stepped through my gate. He grabs her hips and pulls her against him.

I take a breath and try to swallow the bile creeping up my throat. It's fine, they're just dancing.

But then his palm slides up her stomach, settling on her chest, and I snap. I cross the room and grab Tad by the collar of his shirt, pulling him away from Piper. She stumbles back, having relied on him for balance, but finds her footing again.

I narrow my eyes at him. "Leave."

Tad chuckles, ignoring me. It's clear as day that Piper is drunk, and the fact that he thinks it's okay to grope a girl when she's drunk puts him lower than dirt in my book.

Tad wraps his arms around her waist again and dips his head, lips pressing against the smooth skin of Piper's neck. Her head tips back, and a moan escapes her. A moan that almost sounds like my name. I'd be thrilled if it were me causing those sounds, but it's not.

"Last chance, Tad."

"Screw you, Montgomery," he says, nipping at her. "You had your fun last weekend. It's my turn."

I'm going to kill him!

I grab Tad's shirt collar again and yank him back once more. Piper loses her balance this time and falls to the floor, and throws up all over her legs. She's more drunk than I realized. All the more reason no one should be touching her tonight, especially him.

My instinct is to go to her side, but Tad swings at me. He's a shit fighter, barely able to make a dent in the punching bag in the school's gym, and slow. I dodge his right hook and sock him in the nose with a jab. He throws another punch that hits me in the ear. It's a lucky shot. If I hadn't taken my eyes off him to glance at Piper, he never would have landed a hand on me. My ear throbs, but it doesn't slow me down. I live for this shit. Getting to beat the crap out of people is part of what I love about playing hockey, and I'm a damn good fighter.

I throw a combo—jab to the face, left hook to the ribs, right hook to the ribs, uppercut to the jaw. Tad's balance wavers, and he falls. I straddle him and punch him some more. Hit, after hit, after hit, until his face is a bloody mess.

Tad raises his arms to block, but it doesn't make a difference. My fists slam into his arms, and his arms hit his face. The fucker should have learned the first time not to touch my girl.

A set of hands snake up my chest and yank me off before I do lasting damage. "You good, Bro?"

Logan watches me like I'm a rabid dog. He's probably worried I will attack again, and depending on Tad's next move, I just might.

Tad groans and rolls onto his knees. His lip is busted, nose is broken and twisted to the side, and one eye is already swelling shut. Two guys from the football team come to his side, helping him onto his fat hobbit feet.

I point to the gate, my chest heaving as I try to calm down. "Get the fuck out. Everyone."

Within minutes, the deck is cleared. I only threw tonight's party because Logan overheard my conversation with Piper. I would have been more than happy to call it an early night after this morning's redeye, but on the off chance Piper decided to come by, I went ahead and threw the party. I'm glad I did. I wouldn't want her drunk like this anywhere else.

I bend down and swoop Piper into my arms, puke and all. She leans into my chest, nuzzling her cheek against my shirt. I open one of the double doors with the hand under her legs. Piper groans and twists into my arms, turning away from me.

"It's okay, beautiful. I've got you."

My head is killing me. I swear Thor is beating against it with a million tiny hammers, and my skin feels like it's being ripped off. Each movement, even in the smallest of ways, hurts. It's been almost a year since my last hangover, and I could easily go another year without one. Why did I drink again?

Because it made you forget.

Oh yeah.

I rub my hands down my face and open my eyes and the room comes into view—tan walls, navy sheets, and a large window that lets in too much light. This isn't Cooper's room. Shit, this isn't any room in the Harris house.

Where am I?

I kick the covers off and sit up. The world spins around me like it does when you're on a carnival ride, but his ride sucks. I want off. I press my palm to my head, hoping to halt the movement inside my brain. It helps a little, but not nearly enough to make the day tolerable.

I take a breath and cross my legs, placing my hands on the mattress, trying to balance while looking down at myself. I'm in a green shirt that has a deer wearing silver glasses and red and black striped boxers. Last time I checked, I was in jeans and a T-shirt.

Where the hell did this shit come from?

I groan and throw myself back onto the pillow. Last night comes flickering back in pieces. Kissing Rex. Dancing with Tad. Letting Tad kiss my neck. *Fuck.*

None of last night was normal for me. I hate that I drank so much and that I can't remember what I did or didn't do beyond that kiss. I squeeze my eyes shut and press my fingers to my temples.

Think.

Think.

Think.

I've got nothing. Everything after Tad nipping at my neck is gone, sucked into a black hole. I shudder at the thought of what might have happened.

I hate him.

Although right now, I hate myself more. Tad is the last person on Earth that I'd give my firsts to. My real firsts, I don't count the ones that were stolen from me.

I sit up, slower this time, and tip-toe out of the bed, hoping to find a clue as to where I am. I look around the room. It's simple, with a desk and chair, a lamp, and two bedside tables. But there are no pictures to indicate whose room this is. No art to make the place feel homey. Hell, there isn't even a TV.

Something else I don't see... My clothes.

I pad across the hardwood floors, cautious that someone will know I'm awake. That would be my luck. My hand barely touches the knob on the bathroom door when there's a knock at the door.

I freeze. Do I answer? What if it's Tad? It didn't even occur to me until now that this could be *his* house.

What if he wants to do whatever we did last night again? I swallow hard, my mind veering into darker directions, like what if I went home with someone completely different? Someone I can't remember because I was drugged? I stole that bottle of Rum. Who knows what could have been in it?

Shit. Shit. *Shit*!

They knock again. Whoever it is knows I'm here. It's not like I can hide in the closet and pretend like I left. But maybe the window...

I run back to the bed and look out the panes. I'm on the second story, overlooking the neighbor's house. There's no way to get down without breaking my ankle or scaling the roof, and even then, I might still be stuck.

Begrudgingly, I slip back into the bed and pull the covers to my chest. "Come in."

Barely a second passes, but it feels like a lifetime. The hairs on my arms stand on edge, and tiny tremors make their way through my body as my anticipation grows. Last night is a new phantom haunting my thoughts, but what's done is done. One thing's for certain, I am *not* doing anything with anybody this morning.

The door creeps open. I suck in a breath and wait. The tip of a black flip-flop comes into the room, followed by a leg and then finally, the face. A sigh of relief escapes me when I see who it is.

Rex.

As crazy as it sounds, I don't think Rex would have let me do anything I'd regret, and for that I'm grateful. If ever there was a strange bed I'd want to wake up in, it would be his.

He walks into the room with a glass of water in one hand and a plate with a large blueberry muffin in the other. He sets everything on the nightstand closest to me, pulls the curtains shut, and then sits on the edge of the bed. "Good morning, beautiful."

"Morning."

Rex looks crisp. Even in a faded T-shirt and shorts, he could pass for a model. I don't know why his parents didn't get him into that business. Rich people always try to get richer off their kids. Wait. Maybe that's poor people. Is it that the rich and famous try to keep their kids out of the spotlight? I don't know. It doesn't matter. Rex isn't famous, and I'm never going to have his kids.

"Here," he says, unzipping the singular side pocket on his shorts, pulling out a small bottle of aspirin. "Take these. You'll feel better in about an hour."

I hold out my hand. "Thanks."

Rex shakes two pills loose. I toss them into my mouth and grab the water off the nightstand. After a quick swallow, I set the cup back beside me, expecting him to leave, but he doesn't. He stares at me, brows knitted together, worry painted on his face.

Worry swirls in my stomach. Is he going to tell me that *we* did something last night? I try to scan my thoughts again, but all I could find is a kiss. One glorious kiss that sends my pulse into warp speed just thinking about. "Everything okay?"

"You threw up on yourself last night..." Rex pauses and runs his hand through his hair, pushing those dark locks away from his eyes. They fall back into place a moment later, looking better than ever. "I put you in the shower and changed you., but don't worry. You weren't naked, I kept your bra and panties on."

"Oh. Um. Thanks." That explains why I can't find my clothes. Rex probably put them to wash. Now that he mentions it, I notice the rancid scent of puke on myself. He must not have scrubbed me clean, only ran water over my body. As grateful as I am for his respect, I'm a little disappointed. I need a reason *not* to like Rex. A pervy, horny teenager is the perfect excuse, but he's a true gentleman.

"You should probably take another shower, though. All I did was rinse you off. Towels are in the bathroom already." Rex stands and hitches his thumb over his shoulder. "I'm gonna head downstairs. Eat something. Maybe sleep some more, too. I promise if you do, you'll feel better in a few hours."

"Thanks," I mumble as he walks out.

Four hours pass before I hear a pitter-patter on the stairs. I close my team's playbook and walk toward the front entryway. There are only so many stairs, and by the time I reach the hallway, Piper is at the bottom.

She's stunning. Her long hair is tucked behind her ears, falling in damp spirals past her shoulders. She's found a clean shirt of mine and a pair of basketball shorts that I forgot I hid in that closet.

Who did I hide my clean clothes from?

Myself.

I hate doing laundry.

"Morning, beautiful."

Piper leans one arm on the banister and smiles. I know I shouldn't get used to this. She's a guarded girl who tries to hide her emotions, but damn she's radiant when she lets her guard down.

"Hey."

"Feeling better?"

She nods. We stare at each other. Piper shamelessly eyeing me in my shorts. Me taking every inch of her perfect body. I'm mentally cataloging each detail so I can recall it later. If I had my phone, I'd snap a picture, but it's back in the living room on the couch and I don't want to spook her. "It's nearly two. Are you hungry?"

Piper's eyes widen. "Oh my God!"

I rack my brain, trying to come up with possible scenarios of what could be wrong now. I've got nothing. "What?"

"I slept through my history final." One hand pushes her long, damp bangs back. "Shit, Cherrybroom is gonna kill me."

I shake my head, trying to keep a laugh hidden. Mrs. Cherrybroom is a joke. Like most school counselors, her hands are tied in a bunch of legal mumbo-jumbo. She can't sneeze, much less do anything regarding Piper without jumping through yards of red tape. "You'll be fine, don't worry. Come on, let's have some lunch."

Piper mulls over my words for a minute and then takes my outstretched hand. She slides onto a barstool in the kitchen while I grab some sandwich materials from the fridge. "Mayonnaise, mustard, relish... Pick your poison."

"Mayo only please."

"You got it." A few minutes later, we're both eating inch-thick, deli-worthy sandwiches off paper plates. My phone vibrates on the counter, the ding of an alert sounding a half second later that a notification that a deposit of twenty-thousand dollars has been added to my account.

Another ding.

Mom: Happy birthday!

I set my phone back on the counter, face down. Every year, it's the same. No call. No card. Just a deposit and a text. My mom and Dad mean well, but at some point, they forgot what it takes to be a parent. I don't want their money. I want them to spend time with me, but since I can't have one I might as well take the other.

"You alright?" Piper asks, throwing her plate in the trash.

"I'm fine." My phone rings and for a second I think it might be my parents. They never call, let alone FaceTime, but today is special. It's not every birthday your only child turns eighteen. My heart drops the moment I see it's Jenny.

Jenny is to me what Piper is to Cooper. A girl who needs protecting, one of my best friends, and the only person from my last school to make an effort to stay in touch after I moved. While Jenny is as beautiful as the day is long, with her Barbie blonde hair and legs that go on for days, we were just friends.

Why? For starters, she's dated Ambrose since the seventh grade, but even if she was single, Jenny is too high maintenance for me. As her friend, I can tell her to stick it where the sun doesn't shine when she's being a brat. As her boyfriend, I'd have to suck it up and play nice, and I'm not about pretending when I'm in a relationship.

"Happy birthday, Rexy-Roo!" Jenny yells as soon as her face pops onto the screen.

I chuckle, her nickname bringing back a horde of drunken memories. Jenny nicknamed me Rexy-Roo after some party game last year. I guess I reminded her of a kangaroo or something. I don't know, but it stuck, and she's the only one allowed to use it. "Thanks, Jen. How are things going?"

Jenny rolls her big green eyes—always lined—lashes fluttering like butterfly wings. "It's going. My parents' divorce settled. Mom got everything. Dad and I had to move out to Southside."

Jenny had every girl's dream life—big house, fancy car, perfect boyfriend. She spent money like it grew on trees without a care in the world. Her mom was an heiress or something. I don't really know. Jenny was always vague on the details.

Life for her was good until her mom ran away with the plastic surgeon that brought her store-bought C's to D's. Jenny's dad is in construction and makes enough to survive, but not support his daughter's lavish ways. Everyone knew her mom would take them to the cleaners, not that he was Mr. Moneybags, she was just *that* kind of woman.

"Shit, that sucks."

"It's not too bad. I get to finish out the year on a scholarship, and Lula's parents said I could stay with them during the week until graduation. Dad didn't like it at first, but he came around when I got mugged on the subway."

She's riding the subway? Staying with Lula? What the hell? We have an empty house with two cars minutes from where she used to live. "Shit, Jenny! Why didn't you call me? I could have helped you."

She rolls her big eyes. "Because, Rex, I'm not your responsibility. Everything will work itself out."

I point at her through the phone. She may not be my responsibility, but she's my friend. I don't have too many of those, so I try to take care of the ones I've got. Besides, Jenny's not a user. She'd cut off her left hand before taking a handout, but knowing this doesn't stop me from offering. "Promise me you'll come to me if shit goes south. I'm only a phone call away. You know I've always got your back."

Jenny smiles, and this time, it's not one of her show-pony smiles, but a genuinely grateful grin. "I know, and that's why I love you." She flicks her hand. "Enough about me. What are you doing today? Please don't tell me you've ditched school on your birthday to wallow in self-pity. Swear to God, I'll hitchhike my way down there if you are."

I chuckle. Always a flair for the dramatics. "First of all, you will never hitchhike, and secondly..." I flip the camera around to show her Piper. "I'm spending the day with this pretty lady."

"Hi!" Jenny squeals, waving at the camera like a lunatic, which is facing me again.

"That's Piper." Beautiful, wonderful, sweet Piper. I've never mentioned a girl to Jenny. While I've had my share of beautiful women, none of them have struck me as anything more than a fling.

Until Piper.

I can't explain it, and I don't try to understand it, but being with Piper feels right.

"Well, I'm not gonna keep you any longer. Be good!" Jenny wiggles her eyebrows and then hangs up. I set my phone face down on the counter and pick at the chips on my plate.

"So, it's your birthday?" Piper asks, a sly smile on her face.

"Yup."

She leans onto the counter, a long tendril of hair falling over her shoulders. "Any big plans tonight?"

Gretchen used to make a big deal out of my birthday—surprise decorations that stopped being a surprise when I was ten, cake, presents, some fun activities with my friends. Now she's gone, and today is just another day. "You're looking at them."

Piper nods, the sparkle in her eyes fading. "My mom never celebrated my birthday. I'd never had cake until I went to live with Mamma T."

If not for Gretchen, I probably wouldn't have had cake either, but it doesn't make me any less sad for Piper. Birthdays are supposed to be fun. When I have kids, I'm going all out for them, every year. Bounce houses. Bands. Balloon-shaping clowns. You name it, they'll have it. No child should ever feel the disappointment of their parents forgetting the day they were born.

"Who is Mamma T?"

"Cooper and Logan's mom. She took me in for a few years." Piper flicks her hand, dismissing the fact like it's no big deal, but for me it's a bit of clarity. If she grew up with the Harris's, it's likely she thinks of the twins as family.

"Let's do something. It's not like we can go to school today anyway," she says suddenly.

"For a girl who skipped yesterday afternoon, you're all about your education. Aren't you?"

Piper reaches across the table and steals the other half of my sandwich. "Something's gotta get me out of this town. It sure ain't gonna be my looks."

The leather seats of Rex's Range Rover are comfy, but after two hours, I'm itching to get out of them. Sitting still with the seat belt holding me down, only able to move a few inches, is getting to me. The more I think about being trapped in the car, the worse my anxiety gets.

It's nothing against Rex. He's been great, singing along with everything from Dropkick Murphy's to Brooks and Dunn. Not surprisingly, he's got a set of pipes on him, but it's the feeling of being restrained that's bothering me. I shift in my seat for the millionth time, trying to get comfortable.

Rex hits his blinker, merging onto Interstate 75. "Fifteen more minutes, babe."

I nod, pulling at the strap across my chest. If not for the alarm signaling the seatbelt isn't fastened, I would have unbuckled ages ago, but the beeping noise it makes every three minutes drives me crazy.

After what feels like a lifetime, Rex parks along the side of a massive, tan, dome-like building with a bright yellow accent streak across its top half, ignoring the obviously marked front entrance. He gets out and runs around the front of the vehicle to open the door for me.

"I was gonna get that." Contrary to what Cooper and Bane think, I can take care of myself but I won't pass up a chance to touch this man. "I'm not a damsel in distress. You don't have to do all this."

Rex laces his fingers with mine, bumping the door shut with his hip. "All what?"

"You know. Opening doors. Helping me out."

"Ah," he says, those glorious dimples coming out to play. "You mean being a gentleman."

I twist the strap of my bag. It's been weeks since our first encounter and Rex still makes me nervous—a good, fluttery stomach, racing heart, on my toes, kind of nervous; but nervous nonetheless. He's just too sweet. I'm still not used to it. "Guys our age don't do shit like that."

Rex chuckles and pulls a key from his pocket when we reach the building. He swipes a badge against a reader beside the door marked *team members only* and then lets us into the building. His free hand goes to the small of my back, pinky dipping beneath the band of my pants, guiding me down a dimly lit hallway so cold it could be made of ice.

"Guys our age are douchebags. I'm one of a kind."

That you are, Rex. That you are.

We are in a freaking hockey arena. A cold-ass hockey arena, might I add. Rex practically skips as he guides me past the lockers to a viewing room reserved exclusively for post-game mingling. The room is a good twenty degrees warmer with four large flat-screen TVs hanging on the wall, an L-shaped sectional, and a cabinet next to the fridge. He unlocks the cabinet and grabs a green blanket from inside. "Here. This should help keep you warm."

"Thanks." I lean back against Rex's chest. He kisses the side of my head, then steadies me with his hands as he steps back.

A moment later, we're walking through a maze of hallways and entering the stadium. I've never been to a game before and am shocked upon seeing the arena's size. From the outside, it didn't look nearly this big. Distant voices of people yelling drills bounce off seemingly endless rows of empty chairs surrounding the ice.

Rex slips his hand in mine again, the familiar tingle warming my body from the inside out. "Isn't this amazing?" he asks sitting us center ice behind the penalty box.

I nod. I'm not sure what's so amazing about a bunch of guys on skates passing a puck around, but Rex looks like a kid in a candy shop, his eyes practically glistening with joy.

He whispers jargon I don't understand, trying to explain what's happening in real time, but I've zoned out. My eyes are open, I look like I'm listening, but I'm half asleep. I think it's called micro-napping. After so many hours awake, my brain needs to shut down, and this is one way it does.

The whistle blows. I blink a few times, awake again, and try to figure out what's happening on the ice. A man, presumably the coach and the only person in the rink without a helmet, skates toward us. "Montgomery, is that you out there?"

Rex holds up his hand. "Yes, sir."

"Good timing," the coach yells. "Suit up. We're about to scrimmage."

I'VE NEVER SEEN SOMETHING SO THRILLING YET TERRIFYING IN MY life. A scrimmage is basically a fight on ice. I don't even know what to call Rex's position. A hunter? Is that a thing in hockey? His job is to chase the puck while everyone else chases him and shoves him into the plexiglass wall surrounding the rink. And sometimes their sticks hit his, making a god-awful slamming sound.

I chew my nails, sitting on the edge of my seat. Rex is on the green team, competing against white. They are neck and neck, white leading by one point, and there are three minutes left in the third quarter. Are there quarters in hockey? I don't even know, but the giant timer above the ice is counting down to zero, and Rex has the puck.

Rex spins on the ice with the grace of a ballerina, dodging a defensive attack from the other team. He passes the puck just as someone from the white team rams him from the right. His helmet slams into the glass with a cracking sound. I suck in a breath, terrified that he's hurt, but he seems fine. He shoves the guy off and goes after the puck.

Green number thirteen has the puck and lines up to shoot again. White number seven heads straight for him, but Rex ducks down low and hits his opponent in the stomach with his shoulder, sending them both to the ice, while a red light spins above the net just as the timer sounds.

"Yes!" I yell, jumping up and down in my seat. Never in a million years would I have pegged myself as a hockey girl, but watching Rex out there, killing it, has made me a fan.

Coach blows his whistle and everyone skates into a line. He gives a speech I can't hear, pointing and nodding, and then blows his whistle again.

The team skates off toward the locker room, but Rex skates to me. I step onto my seat and curl my fingers over the top of the penalty box glass. He skates into the box and stands directly under me, his face about a foot beneath mine.

He takes his gloves and helmet off and sets them beside him on the bench that the players sit on when they get in trouble during the game. "So? What did you think?"

"That has to be the most amazing thing I've seen. Ever! Did you know you were going to play?"

"No, but I knew it was a good possibility." He beams. "I have an open invitation to the practices."

"Please tell me you're joking because if you're not I need to be at every one." There is something morbidly hot about watching Rex beat the living shit out of people.

He shakes his head, that grin stretching wider. "I signed a contract in February to start next season. Coach knows I'm still in school, so anytime I get to train this season is a bonus. Hey, wanna see my stick?"

He winks ant I roll my eyes and feign annoyance, but yes. Hell yes! I want to touch it, too. Rex holds his hockey stick up and I bite back a grin as I reach out to stroke it. "Looks big."

Rex's cheeks flush and I swear it's the hottest thing I've seen all day. He clears his throat and hitches his thumb behind him. "I'm gonna shower up and get changed. Meet me in the room we got your blanket from in thirty?"

"I doubt I'll find it again, but I did notice a gift shop that I can easily get to."

"Okay, let's meet there."

REX

There's nothing I love more than hockey. My stick is an extension of me, maneuvering the puck with precision. I love the feel of the cool wind kissing my face as I speed around the rink, and did I mention how much I love ramming into people who piss me off? Best of all, I'm about to get paid for it. Minor leagues pay crap, but the goal is to do a year, or two, then hit the major leagues.

But Piper sitting on the edge of her seat, talking with her hands, full of life, has become my new favorite thing. I love seeing her like this.

"And it didn't even matter that you didn't score the final goal," she continues, "because you took that guy down. Doesn't it hurt, hitting people like that?"

I chuckle, completely enamored with her. At first, I wasn't sure how Piper would like the game but now I can't wait to take her to another. Too bad the season is about to end. "It can, but we've got gear on. I also have years of practice under my belt. If I'm doing the hitting, I'm generally alright. It's the other guy's blows I've got to watch out for."

"Is that why you're so good at football?"

"What do you mean? I don't play football."

I watch Piper from the corner of my eye. Her fingers twist the strap of her shoulder bag, over and over. She closes her eyes, takes a deep breath, and then lets it out slowly. Her anxiety is getting to her. We aren't even touching and she's winding up tighter than a gnat's ass. I fight a frown. I thought we were making progress. What could she possibly be nervous about?

Piper opens her eyes but turns her gaze to the window. "P.E. You barrel through anyone that gets in your way. I'm sure Coach kicks himself in the ass for not letting you join mid-year each time you play."

I knew she watched me play. It's hard to miss her in all that black at the top of the stands, but I wanted her to admit she liked me all along. You know, ego and all. "So, she is interested," I tease.

Piper's cheeks flush and her reflection gives away the smile she's trying to hide. "I don't know what you're talking about."

"Face it, Piper. You like me. As much as you try to fight this, fight us, you want this to happen just as much as I do."

A FEW HOURS LATER, THE GARAGE DOOR CLOSES BEHIND US. PIPER enters the house first, dropping her bag on the kitchen counter.

"I've got to pee," she says, darting around the corner. She comes back a few minutes later. Hair pulled into a messy bun—shoes off—and sits on a barstool. "Now what, birthday boy?"

I lean against the edge of the counter nearest Piper. I take her hand, my thumb brushing soft circles across her palm. "Well, it's getting late. You can go back up to the guest room tonight and crash or we can fall asleep to a movie on the couch again. Your call."

Piper looks off into the distance, thinking. Each second that ticks by takes a lifetime. I study the subtleties of her face—tiny laugh lines around her eyes, divots in her skin from blemishes she probably had years ago, the seventeen freckles across her cheeks, and one that's almost too light to see just above her lips. Dark, pouty lips that I dream about every night.

I lean in, expecting to be shot down, but Piper presses into me. Our lips touch softly at first but then I feel her mouth open. She reaches for me, her hand going to the back of my head, fingers curling in my hair. I lift her onto the counter and step between her legs, eliminating the space between our bodies. The kiss is hot and needy, and it takes every inch of willpower I have not to lay her on the counter and explore the rest of her body with my tongue.

Piper pulls back, gasping for air, but I need more. My mouth finds the soft skin of her shoulder. I kiss my way up the side of her neck to her ear, taking the lobe and tiny earrings in my mouth. She gasps again, pressing her legs tighter to my sides. She tugs at my hair, demanding my lips against hers again, and I give her what she wants.

Piper pulls away a little while later, her breaths sharp and short, matching mine and those perfect lips of hers curl into a grin. "I've wanted to do that since the scrimmage. Happy birthday, Rex."

Cooper: Meet me in the stairwell

I groan and slide my phone back into my shoulder bag. As if this morning wasn't bad enough with Mrs. Cherrybroom being on my ass again about college, now I've got to deal with Cooper and whatever his problem is. I wish I could go back to last night, to kissing in the kitchen. I know Rex and I've kissed before, but I was drunk and couldn't fully appreciate it for what it was. Last night's kiss wipes the memory of the first one out of the water. Hands down!

My phone dings again.

Cooper: NOW

Ugh. I beat my head against my closed locker. Today. Sucks. Balls.

I have to stay after school to retake the history final I missed yesterday, which wouldn't be a big deal if I were allowed to make it up in my free period. But no, Mr. Burgess is making me wait until after the last bell at 2:15. Again, not a big deal if I didn't have to work tonight, and if I didn't have to catch the bus, and if I knew I could finish the test in under two hours. But all these things stacked against me, plus Cooper's shit attitude, is a vortex of bad karma that I can't swim my way out of.

Add to it that I'm going to be late for work, which is going to make him even madder at me—not that I have any clue what I've done to piss him off to begin with— and yeah...

Hands settle on my hips behind me. I should be freaking out, but I recognized Rex's cologne before his hands even found my body. I smile, taking in the scent that is Rex.

"Hey, beautiful."

I spin in Rex's arms and lean against the cold metal of my locker. His lips find mine for a chaste kiss that makes me want to skip the rest of the day and explore how he can make the rest of my body feel. He reaches behind him and pulls a small daisy from his back pocket and holds it out to me. I take the flower and bring it to my nose. The fragrance is sweet, making an unintentional smile appear. He's been doing that a lot lately, making me smile. Being together like this feels right. Like I'm supposed to be happy again.

"Here," Rex says, taking the flower from between my fingers. He snaps the stem and then tucks it behind my ear. White against black. A light in the darkness that is my life, just like him. "Much better."

"Could you be any more cliché?" I roll my eyes, pretending to be annoyed but the truth is, I love it. The gestures, the kindness, the attention. He's meeting and exceeding my expectations of what a boyfriend should be. The only part that's missing? We're not actually dating. I really don't know what we are yet.

Rex shrugs. "Probably. I can go full Prince Charming on you, if you want."

I turn and lean my back against the cold metal. He places one foot on either side of me and hooks his fingers onto my belt loops.

He dips his head, nose brushing against my cheek until his lips find my ear. "Let me make you mine and I'll treat you like a queen."

My phone dings again from my shoulder bag, saving me from a question I'm not sure how to answer. Do I want Rex to be my boyfriend? Yes, absolutely! But there's that lingering black cloud reminding me our time together is limited.

Is breaking his heart and possibly mine for a few weeks of bliss worth it? Or will it be less tortuous in the end to remain in this weird friend-dating-limbo? "I've got to meet Cooper. He's pissed off about something."

"Want me to walk you?"

I look up into those perfect blues.

So beautiful.

So full of hope.

Everything about Rex is too good to be true. Sooner or later, the shoe will drop, and by the way he's got me feeling, I'm not going to land on my feet. "If you keep hanging out with me, Rex, people are gonna start talking."

He shrugs, slipping his hand in mine. He brings my palm to his lips and softly kisses my knuckles. "They already are. I don't care what anyone thinks, Piper. I like you."

"You shouldn't." The words taste like crow because I want Rex to like me. God, I want him to like me. "Whatever this is between us, it will only end in heartbreak."

"You don't know that."

But I do. There are only four weeks until Gerald is released. I shouldn't let myself get used to having Rex around. Shouldn't like the way my hand feels in his, but I do. God, I do.

"Nice flower," Cooper chides. He leans against the navy blue handrail in the stairwell, his arms crossed, eyes narrowed. If looks could kill, I'd be dead already, but Death is a finicky bitch.

I pluck the daisy from behind my ear and let it fall to the floor. I try to keep my voice steady, but inside, I'm shaking. Things have been off between Cooper and me this year, and they are progressively getting worse. He is, and forever will be, my best friend, but still... "What's up, Coop?"

He stands straight and steps towards me, stopping inches from my face. Cooper is not aggressive. On the football field, he does what he needs to do to win the game, but he's a teddy bear off the field. This new side of him is a little scary. "You tell me, Piper."

"I don't know what you're talking about." I take a step back. Even with a few inches between us, I'm trembling. I'm not afraid of Cooper. He won't hurt me. He's just angry.

Cooper reaches into his pocket and pulls out his phone. He swipes the screen several times before shoving a group Snap story in my face. *Fucking Snapchat.*

There is a frame of me pressed against Tad with a *play* triangle at its center. I take his phone and start the video. It backs up a few seconds, to where I'm dancing like an uncoordinated stripper, and then Tad comes up behind me.

Bits of fragmented memories come together as I watch two minutes of my life play out for the world to see. My head falling back against Tad's chest. His lips finding the soft skin of my neck. I reach up and touch where I think they've been, where Rex's were last night, and then it stops.

My gaze falls to my feet. I can't look Cooper in the eye. The last time I drank like that was over a year ago, when I kissed him. I can only imagine what he thinks of me, of my reputation. *Poor, broken, Piper, seeking attention from all the wrong people.*

That's not the case, but I know Cooper. The pessimist in him will assume the worst. I scroll through the group, looking for Rex's name. I find Logan's and a few others I recognize, but not his. Satisfied, I hand Cooper back his phone. "How many people have seen this?"

"There's at least a hundred in the chat and I don't know how many comments." He shakes his head in disgust. "So much for your reputation being bullshit, Piper."

There it is.

My reputation, the one I'm trying hard as hell to get rid of, has bitten me in the ass once again. Cooper knows the truth about what I did and didn't do this year. Through it all, he's stood by my side, never batting an eye at the rumors. Now, it looks like he's second-guessing everything that's ever been said about me.

Cooper puts the phone to sleep and shoves it back into his pocket. "What were you thinking?"

That I needed to make the memories go away.

That, for one stupid night in my life, I wanted to feel normal and have a little fun. "I don't know, I guess I wasn't. What does it matter? Girls get drunk and hook up all the time."

Cooper's brows furrow. "So, you hooked up with Tad?"

The disappointment etched on his face burns a hole in me. Even though I didn't do anything wrong, I feel guilty. Dirty.

Does kissing Rex count? "No. Of course not. I'm just saying, having a good time isn't a big deal."

"That's bullshit, Piper, and you know it." Cooper pauses, chewing on the inside of his cheek, mulling over his words. He's right. It's a huge deal. A monstrous step in my long-awaited recovery. A moment Cooper is probably upset that he missed. "This was at Rex's house, wasn't it?"

I groan. Somehow, I knew this would circle back to Rex. For reasons I can't fathom, Cooper has hated the guy since he moved here. Although, because of how friendly Cooper is to everyone, you'd never know it. Not until he let you in enough to show his true colors.

"Does that even matter?"

"I knew it was just a matter of time until Rex sucked you in. This whole nice guy thing that he's got going on, it's just an act. A fucking act that you're stupid enough to fall for, like every other girl in the school. At least they aren't changing themselves to get his attention."

"Really? That's the angle you're working? That I'm different? Sorry to rock your world there, Coop, but I don't have to be moody and pissed off all the time. I'm eighteen years old! I can laugh and have fun once in a blue moon! But I forgot, I can only be happy when you're around."

"You're partying and letting people touch you." Cooper's voice echoes in the small space. He's not yelling yet, but as tensions rise between us, I can feel it coming.

We've never fought before. It's like riding a bike for the first time, knowing you're going to fall. My adrenaline's pumping. It's only a matter of time until I lose control and hit the pavement, so to speak.

"Maybe I'm getting better," I say, my voice growing to match his. I'm trying my hardest to stay strong, but I'm struggling. I want to scream and cry at the same time. I need to focus on my frustration towards Cooper if I'm going to make it through this. If not, I'll be a mess of tears before it's over. "Did you ever think of that?"

"No, Piper, I didn't. You don't just magically get better over the weekend. That's not how your shit works."

"Really? My shit." I cross my arms, tears morphing into fire.

How dare he. Cooper doesn't have the faintest clue about what I cope with daily. If he did, he'd try harder to understand my boundary issues and not push me damn near my breaking point by forcing me to hug him every fucking day. "What exactly is my shit, Cooper?"

He groans and rubs the back of his head. "I don't know. Depression?"

I snort. "I'm not depressed."

This summer, yeah, I abso-fucking-lutely was. The only good thing about depression is that eventually you go numb and nothing matters anymore. I found that stage in August. After the overdose and the blood, when I realized the Harris family wasn't going to let me die. I needed to numb the pain to make things better for them.

But I feel again. Every time Rex touches me, I'm brought back to life. Is it wrong to rely on someone else to help me get better? Yes, but accepting help, even when unwanted and unexpected, is better than wallowing.

Mrs. Cherrybroom said that sooner or later, it would happen. Something would change, propelling me into recovery. Never in my wildest dreams did I think that something would be Rex, but I'm grateful for him. Even if I don't know exactly what we are.

"Then why did you try to kill yourself? The only reason I could come up with was because I shot you down at the party last summer."

My jaw drops. He can't possibly be that narcissistic. Cooper has always been full of himself. His ego is bigger than the moon, but he downplays it in public. And girls flock to him, eating up the sweet boy-next-door persona he puts off. "Seriously? You think that was about you?"

"What else am I supposed to think? You kiss me. I have a minor freak out and then, a few weeks later, I find you in a puddle of blood in my bathtub."

"Jesus Christ, Cooper. I'm not getting into this with you." Tears pool behind my lashes. I'm trying my hardest to hold them back, but it's a losing battle. This is too much. I close my eyes and try to slow my breathing. Steady my thoughts, but it all comes back.

Gerald takes my chin between his thumb and forefinger and forces me to look at him. "You will watch, you will scream, and you will remember that I own you."

He unzips himself, fumbling with the button on his jeans. I pull and pull on my bindings until, finally, the knot around my wrists loosens. This is my chance. A split second is all I have to try and get away, and I take it. I yank my right arm as hard as I can, and my wrists slip from between the fabric.

Gerald doesn't notice. His mind is too fucked up, too focused on the button that won't let go of his pants.

I reach for my bedside table. Somewhere, there is a pair of scissors beside my journal. I stretch, trying to be as discreet as possible.

Just a little closer...

Gerald's button gives and he pulls himself out of his pants, his eyes back on me. "What do you think you're doing?"

I panic and grab the only thing I can reach—a ballpoint pen. With every bit of strength I have, I stab him in the neck. The pen pierces his skin with ease. Sobs muffle my screams as I pull the pen out and stab him again, and again, over and over until we're both covered in blood.

Gerald falls onto me, groaning, and I push his limp—but not lifeless—body on the floor and run. I don't think about the blood on my hands or the fact that my shirt is ripped open. I don't think about where I'm going until my hand beats against the cherry wood, staining its grains with fist prints.

Bane cracks the door open, the end of a pistol greeting me. I should have expected it. In this neighborhood, anyone beating on your door at three in the morning is asking for trouble. I don't flinch, or cry, or scream.

I'm numb. Shaking from the fleeting adrenaline.

Bane yanks the door open and tugs me inside. He slams it shut behind him, his eyes trailing over my body, worry etched on his face. "Jesus, Piper."

He leaves me in the entryway and I don't know how long he's gone. A minute? An hour? A day? Time is stuck, forcing me to stay in the room I escaped from, Gerald's voice playing on a loop in my mind. I squeeze my eyes shut, hoping to chase the sounds away, but am met with his face.

A hand touches my arm. I open my eyes, yanking the trembling limb from Bane's grasp. "It's okay," he assures me. "You're safe now."

I suck in a staggering breath and open my eyes. Salty, wet pain runs down my cheeks. I turn to leave, but Cooper grabs my arm. As if having the worst day of my life flood my conscious thoughts wasn't enough, my body chooses this moment to remember what a panic attack is. My heart hammers in my chest.

One Mississippi.

"Yes, you are." Cooper reels.

I am what? I barely remember what we're talking about. My brain is lost in a fog of memories and pain.

"You've shut me out for almost a year," Cooper continues, "and now you're acting out. I don't want to find you dead somewhere because I almost missed the signs again."

Two Mississippi.

I snatch my arm out of his hand and take three breaths. One to steady my heart. One to clear my head. And one to try and control the fire simmering inside me. Using the calmest, most monotone voice I can muster, I say, "There are no signs, Cooper. I'm fine."

"You're far from fine. You had another panic attack, just now, because I touched you. I can't even hug you anymore without your body freaking out, but Rex can." There's pain in his eyes. I almost feel bad, but he's forcing me to talk about things he's not ready to deal with. "Why is that?"

"You want to know why, Cooper?"

That's it. He's pushed me to the edge. I shouldn't lay it all on the line. I'm too emotional, but I don't care anymore. Everything was bound to come out sooner or later. Might as well be today.

"Because you're a before. Me wanting to die had nothing to do with you. It has everything to do with how Gerald, Bane's dad, broke into my room the night of that party, after I stumbled home with a bruised ego, and how he forced himself on me."

"Fuck, Piper. I..." Cooper looks around as if the word he is searching for will magically appear on the walls. "Did he...you know?"

"Rape me?" My voice breaks, barely able to utter the words.

The two-minute warning bell rings. "Maybe we should talk about this at home. With Mom," Cooper says, clearly uncomfortable with the conversation.

"You backed yourself into this corner, Coop." My adrenaline is running rampant. I'm angry and upset all at once. It's a lethal combination. "No, I wasn't raped."

Cooper lets out a sigh of relief. "Oh, thank God. I mean—"

I don't let him finish. There's no relief in what happened to me. No, *it could have been worse*. In either situation, what could have happened and what did happen, I died on the inside. The tiny bit of fire I had left in me to survive was snuffed out the moment Gerald's hands touched me. "I stabbed him in the neck and ran away before he got the chance."

Cooper stares, eyes wide. He's finally seeing me for what I am—a monster. I snort-laugh through my tears. "I stabbed him in the neck until he'd lost too much blood to fight back and then I pushed Gerald's heavy body off me and ran to Bane's house."

Cooper takes a step, literally backing himself into a corner. What little spark of life that had been ignited this week is gone. I don't know why I'm still crying. I'm not upset about what I did or even what happened anymore. This is my life.

Cooper looks at me like I'm a rabid beast, like he's afraid to get too close. "Did Bane hurt you too?"

"Fuck you for even suggesting that. He saved me. I know you hate Bane, Cooper, but without him that night, I'd probably be dead."

Cooper's legs give out, unable to handle anymore. He slides down the wall, his body slouching when it hits the floor. "Fucking hell, Piper. Why didn't you tell me?"

I crouch down to Cooper's level and look him dead in the eye. He needs to understand that I'm in a hole so deep, no one can dig me out of it. "Because if Gerald and his gang found out you knew what happened, they could come for you too."

Fear dances across his face. "What are you talking about?"

Someone knocks.

No one knocks on a stairwell door. I already know who's coming before the door creeps open. I stand and take a step back.

Rex peeks his head in, "Piper, we should—" his words cut off, probably because I look like a dying raccoon with mascara running down my cheeks. He steps in and closes the door, then pulls me into his chest, arms protectively wrapping around me. "Are you okay?"

The tension in my lungs fades almost instantly. I close my eyes and bury my face in his chest. Somehow, even when I'm at my darkest, Rex makes me feel alive again. I know I should hold on to the emptiness, it'll make leaving that much easier, but I can't. Being in his arms is like curling up with a good book and a cozy blanket on a rainy Sunday afternoon. Pure perfection.

I nod.

"This!" Cooper bellows in frustration. He stands and waves a hand in Rex's direction. "Why is it that he can do this and I can't? Goddamn it, I should be the one comforting you. I'm your best friend. I fucking love you, Piper!"

I wipe my nose on the back of my hand. "Because every time I look at you, at anyone from this school, memories of that night come flooding back. The good and the bad. You're a before. The only reason I think I'm okay with Rex touching me is because he's an after."

Cooper storms past us, pushing the door behind me open with enough force that it slams against the wall and echoes in the stairwell. I feel bad for the guy. It's obvious he likes Piper. Hell, with everything they've been through, he probably loves her as more than a friend, too.

Cooper doubles back and glares at me. He's a big boy, nearly as tall as me and built like a brick house, but if need be, I could take him. "I swear to God, Rex, if you hurt her I'll kill you."

I ignore his comment and look down at Piper. "Are you okay?"

She lets out a sound that mixes a laugh and a cry. "Not even close."

I expected as much. I didn't mean to eavesdrop on her conversation, but it was hard not to hear. I get it now, why Piper hates to sleep—closing her eyes only to relive the worst day of her life. I can't begin to imagine the pain she deals with daily. "Do you want to get lunch?"

"It's ten-forty-five."

"Yeah, and lunch is next period. We're just getting a jump on it."

"Sure," Piper agrees, but there's no happiness in her tone. She's a shell of the person I had last night, but it's okay. Everything will be alright because I'll breathe life into her again. Now more than ever, I feel like I was brought here to save her. I hold my hand out, but Piper crosses her arms, hugging herself.

"So, I'm an *after*?" I say as we walk down the hallway, not giving two shits if a teacher sees us ditching. "Do you want to talk about that?"

"No."

I nod, respecting her decision.

Outside, the senior lot is not gated. I guess the school's administration doesn't care enough to stop kids who skip, or there are too many goody-two-shoes who don't.

"Do you want to drive?" I ask, nearing my Range Rover.

Piper perks up a little. "Really?"

I toss her my wireless key fob. She catches it with one hand and stares at it like it's magic. "Sure. Why not? I've got insurance. You've got a license, right?"

Her face falls. "No."

I'm not surprised. A mom who nearly lets her daughter be raped doesn't sound like the kind of person to take Piper to the DMV. "No biggie. Just don't get pulled over."

Piper pushes the start button on the key fob and grins when the engine roars to life. The car automatically unlocks, and we get in. She spends a solid minute adjusting the seat and mirrors, then asks, "Where to?"

"You're the captain. Whatever you want, I'm buying."

"Good, because I'm broke," Piper jokes, putting the car in reverse. "This isn't a stick, right?"

"No. Why?"

"Because I have no clue how to drive one. I'd probably fuck up your transmission."

PIPER

We skip the rest of the day. Somehow, time always flies away from me when I'm with Rex. We don't even do much of anything, just eat Subway, then drive around. I make it back to school by the skin of my teeth for my final.

Now, two and a half hours later, I've got to catch a bus to the beachside so I don't miss all of my shift tonight. Although, I wouldn't mind skipping it to avoid Cooper.

I walk out of the school's main entrance and don't bother to fight the grin that takes over my face when I see him. Rex is parked in the parent-pick-up circle, waiting for me. He leans against the shiny black paint of his Range Rover, looking like he just popped out of a magazine.

"Thought you might need a ride." He opens the passenger door for me and I climb in.

The car is already running, air on, and ready to go. "What? I don't get to drive this time?"

Rex shakes his head, chuckling. My door shuts and he runs around to get in on his side. He shifts into drive and pulls out of school. "No. You're great and all, but you're a terrible driver."

"I'm not that bad."

"You almost took out a stop sign," he says, amusement dancing in his tone.

"That was one time, and it came out of nowhere!"

"One time is all it takes, babe." The blinker clicks as he turns onto Highway One. "How late do you work tonight?"

"We close at nine, but clean up takes about an hour."

"Is it cool if I come back and get you around nine-thirty? I can wait outside until you're done."

I try to hide my surprise. Rex must not have heard my conversation. If he had, he wouldn't want to be alone with me again. Hell, most days, I don't want to be alone with me. "Why would you do that?"

"We were gonna watch *Aladdin* tonight. Remember?"

"But tonight's a school night." My rebuttal is weak, but it's the only excuse I can come up with. I love hanging out with Rex, which is all the more reason I should stop. If things keep going the way they are, I'm going to have a hard time leaving in a few weeks.

Rex rolls his eyes. "So was last night and the night before. I promise we won't be up too late."

"I should go home tonight. Mamma T will start to worry."

Rex pulls into the front parking space at the Red Onion. It's four-fifty-five. We made it to the diner with five minutes to spare before my shift starts.

"It's okay, I understand. See you tomorrow?"

"Definitely." I un-click my seatbelt but don't open the door. I should go, but I'm not ready. I want a few more minutes of heaven before having to deal with Cooper. "Thanks for the ride, Rex."

"Anytime, babe. It's what I'm here for."

That's the second time Rex has called me *babe*. I kind of like it. I lean over and give him a quick kiss on the cheek. He slips his fingers through my hair, bringing my lips to his before I can pull away, not that I would. His tongue slides into my mouth, dancing with mine just long enough to make me want more.

Rex pulls back and tips his forehead to mine. "Just a reminder of what you're missing out on tonight."

I swallow hard and lean back in my seat. It's four-fifty-nine. "I should go," I tell him before I say something stupid, like admit I want to go to his house after work.

I climb out of the car, and Rex's Range Rover is gone from the parking space and around the corner before I can get inside to peek out the window.

"Him again?" Cooper growls.

I grab a rag and the spray bottle from behind the counter and wipe down tables, even though they don't look dirty. "Jealousy isn't a good look on you, Coop."

"Yeah, well, gold digger isn't a good look on you," he says under his breath.

"Excuse me?" I rear back.

"I can't think of any other reason you'd be with Rex besides the fact that he's loaded and can take care of you." Cooper throws the napkin container on the counter at the wall. Thank God the place is empty. Mamma T would have a fit if he acted this way in front of customers.

"Fuck you, Cooper." I've never said that to him before. Not in a meaningful way.

Cooper's mouth hangs open. He promptly shuts it and picks up the napkin holder and the napkins that have flown across the floor. I thought telling Cooper what happened last summer would have made him a little more understanding of what I cope with every day.

Apparently, I was wrong.

R oses.

Dark red.

Long stemmed, with trimmed thorns that are wrapped in deep purple tissue paper, wait for me. I've never been given roses, or any bouquet of flowers for that matter.

In the land of the wealthy, flowers are reserved for Valentine's Day and romantic gestures. Both of which require having someone who likes you, and up until recently, I have either been friend-zoned or danger-zoned.

However, on the other side of the tracks, flowers are reserved for funerals. A sign of condolence to help decorate the grieving family's home because after the cost of a casket and the service, they usually don't have anything left.

"What am I supposed to do with these?"

Rex extends the bouquet to me and then sticks his hands in the pockets of his khakis. The muscles of his arms flex underneath the short-sleeved navy polo, the sleeves tightening around his bicep. "I think the words you're looking for are 'Oh, my gosh, Rex! Thank you!'"

Cheeky bastard. I bat my dark-lined lashes and flash the cheesiest smile. I should get an award for this one. I don't think I've ever done anything so fake. "Thank you."

"You're welcome," he says with a shit-eating grin.

I look down at my roses. Their fragrance fills the space between us. Their soft petals waiting to be touched. *If I plucked each one, would they say that he loves me? Or that he loves me not?* "Seriously though, what do I do with them?"

"Stuff 'em in your locker. Braid them into a crown. I don't care. After everything that happened yesterday, I just thought you could use a smile. Gretchen would always smile when her oldest son had flowers delivered."

"So, I remind you of Gretchen?"

"Fuck, no. You're way hotter."

"You're not supposed to think your nanny is hot."

"Have you seen my nanny?" He shakes his head and whistles. "Just kidding."

"You're weird."

"And you're pretty."

The bell rings. I look up at the ceiling tiles. I want more time together. I like how easy things are with Rex. How talking and touching and existing come without fail when we're together, but we only have two minutes.

I hand Rex back the flowers and open my locker. Everything is organized to a fault. Last year, I bought a pink wire shelf from Target to help me get the most out of my available space—books and notebooks on top, a toiletry bag with shampoo, a hairbrush, a toothbrush, toothpaste, and a bag of makeup on the bottom.

At one point, I practically lived out of my locker and my shoulder bag. This was before Mamma T made me move back in with her, before the party, when my life was normal teenage sucky.

A mirror and a matching pink wire basket filled with pens are stuck to the back of the door. Underneath it is my favorite picture.

Mamma T snapped it on my tenth birthday. I'm in the middle in my bright yellow bathing suit, one arm around Logan, the other around Cooper. It was the first birthday party I'd ever had and the most memorable.

After grabbing the books for my next two classes, I quickly rearrange everything to make the flowers fit inside.

"Want me to walk you?" he asks when I close the door.

"Won't you be late?"

"Maybe, but I'll take fifteen minutes of detention if it gets me one more minute with you."

Feeling my cheeks heat, I nod because I don't trust my words. They might tell him he's the best thing to happen to me. They might ask if he has a burger to go with that cheese. Or worse, there might not be any words. It wouldn't be the first time they've left me when I needed them most.

I slide into class just as the door is closing. My professor, Mr. Greene, grunts in disapproval but lets me in without causing a scene.

I take a seat at the only open table at the front of the room. The table no one likes because you're a target. Not only from Mr. Greene but from our classmates, too.

Two minutes later, the door opens again. I take my book out of my bag and duck my head, thankful the attention is off me, even if it's only for a few minutes.

"You're late," Mr. Greene growls.

Silently, a body finds its way into the stool next to mine. The person, who I'm trying my hardest not to look at, nudges my arm with his elbow. His cologne closes the space between us, swirling in my nostrils. My gaze snaps up immediately.

"What are you doing here?" I whisper yell.

"Trying to pass physics. Can we share?" Rex points at my book. "I didn't have time to run and get mine."

I pull the inch-thick text from my bag, open it to today's assignment, and then push it between us. "Since when do you have physics first period?"

He shrugs, the corner of his lips tugging to the ceiling. "I transferred in last month."

"Have I not noticed you all this time? You're kind of hard to miss."

"I'll take that as a compliment." Rex looks up at the board and nods, like he's paying attention to Mr. Greene's lecture when he walks in front of us. As soon as his back is to us, Rex says, "You usually come in just before the bell and sit right here." He points to our table. "And keep your head low. I used to hang out in the back and stare at you."

"Weirdo."

"Am I interrupting something?" Mr. Greene asks from behind us and the room fills with whispers and giggles. I duck my head, creating a curtain with my hair.

"Just discussing nonlinear dynamics, sir," Rex replies with a smile as wide as Texas.

"That's not what we are reviewing," Mr. Greene says, with an I'm-growing-tired-of-you tone.

"You didn't ask what *you* were discussing, sir. You asked if you were interrupting what we were discussing."

The class erupts in a fit of "oohs." I hide my face in my hands, my cheeks burning from embarrassment. Today is going to be a long day.

"Spill." Melody sets her tray, the same color blue as the sweater draped over her shoulders, on the table in front of her.

In front of me.

Melody flicks her wrist, casually tossing bleached hair over her shoulder. Like clockwork, Sarah and Rachel, who are only seconds behind, sit down, too. My table of one is once again a table of four, and I can't figure out why these girls haven't moved on yet.

"If you're going to sit with us," Melody starts, sliding the straw into her soda. "We need to know how you bagged Rex Montgomery."

"Pretty sure you sat down at my table."

Melody rolls her eyes. "Potato. Tomato. I'm risking my prom queen nomination by sitting with you as often as I do. The least you could do is tell me how you did it. Was it back door? He looks like a back door kind of guy."

"And you look like the type of girl to give it, Melody," Rex says, walking up to us.

Sarah chokes on her orange soda, earning her dirty looks from both Rachel and Melody. She wipes her mouth with the back of her hand, mumbling, "Sorry."

"You never gave me the chance to show you if I was," Melody adds. She shimmies her shoulders in a proud you-would-have-loved-it way.

Rex sits beside me, one leg on each side of the bench. He slips his arms around my waist and pulls me into him. He's claiming me for all of the cafeteria to see. Not that anyone else wants me. In reality, he's letting everyone know he's off the market.

Of course though, this is the moment that Cooper walks up to the table. Most days, he'd sit down without question, but the way things are between us, I don't know what he's planning. We haven't talked since work last night and it's killing me. We've never gone this long without speaking. No texts, no notes, nothing. Twenty-four hours with no communication is twenty too long.

Cooper stops at the head of the table and stares at us for a solid five seconds. Each beat of my heart, each breath I take waiting for him to speak is a lifetime of their own. My stomach flips, sending the few bites of my chicken sandwich into my throat when he turns, tosses his untouched food tray in the nearby trash can and leaves. Leaves his friends.

Leaves the cafeteria.

Leaves me.

"Now I've seen everything," Rachel says, shaking her head.

Rex's arms fall to his lap when I jump up. I run—literally run—after Cooper. Rex will understand, he has to. I know being in the cafeteria today with me is a big moment for us—whatever we are— but Cooper comes first, especially if he's upset.

My fingers grasp the metal bar of the cafeteria door, pushing it open, hitting the wall with a loud *whack,* as I run into the long hallway. "Cooper!"

He stops walking, his hand on the door that leads out to the parking lot. He's not just leaving the cafeteria, he's leaving school. My heart breaks because it genuinely feels like he's *leaving* me. My protector—my hero in these halls—is giving up on me.

I shouldn't be surprised, everyone does eventually, but I never thought he would.

I'm panting when I reach him. Each breath is pained and almost as difficult as it is with a panic attack. I know we've drifted apart the past few months, but I thought him going out at night was his way of giving me the space I needed—wanted—but now I worry that the distance I equated with trust had been the beginning of the end for us. "Where are you going?"

"Does it matter?" He asks, his voice devoid of emotion. "It's not like you care anymore."

"What are you talking about, Coop? Of course I care. I love you."

"No!" he booms. "You don't love me, Piper and that's the problem. I love you. I always have and probably always fucking will, but you, you won't love me. You can't love me because I'm a *before*."

Oh, God... How could I have missed it? All these years, the late-night texts after I moved out, the lunch dates in the cafeteria, the looking out for me. I always thought it was brotherly.

"I kissed you, and you ran."

Cooper bolted so fast that night, he tripped over the beach chairs we were sitting in. I was left alone by a dying fire in the Harris's backyard, heartbroken and confused.

After swallowing a lump of tears, I mustered up the courage to go after him. The plan was to apologize and tell him I was drunk and it was a mistake. I pushed open his bedroom door without knocking and froze.

Sarah Archer had her legs around him, her lips against his. I didn't think I had taken that much time outside, but apparently I did. I ran from that room as fast as my legs could take me, tears running down my cheeks, and bumped into Logan on my way out—who promptly told me not to let the door hit my ass. The shit thing is, the night only got worse from there.

Cooper shrugs. "And I freaked."

"Enough to swap spit with Sarah?"

"That was a mistake. When you saw us, I threw her off me and ran after you. Kissing her made me realize how much I wanted to be kissing you!"

"You realize how cliché that sounds, right?"

Silence falls between us. Cooper's eyes are bloodshot, sleepless from his night on the couch and maybe even brimmed with tears. My heart hurts because, for a moment, I wish I could have been his. I wish I could be the girl he deserves but there's no changing what happened. Even if there was a way to forget the way my heart hurt that night, I can't forget everything that happened after. I can't force my body to react to him like it does with Rex.

Cooper smiles, but it doesn't reach his ears. "I can't watch you with him, Piper. I'm glad he makes you better and I'm glad you're happy. It just kills me that everything that happened to you is my fault."

"Cooper—"

"No, Piper. Gerald wouldn't have hurt you if I had kissed you back, pulled you into my arms, and told you I loved you like I should have. You wouldn't have almost overdosed in Bane's apartment and I wouldn't have found you in a bathtub of blood two weeks later, either."

I'm trembling. The shakes from the pounding of my heart vibrate throughout my body. I suck in a breath and reach for Cooper. His touch burns, a fire ignited under my skin in the worst of ways, but I take the pain. I swallow the bile and let him hold me as long as he needs. By the time Cooper lets go, I'm lightheaded. I cough on an inhale from the pressure in my chest.

"I can't even hold you without hurting you, Pipes," he says, tears in his eyes as he turns away.

Chapter 19
PIPER

It's been a week since my fight with Cooper and my breakdown in the hallway. To make things easier, I haven't been home. Rex and I hang out after school, watching movies or chilling at the beach until my pretend curfew of midnight, to which I pretend to text Mamma T and tell her I'm not coming home.

I've pretty much taken up residency in Rex's guest room. The reason being—I don't trust myself with Rex. He's handsome and sweet and patient. Most importantly, he turns me on and I'm scared I won't be able to control myself if we share a bed.

Rex pulls me into him when my shift at the Red Onion is over, swallowing me with his massive frame. I nuzzle my nose into his chest, breathing in the scent of his cologne. "Ready to go?"

Cooper finishes locking up and turns around, a scowl on his face. "You're not coming home tonight?"

"I promised Rex I'd watch a movie for a bit." Lie. Why am I lying to him? All I'm doing is creating more walls, encouraging the space to grow between us. I wish we could go back to last week. I wouldn't have chased after Cooper. He wouldn't have opened his heart to me and things would be normal...ish. "I'll probably be home late."

"Whatever," Cooper mumbles, walking past us.

"I'll drop her off as soon as she's ready," Rex says cautiously.

I never made it back to the cafeteria that day. I fell to my knees when Cooper left and cried. I cried until I couldn't breathe, couldn't move. My heart broke with each inhale. I lost my best friend because I couldn't love him, because he couldn't heal me, and ultimately because I chose someone else.

Rex found me curled in a corner and carried me to the nurse's office. She gave us a pass for the day and he brought me back to the Horizon Hotel. We laid under an umbrella until the sun set and I was calm again. He didn't ask what happened. I think he knew something monumental passed between Cooper and me, and he understood. There was no jealousy or bitterness, just compassion and understanding.

My phone dings an hour into tonight's movie. Rex reaches over the side of the couch with one arm and hands me my bag. I sit up, leaving the warmth of his chest, and rummage through the oversized messenger satchel until I find it.

I pull out my life—a pair of jeans, two extra shirts, a school skirt, my bag of makeup, and two handfuls of random pens—until finally finding my phone zipped in a pocket it doesn't belong in.

> Bane: Your boy is here.

> Me:?

What does he mean my boy is there? I don't have any...oh no.
Cooper.

I chew the inside of my cheek, using the pain to keep the tears welling behind my eyes at bay. Cooper *hates* Bane. Nothing good can come from him being there.

If it weren't for my *almost* overdose, Cooper wouldn't even know where Bane lived. By that point, I'd been hiding out at Bane's for a little over a week. We both knew Gerald would eventually figure out where I was. The man is dumb, but he's not stupid. It was just a matter of time until he had someone camp out in front of the apartment complex, waiting to snatch me up when I left for school, but the thought of leaving, being seen or taken, was too much.

I weighed my options. No matter which way I figured it, I was going to get caught, raped, and probably killed. No one stabs a mob boss, or drug lord, or whatever Gerald is and gets away with it. Bad guys don't keep their tough reputation by letting scrawny eighteen-year-old girls get the best of them. The only question was how many people would be hurt in the process.

My decision? One.

Bane had a stash of pills in his bathroom. He wasn't dealing, never had, but his recreational stash was stout. I locked the bathroom door and dumped a few of each in my hand. I had no clue what I was taking, but I figured something would work. I just hoped they'd put me to sleep and it would be an easy death.

Everything after that is a blur. Somehow, I woke up in Cooper's bathroom, throwing up everything in my stomach. It couldn't have been the first time I puked, either. My chest ached, my stomach knotted, and my head was pounding. Next thing I know, I'm in his bed with a wet rag on my head, being told I was moving in.

> Bane: Come to my house.
>
> Me: Is it safe?

Not that safety matters at this point. Cooper is family. Even if we are fighting, I'd give my life for him.

> Bane: Honestly, no. Dad's crew is out tonight, but he can't stay.
>
> Me: Fuck. Okay, be there as soon as I can.

I drop my phone in my lap and pull the elastic from my hair, just to tie it up again. I pick up my phone, scrolling through the contacts, and stop at Logan's name. My thumb hovers over it before hitting the home button. I can't bring Logan into this. He'll lose his temper, draw attention to us, and then we'll all be in trouble. I drop my phone beside my leg, between Rex and me.

Think.

Think

Think.

"You good?"

"No. I need to go." I pick my phone up again and download the Uber app. I've never used it before, but I don't have time to wait for the bus tonight. I go through the motions, answering what feels like a million questions about myself and clicking through stupid informational messages without reading them.

"I can drive, you know."

"No." I don't bother to look up. I'm too busy linking my debit card. Besides, this isn't his mess. It's mine.

"Piper." Rex puts his hand on mine, covering my phone.

I sigh, my body shaking in fear. This, Cooper being at Bane's house, is all my fault. I don't know why he's there, but if Cooper is torn up enough to go to *him,* he must be in bad shape. "I need to go home."

"It's not a big deal. I'll take you."

I shake my head. "Not that home. My old one. Cooper is in trouble."

"And it's your job to save him, why? He's a grown-ass man, Piper."

Rex can't understand. From the first night terror when I was eight years old, Cooper was there, rushing into my room before his parents. He held my hand in the hallway at school every day that year, not giving a damn about spiteful third graders, who quickly learned to keep their mouths shut. He's had my back time after time. He knows everything I went through as a kid and never once judged me. In fact, I think my hardships made him love me more. He loved me because I was broken.

"Because he's always had my back when I needed it. Even when I didn't want him to. It's my turn."

Rex mulls over my words a few moments, then nods. Whatever it is that makes him understand, I'm glad. I don't have the energy to argue. "I'm driving."

"No, Rex. It's not safe."

"And that's exactly why you're not going alone."

Twenty minutes later, we're parked in front of apartment 2A. Bane's building is nicer than Monica's. The paint outside is fresh powder blue with only a handful of spray-painted tags. The potholes in the parking lot were filled last spring and the landlord attempted to landscape the first floor with shrubs. They died because no one watered them and now they're just twigs out front, but at least he tried. Still, for the area, it's the nicest complex around.

I turn the knob without knocking, a death wish in this part of town. When I open the door, Bane is frozen in the hallway, one foot behind the other at an angle, a pistol pointed at us.

Rex notices the gun before I do. His hand curls around my waist, pulling me three steps backward. He steps in front of me, physically shielding me in case things go wrong. Brave, but stupid. Rex is going places; he can't be putting his life on the line for me like that.

"Fucking hell, Piper," Bane says, slipping the pistol beneath the band of his pants again. "I could have killed you."

I step around Rex and fist-bump Bane. "You wouldn't have shot me."

"No, but I damn sure would have shot this one," he says, looking at Rex. "The fucker is huge."

"I'll take that as a compliment." Rex chuckles and holds out his hand. "Rex."

"Bane."

"And I'm Piper," I say sarcastically.

Bane smirks and flips me the bird. I wrinkle my nose and stick my tongue out at him. We both laugh, remembering a time when life was simpler, when all we had to worry about was staying out of gang turf and not getting mud on his mamma's carpet.

Silence slips its way into the room until the *cha-ching* of a cash register sounds. Bane pulls his phone from his pocket and frowns. "We gotta move fast, Piper. Someone saw you."

Piper is an idiot.

No girl, especially one as beautiful as she is, should be alone in this part of town. She could get mugged, or raped, or even killed. As much as I hate knowing she shares a bed with Cooper at night, I'm glad she's not living here anymore.

I look out Bane's front door for this *supposed* threat. The street is dead, illuminated by a single lamp with three women standing under it. Skinny, frail-looking women who need to put some clothes on. I don't care who you are, a lady should have more respect for herself than to walk around in their bra and a scrap of fabric that's supposed to be a skirt if she's not at the beach. Outside of them, I don't see anyone. I think Bane is full of shit. No one saw us arrive, and even if they did I don't see how it matters. We're here to collect Cooper.

Nothing more.

I shut the front door and then follow Piper and Bane to the bedroom. She leads the way, twisting the knob of the room, opening doors like she owns the place. I don't like how comfortable Piper is here. She and Bane have a history and I can't help but wonder how far it goes.

I give Bane a once over, sizing him up. The dude is tall, but not as tall as me. Every inch of his arms is covered in colorful ink, making his muscles even more defined. I could take him, but it would be a close fight. I push those thoughts away. For now, Bane and I are on the same team—team Piper—and until he becomes a threat I will just have to deal.

Piper kneels beside his queen-sized bed. "What happened?"

Cooper is passed out, one hand down his pants, drool leaking out his mouth.

Bane shakes his head. "No. Fucking. Clue. He came here with a purpose, pounding on my door, yelling things I couldn't understand, and then asked to take a piss. When I checked on him a few minutes later, he was asleep." He holds his hand out. "Like this."

"And he can't sleep it off here, why?" I ask.

Piper wipes Cooper's mouth with the bottom of her shirt. His lips press together a time or two before falling open again with a snore.

"His car is too expensive. Parked out front for a few minutes, not a big deal, but unmoved for this long, people take notice. They talk. This isn't the kind of place you want to stand out in." Piper looks from Bane to me to Cooper and then back to me. "Let's load him in the back of your car. It's bigger. I'll follow you in his."

"You can't take him home," Bane says, a worry line between his brows. "Where are you gonna go?"

Piper looks at me, her big eyes begging without words.

"He can sleep in the guest room," I suggest, even though having Cooper in my house is the last thing I want, but at least if he's with us Piper won't worry so much.

She smiles, relief written all over her face. "Thanks."

"You grab his arms," I tell Bane. "I'll take his feet."

Five minutes later, Cooper's drooling on my leather seats. He's going to pay to get my backseat detailed after this shit. Piper faces Bane, her back to me, saying a goodbye I can't hear. He bends low and whispers into her ear. She nods, her shoulders slumping forward, then raises her hand for a fist bump before walking in my direction.

Bane raises his hand, a silent goodbye to me. I give a two-fingered salute and turn my attention to Piper when suddenly there's a loud popping sound.

Bang. Bang. Bang.

The shots echo in the night—one pop of a gun bouncing off the other, milliseconds apart. I hurl myself onto Piper, knocking her to the ground. We lay there until the sound of tires squealing against the pavement fades into silence.

"Sorry," I say, getting to my feet. I extend a hand to Piper and she takes it, letting me help her up. "I heard the first pop and didn't think about the fall, I just wanted you out of harm's way."

"It's fine," she says, brushing dirt off her ass. "Bane?" Piper looks over her shoulder and shrieks. "Bane!" She runs the ten steps to him. He leans against his door, a trail of blood leading down to his spot on the ground.

"I'm good," he grunts.

"The fuck you are!" Piper tugs at his hand. "Get up! You're going to the hospital!"

Bane pushes against the ground with his good arm and stands. His left arm covers his side, a puddle of blood seeping from the hole, drenching his shirt. "It's not like I have a few grand lying around to cover the bill, Pipes."

"Screw the money, Bane! You can't die on me!" Piper shoves him in the chest. He winces, but she's too emotional to notice.

"I'll be fine!" he insists. "Rita can stitch me up."

"With what? Her heroine needles?"

I exhale through my nose. Piper's becoming more frantic by the minute and we can't risk the shooters circling back. "Get in the car, Bane."

"You too?" he says, his brows drawing tight.

I step forward until we're nose to nose. "This can go two ways. One, you get in and let a real doctor fix your gut—my treat—or two, I knock your ass out and they treat you for a concussion, too. Either way, your ass is going to the hospital."

Four hours, eight thousand dollars, and one pissed-off doctor later, Bane is passed out in the upstairs guest room. The one Piper usually sleeps in.

Cooper is still knocked out in the downstairs room. Reason for their placement? Bane, while groggy, can walk. I didn't want to carry Cooper's heavy ass up the stairs by myself.

"Hell of a night," Piper says, sliding the plate across the kitchen counter to me.

I grab two cups from the cabinet, fill them with water, then sit beside her. "You're telling me." We sit in silence, eating our sandwiches until our bellies are full and the plates are in the dishwasher. "So."

"So," she says, with a smile.

"I don't know about you, but I'm beat."

Piper pulls her hair from her ponytail and slips the tie around her wrists. Her fingers run across her scalp, pushing her long bangs from her eyes. "Yeah, I'm exhausted. I should go to bed."

"I'm out of guest rooms," I lie, "but you can take my parents' room if you want. Or..."

"Or what?"

"Or you could stay with me." I'm half joking, but the moment the words leave my mouth, I regret them.

Piper's not that kind of girl. I like that she's different, guarded. Timid yet fierce. Sometimes I feel like I'm walking on eggshells with her, terrified that with one wrong move she'll pull away. In the past couple of weeks, I've made progress in leaps and bounds, crossing from nonexistent semi-stalker to friend with the potential for more. Now I may have screwed it all up with one stupid comment.

"You could always sleep on the floor beside me," Piper says, a glint of playfulness in her eyes. She's got a come-and-get-me look mixed with a hint of terrified.

"Ouch. Way to secure my seat in the friend zone." I tease. *Damn. I did screw up.* "But if that's what you want."

She tucks her hair behind her ear and chews on her cheek. "No. Definitely not."

We climb the steps together and stop at the top. "What's it gonna be?"

Piper bites her lip, looking left and right before meeting my gaze. Her big grays, which I'm now convinced are secretly blue, stare up at me. "I..."

My heart beats against my chest. If this girl doesn't speak soon, my rib cage will be bruised. *Please stay with me. Please stay with me. Please...*

She exhales loudly. "Can I sleep with you?"

Yes! Hell yes! I smile, hoping it looks natural and not overly excited. I put my arm around her shoulders and kiss her forehead. "Anything you want, babe."

I take Piper to my room and open the door. She steps in and stands in the center, looking around. She walks over to the bookshelf and studies each trophy. I have six in all. She then walks over to my desk and picks up the only picture in the room. My arm is over Jenny's shoulder. I'm looking at the camera and she's sticking her tongue out at me. With a faint smile, Piper sets it down. She does a little spin, taking in the rest of the space, and says, "Your room is spotless."

I close the door out of habit, then wonder if I should have left it open. Not wanting to seem nervous, I shove my hands in my pockets and lean against the edge of my desk. "You're lucky. I just cleaned it yesterday."

Piper looks over her shoulder, her fingers running across the shirts in my closet. "You don't let the maid in here?"

"Nah," I walk to the bed and sit on the end of it, waiting, wondering if Piper will do the same. "I don't want her going through my things."

Piper follows and sits beside me, her tiny frame barely making the mattress dip. "And what kind of things might she find?"

I shrug. "Normal boy stuff. Dirty magazines. Condoms. Maybe a little weed now and then."

Shock dances across Piper's face, but it's gone as quickly as it arrived. "I never pegged you as a smoker."

"It's not something I do often. Under the right circumstances, with the right people, yes, but those people don't live here, so I gave my stash away at one of my parties a while back."

Piper inches closer. "And the condoms?"

I slide my foot underneath me, allowing myself to scoot closer. I'm sitting too close to her for my own good. The smell of her perfume does things to me. Add that we're in my bed...yeah. "Never can be too prepared."

She leans in. Close enough to let me know she wants to kiss but far enough that I have to lean in, too. Her fingers run down my chest, sending a wave of goosebumps over my body. "And who are you preparing for?"

I swallow hard. "No one in particular."

"Too bad," Piper whispers, her hand sliding up the leg of my shorts. "I almost wish they were just for me."

I scoot back a couple of inches and Piper's hand slides off my thigh. My dick is screaming that I'm an idiot. It's pressed tight against my shorts, ready to come out and play. As much as I want it to, God, I want it to; I want us to be more than a one-time fuck. "Piper, just because you're in my bed doesn't mean we have to do anything."

Her eyes widen, her mouth falling open. "You don't want to?"

If a man-card were a thing, mine would be revoked right now. Piper is giving me all the signs, and I've got a damn conscience. "Of course I do, but we should go slow."

She snorts. "You sound like a girl."

"Maybe I want to do things right with you." I brush a strand of hair behind her ear, but Piper pushes my hand away.

"Well, maybe I just want to see how far I can go before my body freaks out on me again. And I thought..." She groans and stands, storming out of my room. "Ugh, never mind."

I slam Rex's bedroom door behind me and run downstairs, out of the kitchen, and shut myself in the pool house.

I slam that door, too, and then throw myself onto the bed. If there were pictures on the walls, they would shake and probably fall to the floor, shattering into a million pieces like my ego.

Why is it that when I get the courage to make a move it doesn't work out? Why do they always turn me down? First Cooper and now Rex. What's wrong with these boys? *What's wrong with me?*

Cooper, I can maybe understand. We're best friends, but Rex? I thought all guys wanted sex. I'm pretty...ish, and Rex looks at me like I'm the only girl in the world. But he doesn't want me.

There's a knock at the door that could only be one person. I lift my head from the pillow, ashamed of my tears, and yell, "Go away!"

Rex ignores my request and opens the door. I don't bother to look; I don't want to see him. My ego can't take the hit again. Hell, my nerves can't handle it. Cooper is a mess, Bane was shot, and now this. Nope. I'm done.

The bed dips beside me and Rex rests his hand on my lower back. "Piper."

I turn my head and look at the wall. I'm having my first girlish-over-reacting teenage moment and the boy I'm freaking out about is the one comforting me. Tell me again how Life isn't out to fuck me?

"Don't be mad, but I overheard your conversation with Cooper the other day."

I groan and curl into the fetal position. No wonder Rex doesn't want me. Even though Gerald didn't penetrate me, he still touched me. Dirtying me. Why would someone as beautiful and perfect as Rex want something a nasty forty-something-year-old man has touched?

"It was kind of hard not to hear. You were practically screaming at Cooper." Rex pauses, probably waiting for me to respond. When I don't, he continues. "But he's got it wrong. You're not depressed. You're traumatized."

"You think?" I chide.

"Look at me." Rex puts his hand on my shoulder and turns me onto my back. He cradles my cheek and rubs black tear stains from my skin. "Do you like me? Or am I some weird experiment you're doing with yourself?"

I suck in a breath and exhale loudly. He's not one for messing around, is he? "I like you, Rex. I like how you make me feel."

"Okay," he says with a grin, leaning down to kiss me.

"But," I add and Rex sits back up, looking at me quizzically. "I don't know my limits. I'm so used to not being able to do anything with anyone. Whatever this is, it terrifies me. Can't we get the big stuff over with so I know how far I can go?"

"No, Piper. We can't just get it over with." Rex takes my arms and pulls me until I'm sitting up. "I'll do whatever you want, but we need to take it in stride. We don't have to go snail slow, but I don't want to try too much at once. I want our firsts to be memorable, in a good way."

His words, while kind, sting. There's the promise of tomorrow in his eyes but my tomorrows are limited. I want everything now, while my body still allows me to enjoy it. "Pretty sure you're not a virgin."

His head bobbles side to side. "True, but I've never had a girlfriend before. So, everything I do with you would be a first."

"Girlfriend?"

"Only if you want to be."

I bite my lip and nod. Rex takes my hand in his and brings it to his lips, kissing my knuckles before pulling me into his arms. I lay my head against his chest, listening to his heart race beneath me. "What man turns down sex? I can't think of anyone at school that would pass this up."

"First of all, I'm not passing anything up. I'm postponing it. Secondly, the guys at school aren't men, they're boys. They think with their dicks. Real men think with their hearts and baby, until you break it, mine's all yours."

REX

Does Piper have my heart?

Eh. She's got some but not all of it. After only a few weeks of hanging out, I'd be stupid to fall in love with someone. But there is something gloriously satisfying about the girl you've been pining after for months giving you a chance.

I run my fingers through Piper's hair a few times. I love how soft it is. Silky black strands that smell like strawberries and cream. She nuzzles into my chest, a quiet moan escaping her. "I should probably sleep upstairs tonight."

Her head lifts, those gray-blue eyes peering into my soul and I swear they crush me. Such beauty. Such pain. "Why?"

Piper runs her hand across my stomach. I'm sure she can hear the beats of my heart in my chest, and see how my shorts are getting tight. I'm going to have to relieve myself soon or it's going to explode. "Um..." *Words, damn it. Use your words.* "Trying to be respectful."

Piper giggles and shifts to straddling me. There's no way she can't feel me underneath her. I'm not porn star huge, but I'm not tiny either. Some guys are show-ers, others are grow-ers. I'm a bit of both. Still, the fact that she's acting like it's not even there is a blow to my ego.

She drags her nails down my chest to my belly button. "You know, you can still be respectful and kiss me. I am your girlfriend now."

I push myself up. Piper's legs wrap around my waist, pressing me tight against her. She pulls her bottom lip between her teeth and it slides out, painfully slow, glistening with saliva.

I don't think.

My hand goes to the back of her head, pulling her lips to mine. Her mouth is soft and warm as I slide my tongue across her bottom lip, and she parts for me. Her hands run down my back, leaving a hot trail behind them. I'm hard everywhere and she's so beautifully soft, molding into me, rocking her hips against my very strained shorts.

After not nearly enough time, Piper breaks the kiss, trailing her lips across my cheek for one last peck. I grunt—*What the fuck? I grunted?*—and clear my throat to cover the sound. Piper rests her forehead on my shoulder. "We should probably go to bed now."

"Yeah, good idea."

She slides off my lap and climbs under the covers. I sit there a minute, weighing my options. If I stay, we'll cuddle. My hand will end up on her boobs, and hers might find its way beneath my pants. Shit could get fun after that, but I don't want to rush things. Then again, tomorrow is a new day. It's not like we'd go from kissing to hand jobs in the same make-out session.

Stop being a dick.

I lay over the covers and drape my arm across Piper's waist. She grabs my hand and scoots back, pressing her ass against my dick again. "Why is there a blanket between us?"

"Because I'm not staying."

Piper turns in my arms and juts out her bottom lip. I lean in and give it a kiss, a chaste kiss that's more restrained than what I'm sporting in my pants.

"I wish you would."

"Next time, I will," I tell her, and she frowns. I lean down and kiss the tip of her nose. "Don't worry. We can spend as many nights together as you want."

Piper nods, her cheeks flushing pink, and presses a soft kiss to my lips again. "Night, boyfriend."

"Good night, girlfriend."

THE ALARM ON MY PHONE RINGS AT SIX. I LAY IN MY BED FOR another fifteen minutes before forcing myself out of it. After a quick shower and shave, I get dressed and head down to the kitchen. I pull the carton of eggs and a pack of bacon out of the fridge, then head to the pantry for some toast and grits. I scramble, fry, toast, and stir. When everything's done, I arrange it all on the kitchen island.

Skipping across the patio, I stop at her door. My heart thrums in my chest. I feel my pulse everywhere, eyes included. I've never cooked a girl breakfast, never tried this hard to be a gentleman. I think I'm doing a good job, but it's not easy.

I close my eyes and take a deep breath. On the exhale, I knock.

Nothing.

I knock again.

Still no answer.

I crack the door open and peek in. Piper is out cold. Her dark hair splayed across the pillows, still wearing yesterday's shirt. She must have slept in it, which means she probably doesn't have anything clean to wear today. That shoulder bag of hers can only hold so much.

I dash upstairs to my mother's closet again. She's got more clothes than a department store, but most of it isn't anything Piper would wear.

Too bright.

Too short.

Too flashy.

I was shocked when Piper chose the white one-piece swimsuit and the *Lilly Pulitzer* dress. Opening and closing drawers, I find a pair of jeans and a black tank top that should fit. It's the closest thing to Piper's style my mom has. I pause at the drawer of my mother's intimates. Should I grab her underwear? Is that weird? Everything still has the tags, but I decide against it. Piper can go commando, which would be totally hot, or figure that business out herself.

I stop at my mother's vanity and put her hair dryer and a brush on the stack of clothes. I don't feel bad taking anything. It's not like she'll know they're missing. That would require her to come home and since Dad is on tour overseas this year, I don't see that happening again anytime soon.

Back at Piper's door, I knock and wait, but there's still no answer. I enter the room and pad across the cold tile to set her things on the desk. I sit on the edge of the bed and put my hand on Piper's back, rubbing small circles like Gretchen used to do for me when I was a kid. "Good morning, beautiful."

Piper groans, then sucks in a breath, her whole body tensing. She opens her eyes, then relaxes. She rolls onto her back and looks up at me. "Hey."

"You okay?"

"Yeah," she says, her voice husky from sleep. "I forgot where I was for a second." She grows quiet for a minute. "About last night...."

I hold my hand up, silencing her. "Don't worry about it."

Rex leans against the marble countertop of the island in the kitchen, a cup of coffee pressed to his lips. He takes a sip and then holds the mug out to me. I shake my head and grab a bottle of water from the fridge instead. My body is burning up just from looking at him. I need to cool it down, not make it hotter. "Breakfast smells great."

Rex sets his cup down and rounds the island. Static bounces between our bodies, pulling us closer together. "I like how you've made yourself at home here."

I turn my back to him and lean against the counter. My skin is humming, desperate to feel his hands on me, but my mind is telling me to slow down. At this point, I'm not sure which one will win.

Rex brushes my hair to one side, exposing my neck, dusting it with featherlight kisses. "You look good in my shirt."

A moan escapes me because, apparently, being someone's girlfriend makes my body create sounds it's never made before. I close my eyes, letting the pleasure flow through me.

"It was in the..." *Fuck that feels good.* "Um, room. I liked it better than your mom's shirt." Tingles spread through my body, down to my core, creating the same need I felt last night. A need I don't know how to control. "Umm...I didn't think you'd mind."

Rex trails across my cheek to my ear. "I don't mind."

He slips my earlobe into his mouth, earrings and all and warm vibrations flutter inside me, making my knees weak. I grip the edge of the counter to keep myself on my feet.

Calloused fingers slip under my shirt, spin me around, and lift me onto the counter. He spreads my legs and steps between them, wrapping his arms around my waist and pulling me flush against his body.

I look into those blue eyes, falling deeper into the abyss. Rex dips his head, the tip of his nose brushing against my cheek. If every touch felt this good, I'd almost welcome my reputation. Not with everyone, just Rex. I suck in a breath, my heart fluttering faster than hummingbird wings. His lips press against mine again. One soft, gentle kiss, followed by another and then another.

Rex opens his mouth, his hot tongue brushing against my lips, silently asking if it's okay. I open mine and let him in. Kissing this morning is even better than it was last night. I grip the sides of his shirt to keep myself from melting into a puddle on the counter. He kisses me harder, threading his fingers in my hair and I can't breathe, but the burn in my chest is a good feeling, one that has me excited for what's to come.

Rex's hands slide under my thighs and he lifts me, carrying me across the room to the table before lying me on my back. I pull at his shirt and tug it over his head with zero coordination. He's a work of art. "Sculpted by the gods."

"What?" Rex pants, mouth finding my neck and then my shoulder. He bites down and my hips rock against the hard length beneath his shorts, friction finding a tender spot that feels like heaven.

Oh, no! Did I say that out loud? I groan, my legs tightening around his waist. I'm dry-humping Rex, but I don't care. Heat and need consume me. I reach for his waist and dip my fingers beneath the band of his pants.

"Fuck, Piper," he says against my neck. I slide my hand deeper, finding coarse, curly hair under his boxers. It feels short, but without actually seeing what's going on down there, it's hard to tell, and then silk. Long, thick silk I can barely wrap my fingers around.

Holy shit it's big!

Someone clears their throat and I yank my hand out of Rex's pants like it's on fire. He grunts and collapses on top of me. *Trust me, I feel your pain.*

"Sorry to interrupt," the voice says with a chuckle, "but where's the bathroom?"

I grit my teeth and swallow. My body is vibrating, desperate to feel more. Rex climbs off of me and sits on the table. I push myself onto my elbows and glare at my friend, who seems to find my frustration hilarious. "You're a fucking cockblock, Bane."

I ADJUST MY SHIRT AND PULL MY HAIR UP WITH THE ELASTIC ON MY wrist. Bane watches, a shit-eating grin plastered on his face.

"Where the hell did you get those?" I ask, looking at the Spiderman pajama pants he's got on.

"Rex laid them out for me. He had a shirt, too, but I didn't want to bleed all over it. Also, I'm not six."

"Why haven't you changed the bandage yet?"

The four-inch by four-inch cotton patch is practically soaked through with dark, dried blood, changing the patch from white to a deep maroon with bright red tape that's barely hanging on. "I was hoping you'd help."

I roll my eyes. "Meaning you want to talk."

He grins. "You know me too well."

"I'm gonna help Bane with his bandage. Be right back!" I yell.

"Okay," Rex replies from the kitchen.

I follow Bane to what, in some ways, is my room. Bane sits on the bed while I pull everything out of his hospital to-go bag—cleansing cloth, tape, and sterile pads—and lay everything on the comforter beside him. I peel back the old bandage and set it on top of the sterile wrapping. Three tiny stitches are oozing blood and yellow gunk. It doesn't look good.

"You can't do this, Pipes."

I ignore him and dab his stitches with a cleansing cloth. "You need to change this more often. I don't want your stitches getting infected."

"Piper," he warns.

I finish cleaning the dried blood off of his skin, then tape a new patch over the wound. Bane was lucky. The bullet missed everything important and lodged itself in one of his ribs. I crumble all the wrappers and dirty bandages together, happily ignoring this conversation when Bane grabs my wrist. Needles crawl up my arm, spiking my blood pressure. I look up, and he lets me go.

"Do you love him?"

"What? No! Rex and I..." We're not just friends anymore, but Bane won't approve. Not because of some unrequited love like Cooper, but because he knows my relationship with Rex will make leaving that much harder. "We are getting to know each other."

"So, you're fucking?"

"Bane!" I smack him on his good side. "First of all, if I was, it's none of your business. But since you must know, no. I'm not."

"Do what you want, Piper. Play house together. Screw each other's brains out. Hell, get pregnant for all I care. Just remember, in four weeks my dad gets released. Rumor has it he could get out early."

I swallow the knot in my throat and focus on the mess of bandages. If I look up at Bane, I might cry. Less than four weeks? Does that mean three? Two? I can't... "How?"

"Good behavior. He sprung for a lawyer this time, and the guy is fucking rank."

"Shit."

"Yeah, shit. Have your fun while you can but the clock is ticking. I've got a buddy with a house in Memphis we can stay at for a few days once we leave, one of Mom's old friends. We'll be safe there until we have a solid plan."

"You're a dead man the moment we leave together. You know that, right?"

Bane shrugs. "Gerald may be my sperm donor, but you're family, Piper. You're all I've got left."

Breakfast was amazing. I rinse my plate in the sink and set it in the dishwasher. Bane and Rex are getting along, which I'd typically be ecstatic about, but Bane's words hang over me like a dark cloud.

Cooper strolls into the kitchen, a hand running through his already disheveled hair as everyone is finishing up. "How the fuck did I get here?"

I wipe my hands on the towel and start fixing him a plate of what's left. There's not much. Rex eats enough for two on his own and Bane is a bottomless pit when food's involved. "Better question, what were you doing at Bane's apartment last night?"

"Piper I—"

"Morning sunshine!" Bane claps his hand on Cooper's shoulder. The timing, which could be a coincidence, is suspicious. Nothing in my life has ever *just happened,* so I can't help but wonder if they're hiding something.

Cooper takes in Bane's shirtless appearance, brows furrowing. "What the hell happened to you?"

Bane shrugs. "It's nothing, just a hazard of crossing the tracks. I've got a great scar from a few years ago." He points to his Spiderman pajama-covered leg. "Wanna see?"

Cooper shakes his head. "Nah, man, I'm good."

"Piper, your meeting with Cherrybroom starts in thirty minutes. Are we skipping today or do you want to go?" Rex asks, bringing the empty serving dishes to the sink.

"We should go. My meeting with her is part of my graduation requirements."

"Speaking of," Bane interjects. "Did you get that situation sorted?"

Cooper eyes me. "What situation?"

"It's nothing, and not yet."

"Piper," Bane warns.

I shoot him a shut-the-hell-up look and change the subject. "Can you take the bus back?"

"I'll take him," Cooper says. I don't like the idea of them spending time together, but as long as it gets him out of Rex's house before I have to answer more questions, I don't care.

Rex runs around the front of his Range Rover and opens the door for me when we park in the school's lot. A few girls stare at us as I take his hand and step out. I bite back a smile, amused by their jealousy.

In the four years I've been in this hell hole, no one has ever wanted anything of mine. Then again, no one has ever looked at me like Rex does, like his world begins and ends with me.

He grabs my bag, puts it on his shoulder, and asks, "Can I walk with you?"

"What do you mean?" I turn and lean against the side of his car. The black paint is warm against my back but not unbearable because the sun hasn't been up long. "You walk inside with me almost every day."

"True." Rex places his hands on either side of me. He whispers into my ear, his breath tickling my cheek. "But I want to walk inside together."

"I'm still confused," I whisper back, my breaths short, my heart fast.

Rex brings his lips to mine, one hand threading through my hair, the other tangling our fingers together. I can't remember what we're talking about. Every thought is lost on how perfect Rex's lips feel.

Someone yells at us to get a room, and Rex pulls away. I whimper, drunk on his kiss, high on his scent, needing more. *Remind me why I agreed to go to school today?* I think I'd prefer to spend the day in his room, exploring each other, then go to counseling this morning.

"Let's go make our first appearance as a *real* couple." He puts his arm over my shoulder and escorts me to the school's entrance.

"I don't remember agreeing to be your girlfriend," I tease. I love being Rex's girlfriend, but I wouldn't be me if I didn't make things difficult.

We stop walking. Rex spins me once, capturing me in his arms. "Should I kiss you again? Would that jog your memory?"

"Only if you promise to push me up against the lockers over there and make a mess of me." All those moments I've read about... yeah... I plan to recreate as many as I can while we're together.

Rex presses his lips against my forehead. "All in good time, Piper. All in good time."

People stare as we walk down the hallway hand in hand. No one bothers to hide their surprise that I snagged the most wanted man at our school, but Rex doesn't seem to notice. He walks with his head held high, showing me off like I'm a prize worth winning.

"Sup, Rex," Jake, one of Logan's friends, says, holding up his hand for a high five.

Rex ignores the hand but grins. "Not much."

Jake's gaze drops to me, "Piper."

My insides squirm in a nervous-get-me-out-of here way. I stretch my fingers, hoping Rex will let go of me so I can make my escape. Instead, he squeezes my hand three times and, in my head, I hear him say *I've got you*. I fake a smile. "Hey, Jake."

"What's good for tomorrow's party?" he asks Rex.

"Not having one this weekend." Rex pulls me closer and then slides his arm over my shoulder. "I'm taking my girl on a date."

A date? Like a real one? All of a sudden, I'm hot. Too hot. Rex's arm over me is heavy and I don't think I can breathe. "Oh, I—"

"She works Friday nights with Cooper," Jake interrupts. "I'll bring the keg this time."

Rex ignores him and looks at me quizzically, sensing the unease brewing. "You okay?"

I take a slow, deep breath. I'm not okay, but I'm trying to be. "Yeah, I'm fine. Um... I work every Monday, Wednesday, and Friday."

"My bad, babe," Rex says with a grin. "I thought you had tomorrow off."

Jake sticks his finger in his mouth and pretends to gag. "Ugh, get a room."

"You ain't seen nothing yet." Rex takes my chin beneath his thumb and forefinger and tilts my face upward. He leans down and kisses me, right in the middle of the hallway. His hands fall to my hips as he backs me into the locker. Every high school romance novel I've ever read has this scene and I *finally* get to know what it feels like.

"How's that?" Rex whispers in my ear.

Amazing. Absolutely amazing.

"Seriously, dude?" Jake asks incredulously. "Do you know where that mouth's been?"

Rex turns to Jake, fire in his eyes, and I feel like someone's gutted me. My first hallway kiss was everything I hoped for and more, only to be ruined by this jerk. *Thanks, Life. Way to ruin everything again.*

"Say one more crude thing about my girlfriend," Rex growls, "and I'll break your fucking jaw."

Jake takes a step back, hands up in surrender. "My bad." He turns to walk away but doesn't get far.

Rex takes a step forward and claps his hand on Jake's shoulder. "You owe her an apology."

Jake groans, barely looking over his shoulder. "Sorry, Piper."

"It's okay," I squeak and scurry down the hallway to my locker. Rex is hot on my heels, forgetting his beef with Jake to be at my side. "You should have your party tomorrow," I tell him, busying myself with the books in my locker.

"I was looking forward to the whole chill, quiet house thing. Our guests put a wrench in last night's plans." He tucks his thumb under my chin and lifts my face to look at him. "Besides, I can't pick you up after work if I have to babysit a bunch of drunk idiots."

"You don't have to pick me up. I can—"

"Sleep with Cooper?" He interrupts. "Not happening."

"Possessive much?" I tease and the idea of Rex being jealous chases away my lingering doubts.

"You have no idea," he says with a chuckle.

I stare at him, not sure what to say. Bane is right. I need to stop this. I've never believed in love, and I still don't, but Rex makes me feel like I've got a shot at something great with him. And maybe I do. I once read that when it's darkest magic happens. My life was a blackhole before Rex. Now, there's light, making me want to give life a chance and that in itself is magical.

"It was a joke, Piper," Rex says, pulling me out of my thoughts. He studies me, a worried expression on his face. He's got that look again, one that says he knows my deepest, darkest secrets—he does—but this time, it's different. "I'm worried if I let you go, you won't come back."

My eyes burn with unshed tears because that's exactly what will happen. Not today, and not tomorrow, but soon. "Why are you worrying about that?"

The warning bell rings and everyone around us starts hurrying to their first class. My question goes unanswered. "Can I walk you?"

I shake my head. "No thanks. That'll open a can of worms I'm not ready to talk about with Mrs. Cherrybroom." I shut my locker door and take a step back. "See you at lunch?"

I don't wait for his response. Knowing Rex, he'll be waiting for me outside of Cherrybroom's office when the bell rings. And I...

I'll bask in the feeling of being loved for as long as I can.

Chapter 23
PIPER

I make it to my counseling session by the skin of my teeth. I've never been late and don't know how it would affect my graduation status. I think it's crap that I have to meet with Cherrybroom as often as I do. It's not like we talk about anything important, which sucks because sometimes I actually want to tell someone about what's going on.

"Cutting it close," Mrs. Cherrybroom says, closing the door behind me. I settle into the chair to the left of her desk and set my bag down. "Although, if I was sporting a hunk like Rex, I'd probably be late too. Granted, my hunk would need to be at least ten years older." She flicks her hand. "I don't care how cute he is. No kid is worth jail time."

This is weird. My guidance counselor just called my boyfriend cute. She might only be twenty-five-ish, but I still don't like it. "Um... Yeah, sorry about that."

"Anyway..." She settles in behind her desk, stacking papers that can't possibly be from today, neatly to one side. She opens the bottom drawer and pulls out another handful of papers. "These are for you."

I lean forward and take her handouts. There are five college applications, all with scholarship information stapled to each. I flip through them, pretending to read each for a second or two, then set the stack on my lap. "I was wondering..."

Mrs. Cherrybroom clasps her hands under her chin. "Yes, dear?"

"Would it be possible to leave a week or two early and still graduate?"

Mrs. Cherrybroom sucks in a breath. "Why on earth would you want to do that?"

"I was thinking of traveling this summer before starting school."

"You mean you're going to enroll somewhere?"

No... "Seems that way."

Mrs. Cherrybroom jumps up from her seat and rushes around the desk. Her long arms wrap around my shoulders as if we're friends as she pulls me into a hug. It's not weird at all. I'm kidding. It's very, very weird.

One Mississippi.

Mrs. Cherrybroom must realize how inappropriate the situation is. She lets go before I can mentally count to two and sits in the chair beside me. "Well, it's probably frowned upon, but if you can finish your final exams, I can work with your professors to sign off on it." She clasps her hands together. "Oh, Piper. I'm so pleased."

"Thank you, ma'am."

Mrs. Cherrybroom stands and walks to her desk. She scribbles something on a pad. "Here." She rips the page free. "I probably shouldn't, but I've written you a pass for the day. There are only a few weeks left. Go, plan your trip. Just promise to make a Facebook profile and add me so I can see what you're up to."

"Thanks, Mrs. Cherrybroom. I will."

As much as I appreciate the day off, I don't skip. If I'm going to get in my professors' good graces, I need to be present as much as possible.

The morning passes in a blur of whispered rumors and too many questions of *"What's going on between you and Rex?"* from people who haven't talked to me since freshman year. I tell them nothing. My life isn't their business. Besides, whatever I say will only fuel the rumor mill. Five minutes left into my third class, my phone buzzes. I slip my bag onto my lap and peek inside.

Rex: Have lunch with me today.

"Miss Lovelace, are you with us?" Mrs. Hale asks.

I nod, and she continues her lecture. It buzzes again.

Eventually, the bell rings and everyone hurries to leave. I close my books and wait for my classmates to exit before getting up, a habit I developed so I don't hear the daily gossip. I shut my notebook and neatly stack it on my textbook while I wait for the last person to leave, then head to my locker.

No matter the time of day, the hallway is still alive with whispers. I smile at the sideways glances, letting everyone know that I see them, I hear them, and, best of all, I'm not stupid.

When I reach my locker, I spin the dial and open it, and a folded paper falls at my feet. I set my books on the top shelf and bend down to pick it up. Inside are two words:

Found you.

The world around me comes to a screeching halt. I think I'm going to be sick. I force my gaze up and look over both of my shoulders. No one in particular stands out, but it doesn't help that I'm a hot topic today, attracting more attention than usual.

I look down at the note again. The paper is a bright white, the words handwritten. I run my thumb over the blue ink, and the letters smudge. It's fresh. Someone dropped this in my locker just before I got here.

"Hey."

"Mercy!" I jump, not expecting anyone to be behind me. I crumple the note and shove it in my pocket. I don't know what I'm going to do with it, but sticking it back in my locker seems like a bad idea.

Slamming the metal door more forcefully than I intended, I look up to see Rex. He's taking this boyfriend thing seriously, leaning one shoulder against the wall of metal, all sexy-like, like Stefan from *The Vampire Diaries*. I think I may be a Netflix junkie now. "Did you get my texts?"

Texts? Oh, right, lunch. "Yeah, sorry. Mrs. Hale caught me while I was reading them. Couldn't respond."

"That's cool." He pushes off the lockers and I look up into his eyes. It's a mistake because those blues are a vortex of beauty and wonder. I get lost in them, counting the colors that swirl within. The only good part of this vortex is that, for a moment, I forget about the note and just appreciate how amazing Rex is. "Are you ready?"

I forgot he was waiting for an answer. Out of the trance that is Rex, worry creeps back. Whoever wrote that note will probably be in the cafeteria watching me, reporting my every move back across the tracks. "I don't know, Rex."

"How about compromise? Let me buy you lunch and we can eat at the big tree you like."

That's doable. No one will see us there and maybe I can relax a little. Rex has a way of calming my nerves; maybe eating together would be a good idea. The worst I'll have to do is brave the lunch line. If we hurry, we can be in and out before it gets too busy. "Okay."

THE ZITI IS DELICIOUS. WHILE MOST CAFETERIA FOOD SUCKS, OUR principal has a top-notch chef in the kitchen. Ziti and prime rib are what's on the menu for today and tomorrow. Heaven forbid rich kids eat typical school food like the taco mush my elementary school had.

My mind races a mile a minute, bursting with questions I don't know the answers to. It's evident now more than ever that I have to leave, and soon. With time ticking away, I want to know everything about Rex. The more information I have, the longer I can hold onto the memories. "I have a question."

"Shoot," he says playfully.

"Why do you think your dad hates you?"

Rex drops his fork on the empty tray and runs a hand through his hair. "Can't start with the easy ones, can you?"

I shake my head and shrug. "The easy stuff is boring. I can probably find your favorite food and color from a Google search."

That annoyingly beautiful grin settles over his face. "Green and chicken cordon bleu, in case you're taking notes." He exhales loudly, his smile falling, and looks down at his hands. "Well, for starters, I don't have a single memory of him and me."

My heart hurts for him. I think back to the photos on the wall. His parents looked so happy, but Rex wasn't in any of them. Their life carries on and he's stuck looking at a family that isn't really his. "What about when he wasn't on tour? Or holidays? Wasn't Kip home?"

Rex pulls at the grass, taking a single green blade between his fingers and ripping it before grabbing another. "Holidays are usually romantic getaways for him and Mom and I can't remember the last birthday my parents spent with me. Any time we happened to be in the house at the same time, Dad would lock himself in his office."

"Shit, that's terrible. I'm sorry." My childhood was crap, for obvious reasons, but I think Rex's might have been worse. I knew what to expect from Monica—nothing. But Rex had two parents who should have loved him.

"Sometimes I wonder if I'm even Kip's kid." Rex stares off into the distance. "I don't look anything like him or my mom. If she cheated, my dad's hatred for me would make sense."

I can't imagine anyone cheating on Kip Montgomery. He's made *sexiest man alive* for the last three years, and he's old as fuck. I can only assume he was just as gorgeous eighteen years ago.

"Enough about me," Rex says, changing the subject. "Tell me something most people don't know about you."

There's plenty that people don't know about me, but I can't tell much of it. "Um. I am terrified of scary movies."

"You're kidding."

"Nope. Zombies are the worst. I tried watching *The Walking Dead* once and had nightmares for weeks." True story. I was thirteen. I thought my usual nightmares were terrible, but no. Take Monica and turn her into a flesh-eating zombie that won't die no matter how many times I shoot her in the head. Yeah... never again.

"So, Halloween Horror Nights at Universal Studios is out this year?" he teases.

"I'd go for you." If I were around... but I won't be. I'll probably be living in the mountains doing God knows what for money. Silence falls between us. I chew on my plastic fork.

"Piper?"

"Hmm?"

"Can we talk about what happened to you?"

"What's there to talk about? You heard everything. Bad guy tried to rape me. I ran away from bad guy. End of story."

"You said someone's after you. Have you thought about going to the cops?"

I toss my fork onto my tray, not necessarily mad at Rex but at our conversation. Gerald is the last person I want to think about, especially with that note burning a hole in my pocket. "I can't. It's been almost a year. There's no evidence anymore and all that will do is piss Gerald off."

"You're well within the statute of limitations. Didn't you hear about the *Me Too* movement a few years ago? Those girls were hurt years ago and their charges stuck."

They stuck because those girls were accusing high-profile people. Lowly, wannabe slum lords are swept under the rug thanks to crooked cops. I wouldn't stand a chance. Besides, all making a report would do is give Gerald a way to find me faster. "Just drop it, Rex."

"That man should be locked up for what he did to you, Piper. You didn't do anything wrong. You shouldn't be afraid to report him."

"I didn't tell the cops when I assaulted him, Rex. By definition, that's doing something wrong."

"But he—"

"No!" I yell. "Conversation over."

First the note and now this. I should have skipped this morning when Mrs. Cherrybroom gave me the pass. I stand and march toward the school, but change my mind. "You can't just ask me to be your girlfriend and expect me to change everything, Rex."

"Change what?"

"Me! My plan. My life." I look at him, frustration building because I want everything to change. I want to stay and figure out what Rex and I could be, and go to college, and enjoy life, but I can't. I just... can't.

Rex stands and takes a step toward me. "What exactly is your plan?"

"Forget it. You wouldn't understand." I turn again and run.

Away from Rex.

Away from it all.

I pushed her too far.

I knew better. I saw the warning signs that she was going to break, but I kept going because I couldn't let it go. The rest of the day dragged. I waited for five minutes at Piper's locker after the last bell, but she never showed up. She wasn't at my car either. After fifteen minutes, I pull out my phone and text her.

> Me: Hey, where are you?
>
> Me: I'm at my car. Want a ride?
>
> Me: I'm sorry, Piper.

Three dots appear. My heart skips until they disappear again, and then there's nothing.

> Me: Text me back. I'm getting worried.

Piper doesn't text me back, so I drive to the Red Onion, but she's not there either. I didn't think she would be. It's her day off, but I hoped. I drive to my house, park in my driveway, and open the front door. It's unlocked, which is strange because I never go out of it.

"Piper?" I call out, running through the house. Searching. Hoping. But she's not here. Not inside. Not outback on the patio. Not in the pool house. She's not here.

My fist hits the wall beside me, leaving a round imprint on the plaster. "Shit!"

You and half the school the first week I was enrolled. Everyone wanted to be my best friend back then. Now, I'm just the party house. I have no real friends, which was fine... until Piper.

Twenty minutes later, there's a knock at my door. I run to it, hoping to God it's Piper. It's not.

"What the hell did you do to her?" Cooper asks, pushing his way inside before I finish opening the door. "Piper!"

"She's not here." I slam it shut and follow him into my kitchen. "Did Logan not tell you anything?"

Cooper whirls around. "He told me you set her off."

My head falls. I can't even argue with him. Anything that happens because of Piper tonight is my fault, and I feel terrible. "He's right, I did."

Cooper's expression softens. We may not be friends, but we want the same thing—for Piper to be safe. "What happened?"

"I tried to talk to her about that night."

"What night?"

"You know...that night."

"Oh," he pauses. "Well, that at least gives us somewhere to start. Grab your keys."

I COULD LIVE MY WHOLE LIFE WITHOUT COMING BACK TO THIS SIDE OF the tracks and this shitty apartment. Cooper knocks on Bane's door, still stained red with blood streaks from a night I'd prefer to forget. There's a pause, then some sliding and clicking of locks until finally, the door opens.

"What the hell are you doing here?" Bane steps back, opening the door wider. "Get in before someone recognizes you two."

We walk inside, but neither Cooper nor I sit.

"Do you have any idea how much you stick out dressed like that?" Bane says to both of us.

I changed into a pair of board shorts and a gray T-shirt. Cooper is still in his school uniform—black slacks, white button-down, but no tie. Compared to Bane's tattered jeans and plain black shirt, I can see what he's talking about. "Next time, I'll be sure to slum it up."

Cooper chuckles even though nothing about why we are here is comical.

Bane flips him the bird, then looks at me. "There shouldn't be a next time. What the fuck are ya'll doing here?"

"Piper's missing," Cooper says, his voice hard and demanding.

"And you think she's here?" Bane looks at us like we've got two heads and I'm lost. Bane and Piper are friends, why wouldn't she come here? Especially if she feels like he can keep her safe. *What am I missing?*

"She disappeared because of something this dimwit said 'bout *that* night."

Something clicks in Bane's head and he runs a hand through his already messy hair. "Fuck."

I get the feeling there's something more than both of them are telling me. "What do you two know that I don't?"

Cooper eyes Bane, who frantically searches through his phone, then exhales. "How much do you know about that night?"

"Only what I overheard in the stairwell."

"The man who did that to her is his dad." Cooper glares at Bane. "But they're not on speaking terms...supposedly."

"Fuck you," Bane retorts. "I hate that man. I hated him before the shit with Piper, but what he did..." Bane pauses and shakes his head.

"Who is he?"

Bane shoves his phone back into his pocket. "A bad motherfucker with plans for Piper that will ruin if not kill her." He looks at Cooper. "I've got the word out with some guys I trust. If Piper shows her face over here, I'll keep her safe."

"And call us," I add.

"Whatever. Get your asses across the tracks before someone puts a mark on you to find her." He points outside and adds, "That car can't come here again."

COOPER CALLS HIS MOM AS WE'RE COMING BACK INTO TOWN AND TELLS her everything—the party, what happened to Piper, and the failed suicide attempts that both he and Bane thwarted.

I sag back into the seat, listening to Piper's secrets. She's had such a shitty year; I can only imagine how bad her life was before it. I wish she would have told me all this herself, but I can understand why she didn't.

Logan, by the orders of his mamma, closes the Red Onion at five and waits at my house in case Piper shows up there.

Cooper and I pull into my driveway after a long night of searching just as the sun peeks over the horizon. "I don't want to go to school."

Cooper runs a hand over his face. "I know, me either, but maybe she'll show up."

Piper has to show up. I won't be able to live with myself if she ran away because of me. I should have known better than to bring that night up. I'm such an idiot.

Cooper's phone dings. He pulls it out of his pocket and reads the message. "She's with Mom."

"Oh, thank God. Let's go get her."

"No," Cooper says in a tone that means this isn't up for discussion. "Give her some time. Whatever's going on, Mom will sort it out."

Mamma T is a tired woman. When Mr. Harris left two years ago, he took everything—the two-story beach house, the cars, her comfort and lifestyle. Sure, she has alimony and child support, but Mamma T says the money is tainted. She'd rather work for what she's got than spend a dime of what that man gives her. It sits in a trust, collecting interest for her boys until they turn twenty-one.

"You gave everyone quite a fright last night," she says, handing me a cup of warm tea.

I place the cup to my lips, exhausted and starving. The drink tastes like heaven and the blueberry muffins she sets on the table are even better. I wolf one down in two seconds, then take another swallow of my drink. "I didn't mean to make anyone worry."

"That boy sure was in a tizzy." Mamma T pulls out a chair and sits at the table across from me. "I think he likes you."

I don't need to ask who she's talking about. Rex blew up my phone last night with a million texts and calls until it died. I'm sure there will be even more messages when I turn it back on. I smile into my cup, hoping Mamma T doesn't notice, but of course, she does.

"Seems like you might like him too."

I shrug and stuff another muffin in my mouth. She sets her cup on the table, holding it with both hands, a worry line between her brows. "Where were you last night?"

A knot twists deep in my stomach. I'm not proud of ghosting everyone, but I needed some time to figure out what to do. I came up with nothing. "On the bus."

"All night?"

"Yeah. Sheila, the driver, she's kind of my friend. I spent more nights on her bus than not last year."

"I see." Mamma T rubs her thumb against the white porcelain of her cup. "You didn't go home when you weren't here, did you?"

"No, ma'am."

Mamma T shakes her head and a disappointed sigh leaves her lips. "Why didn't you tell me you're in trouble, Piper?"

"I'm not," I say instinctively, and she raises her eyes to give me *the look*—the one that says she knows everything. I exhale loudly and hide my face in my hands. "I didn't want you caught up in my shit."

"Language, Piper."

"Sorry."

Mamma T doesn't ask questions. She's already connected the dots and realized why I've done everything I did this year. She might have even figured out that I have to run away, even though I don't want to.

I like the life I'm building. Things between Cooper and I have been tense, but we're still family. I have my family again and a boyfriend. I know that sounds lame, but I don't want to give it all up.

"So, what are you gonna do?"

With no other options and needing some real advice, I tell her the truth. "Run. Change my name. Pray Gerald gets shot, and I can resume normal life someday."

"Gerald, as is in Bane's dad?"

"Yes, ma'am."

"I've got connections, Piper. My life didn't end when Jerry left me. I can help."

I shake my head. "I don't want you involved. This is my mess."

"You are my daughter, Piper. I may not have birthed you, but you're still mine. Your problems are mine by default." Mamma T finishes her drink and then walks to the sink to rinse her cup. "Tell me more about that boy."

"Who? Bane? You've met him before." Once, at the hospital...but we don't talk about that day.

"Not Bane. He's a nice young man, stuck in unfortunate circumstances, but nice. I want to know about the one who rode around with Cooper all night looking for you."

"Rex?"

She nods, an excited grin on her face.

"There's not much to tell. He likes me. I kind of like him, but there's no happy ending for us."

Mamma T shakes her head, a knowing grin lifting her lips. "You never know, dear. Life is full of surprises."

We pull up to the Red Onion a few minutes before my shift starts. I see them both through the window, Rex and Cooper, standing by the counter, chatting like old friends. Aside from those two, the diner is empty, but it won't be for long. Within the next forty-five minutes, the evening rush will start and run full throttle until close, with only a few moments to breathe in between.

"Want me to walk in with you?" Mamma T asks.

I pull at the hem of my shirt, weighing my options. If I go inside alone, Cooper will ream me a new one. But if Mamma T's there, he might not. "It would make things less awkward."

"Oh, honey." She grins. "I live for the awkward moments. Tell you what, let the boys have their outbursts for a few minutes, then I'll get the heat off you."

I raise my brow. "And how exactly are you going to do that?"

Mamma T gives me a crooked grin, one that says she's up to no good. The same grin that's usually plastered on Logan's face. We get out and walk up the steps. She opens the door and the bell dings.

"Piper," Rex says on an exhale. He takes three long strides and pulls me into his arms. "I was so worried."

I suck in a breath, unsure if things changed between us. I'm terrified the switch in my brain has flipped back and the panic attacks will return, but they don't. I wrap my arms around Rex's waist and he squeezes me tighter.

"I'm sorry," I whisper into his shirt.

Cooper clears his throat. Rex takes a step back and I instantly miss him, but our make-up session will have to be finished later. I step around him to Cooper, who stands behind the counter, arms crossed, glaring. "I'm sorry."

"You suck," he says, his tone laced with venom.

I hold my arms out to him. "Hug?"

Cooper's eyes widen. He all but runs around the counter and swoops me into his arms, squeezing me so tight I can barely breathe. My skin pricks beneath his touch, but I do everything I can to keep myself together. He lets go a second later, probably realizing I'm tipping close to a panic attack. "Thanks, Piper. It's been a long time since you've let me hug you like that. Are you okay?"

I nod, taking a deep breath and counting to three as I exhale. My pulse slows enough that I can form a sentence again. "Getting better every day."

Rex slips his hand in mine, and I realize the words couldn't be truer. Little do they know, I'm healing. That hug should have instantly sent my body into shock. Instead, it was a slow build. I want to think my progress is because of Rex, but I'm not naive enough to believe it's all because of him. Whatever the reason, though, I'll take it.

"Piper," Mamma T says, rounding the counter. "Are you going to introduce me to your boyfriend?"

"Oh, my gosh." "I'm Rex," we say at the same time.

Rex chuckles. "Piper doesn't like the label, but she's my girl."

"I see." Mamma T grins and turns her attention to Cooper. "And what about you, dear?"

"What about me?" he asks, thrown off guard by the question.

Mamma T slides the straw dispenser to the middle of the counter. She reaches underneath the counter and pulls out the straw refill box. She opens each container and begins re-stocking, casually bringing him into the conversation. "Is there a lucky lady in your life?"

"Mom," Cooper groans.

"I'm just saying, dear," Mamma T looks up her nose at me and winks. "I never see you with anyone, let alone hear you talk about a special lady. Is there something you'd like to tell me?"

Cooper's cheeks flush, knowing where the conversation is going. "No, Mom."

"What's she doing?" Rex whispers in my ear.

I put my finger to my lips, shushing him. This isn't the first time

Mamma T has brought up Cooper's sexuality. In all fairness, she has good reason to wonder, but while her words are filled with love I don't think she's asking out of the kindness of her heart right now. I think she's trying to distract him. We both know that when Cooper gets stuck in his head, he's a grumpfish, and I have a feeling he's been there all day… worrying about me.

"Darling," Mamma T rounds the counter and takes Cooper's hands. "I'll love you no matter what."

"We all will," Rex chimes in, a shit-eating grin on his face. He's finally caught on to what's happening.

"Bite me, fucker," Cooper growls. "Mom, drop it." He pulls his arms back and starts straightening the already neat tables.

"Just say it, Coop," Mamma T puts her hands on her hips. "You're gay."

"Mom!" Cooper whirls around. "What the hell? I'm not gay."

"Honey," she coos, "it's okay if you're not ready to admit it yet." She rests her hand on his shoulder. "I'll love you no matter what."

"Sorry to disappoint, Mrs. Harris," Rex says, "but Cooper is taking my friend Jenny to prom with us next week."

"Us?" Mamma T asks, her face lighting up as she looks at me. "You're going to prom? Does that mean we get to go dress shopping?"

I'm going to kill Rex. I was *not* planning on going to prom, but I can't crush Mamma T like that. I haven't seen her this gleeful in ages. As much as she's done for me over the years, I guess the least I can do is go dress shopping with her. A shiver runs through me. I *hate* wearing dresses. "It seems that way."

Mamma T squeals and pulls me in for a hug. "Oh, I'm so excited. We haven't had a girl's day since the summer of your freshman year. I'm going to go. I've got to make hair and nail appointments for Saturday morning." She steps back and grabs her keys off the counter, then looks up at Rex. "I'll schedule an appointment for Jenny too. My treat." She walks out, still talking to herself, "We need a *Pinterest* board for hair designs…"

When the door closes, I put my hands on my hips and glare at Rex. "Seriously? Prom?"

He shrugs. "I was meaning to ask you."

"I would have said no."

He grins. "I figured as much, which is why I thought mentioning it in front of Mamma T was perfect."

"Dude," Cooper comes up and gives Rex one of those guy hand-shakes. "Thanks, man. I owe you."

"It's no problem," Rex says, putting his arm around my waist. "Jenny has been bugging me to meet Piper. Now's as good a time as any."

"So," Cooper asks, hopping onto the counter. "Jenny... is she hot?"

Me: I need a favor

Jenny: This could be fun

Me: Come to prom

Jenny: Oh darling I thought you'd never ask

Jenny: lol

Me: I'm serious. I need a wingman

Jenny: Aren't those supposed to be dudes

Me: I'll give you a no-limits shopping spree while you're here

Jenny: Count me in! When is it?

Me: Saturday

Jenny: Same day as ours

Me: Shit. Never mind then. I'll figure something else out

Jenny: Trust me I'd rather be at your prom than mine

Me: Everything ok?

I recline the seat of my Range Rover and drop my phone onto the center console. Piper has ten more minutes before her shift ends. I hope she's coming with me tonight. I don't know where we stand and it kills me. I want her—the good, the bad, the ugly...everything.

The shop's door opens and I sit up. Cooper turns, locking it behind him once Piper is on the sidewalk. They walk down the steps together, laughing like the past few weeks never happened.

Piper stops and her smile falls when she notices my car. My stomach twists, unsure if I should get out to greet her or not. She quickly hugs Cooper and the guy looks like he could reach the moon. Piper's hugs will do that, send you soaring sky-high. I get them all the time but I still remember the first time we touched. It was electric.

She opens the door and gets in the passenger seat. "Hey."

"Hey." I'm elated she's here with me, but I keep my cool. I want to lay into her for ghosting me yesterday and sending us all into a crazed panic, but I also don't want to scare her off again. She left me once. I'm positive she could do it again and that terrifies me.

"Are you ready?" she asks.

"Yup." I put the car into gear, trying desperately not to show her I'm freaking out inside. "Where are we going?"

"Your place." She pulls out her phone and begins texting someone. "I figured we'd watch a movie." She looks up, worry in her eyes. "Is that still okay? That's what we normally do, but I'd get it if you don't want me around."

"Why wouldn't I want you around, Piper? I like you. A lot."

She shrugs. "I don't know. I guess I was worried that running off yesterday meant we broke up."

A noose wraps around my heart. I've never been in a relationship and I hope this isn't how breakups work because I'm not ready to let Piper go. "Is that what you want?"

"No! Not at all!" she says suddenly, dropping her phone in her lap. She looks to me again and all I want to do is pull the car over and make her worries go away. "I...I'm sorry. I shouldn't have disappeared the way I did. I didn't mean to worry you."

"No, Piper, I'm sorry." I pull into a church parking lot and shift into park. I turn to her, giving her my full attention as I say, "I never should have pressured you to talk about that night. You weren't ready and it's none of my business. It's just..." I take her hand in mine. "It kills me that Gerald will get away with hurting you. I want you to know, no matter what—even if you decide to break up with me, which I hope you don't—I'm here for you. If something happens and you're alone, or scared, or anything, just call me, and I'll be there."

She nods and instead of pushing the conversation, I get us back on the road. As much as I want her to say something—anything—placating my feelings comes second to Piper knowing I've got her back.

Fifteen minutes later, we're sitting on the couch together and scrolling through Netflix. Piper's spread out, laying across the length of the cushions with her head in my lap while my fingers trail through her hair, a quiet moan escaping her every now and then.

Her eyes drift shut and a small smile tugs at her lips. Just when I think she's fallen asleep, she says, "How is it that in one night, my life goes back to its fucked up version of normal?" She rolls onto her back and looks up at me. "And then I come here, and all my worries melt away."

I shrug. "Maybe it's because you love me."

I'm joking but then it dawns on me, I like Piper—like, really like her. I'm falling head over heels and there's nothing I can do about it. Hell, I don't even know how much she likes me back. What if this is just a fling for her and I'm over here super attached?

Piper snort-laughs but sadness clouds her features. "I'm not capable of love, Rex, but lust... that's a horse of a different color."

"I thought you hated horses?"

"Who told you that?" she pushes herself up and leans in close. Her lips find my neck and then my ear when she sucks it into her mouth.

"Cooper." Cooper? He is the last person I want to think about right now. I put my arm around her waist and she shifts to sit on my lap. "Um...Last night in the car."

"Cooper's got a big mouth." Her words are a whisper on my skin until she arches back and looks me in the eyes. "I like you. I like the way you make me feel."

"And how do I make you feel?"

"Appreciated." She kisses me once, then lays back down. She gets comfortable, with her head in my lap, and presses play on another movie.

Jenny Cartwright is exactly what I feared she would be—beautiful, posh, and outgoing. She's everything I'm not and a giant reminder that I don't belong with Rex. She looks like a model with her long tan legs, white Daisy-Duke's, and pink crop top. Whereas I look like an early 2000's *Hot Topic* reject. If this girl is Rex's best friend, I can't imagine what the women he's been with look like.

I fiddle with my phone in the front seat of Mamma T's Cadillac, pretending like I have social media or something important to look at because I don't want to talk. I have nothing against Jenny. She's nice-ish. It's just that she's so much like the girls at school; it's hard to separate my hate from them and her. I know it's wrong and judgy, but she's probably judging me too.

"So, Jennifer..." Mamma T starts when we hit the first red light of the day.

The tiny mall we're headed to is a twenty-minute ride from our house. There are a total of thirty-two stoplights on the way, each one bringing me closer to the end of this ridiculous shopping trip. I hate shopping mostly because I've never had the money to waste. Everything I've ever bought has come from a thrift store, and when I shop I'm in and out in fifteen minutes, usually less. In my opinion, there's no point in trying on the whole store if I don't see something I immediately like. But some girls, Mamma T included, fall into a time vortex. Hours are lost with hundreds of dollars are spent, and somehow they only come home with one bag of stuff. I don't get it.

"Oh, no, Mrs. Harris," Jenny giggles from the backseat. "It's Jenny. Only my mother called me Jennifer and that's when I was in trouble."

I roll my eyes and search *Pinterest* for a dress I don't hate. It's a challenging task because I don't wear dresses anymore, not since moving back across the tracks with Monica.

Why?

For starters, my ass was grabbed in passing anytime I wasn't in my room. Monica's Johns tried to get some buy-one-get-one-free action any time they could. Hands over jeans, even for a second, was gross enough. I never wanted to risk their fingers touching me if I were in a dress or skirt. Also, crashing on the bus at night in a skirt or dress would have been asking for trouble. Sheila did a great job at keeping me safe while I slept, but I wasn't about to put her life, or mine, on the line to look cute.

So, pants it was… until I moved back in with the Harris's. I've allowed myself to wear the school's uniform skirts on days when it's warm out, but haven't dared to don a dress.

"Well, Jenny," Mamma T says. "Call me Mamma T. The only time anyone calls me Mrs. Harris is when one of my kids has done something wrong."

"Alright then. Mamma T, it is."

I can practically hear Jenny's smile. It's infuriating. Like seriously, who is this happy all the time? This act has to be as fake as her bleach-blonde hair.

I find myself more and more irritated the longer I listen to her and Mamma T carry on in conversation. Rex doesn't hang out with girls like Jenny at school. Most of the time, he seems irritated around all the plastic, trust fund kids. So why her? What about Jenny sucked him in and earned her the title of best friend? *What am I missing?*

"Now, don't worry about a cent, Jenny. I'm buying." Mamma T turns right on Highway 60. Ten more minutes and we'll be at the mall. Ten more minutes, and this part of the prom fiasco will be that much closer to over.

"Definitely not!" Jenny exclaims. "Rex promised me a no-limits shopping trip and I'm going to find the most expensive shit I can." She giggles and the sound reminds me of champagne bubbles—annoying and dramatic. "It's been a long time since I've been spoiled like this, and he knows damn well I'm gonna take full advantage of the offer."

"Do you even want to go to prom with Cooper or was this just some ploy to get Rex's money?" I ask, not bothering to hide my irritation. I wanted to like Jenny, I really did. Despite my hesitations and inability to separate her from the girls at school, I wanted to find what drew Rex to her. She is, after all, the only friend he's ever mentioned, but I can't play nice if she's a gold digger.

"Piper!" Mamma T scolds.

Jenny giggles again, and I wonder, *Who laughs this much?* No one sane, that's for sure.

"Not in the least. This is my birthday-slash-graduation present. Don't worry, knowing Rexy-Roo, he's got something major planned for you. This shopping trip is going to look like a grain of sand on the beach compared to what he's cooking up."

I don't want anything from Rex for graduation. Not his money, his gifts, or his time. The best present he could give me would be for him to find someone else.

Our time is nearly spent. On Monday, Gerald will be released. This is our last weekend together, and I think that's partly why I'm so bitter. I don't want to say goodbye, but I don't have any other options.

Mamma T pulls into a front-row space in the Hollingdales's parking lot. I jump out of the car, eager to put as much space between Jenny and me as possible. I don't know how long I can play nice if I'm stuck with a fake, gold-digging bitch who is using my boyfriend for his money. I need to keep my earbuds in and my mouth shut. I'd never expect Rex to choose me over her and with the clock ticking I don't want to give Jenny a reason to make him choose.

"This is your mall?" Jenny asks, staring at the mostly empty storefronts once we're inside. "It's pathetic."

"Afraid so," Mamma T says, nodding her head. "Our choices are few and far between unless you want to drive two hours down to Palm Beach, but we won't make it back in time for our salon appointments if we do that."

Jenny reads the mall's directory board and grimaces. "I'd rather do my own hair than settle for whatever's inside these crappy stores."

"Alright then, let's do it," Mamma T says, fishing her keys out of her purse again. "Maybe we'll get lucky and we can snag a few walk-in appointments at one of the salons down there."

Two more hours of driving, plus Lord knows how many hours of shopping, and we're nowhere close to finished. Our mall had maybe twenty stores struggling to survive, but only five that *might* have dresses. This mall has at least forty stores with prom dresses and Jenny insists on looking in every one until we find the perfect dress.

Thirteen stores later, I groan, unable to keep my frustration hidden any longer. I'm tired and hungry, and we still have to get ready for tonight. "Seriously? A dress is a dress. Does it really matter where we get it from?"

Jenny gasps, and I swear this girl could win an Oscar for her goody-two-shoes, southern-belle performance. Perfect, manicured nails cover her heart as she says, "Goodness no! We can't just get some dinosaur dress. This is your senior prom, and mine for that matter."

This bitch doesn't care about prom. She just wants to spend as much of Rex's money as she can. I cross my arms, unfazed by the show Mamma T has eaten up. "It's not like this is your school. What does it matter what you wear?"

"Well, it's yours, and while you might not care about this night, I care about it because Rex does. Which means you should too. He's doing everything he can to make tonight perfect because he likes you." She pokes my shoulder. "Rex doesn't like damn near anyone. So, suck it up, buttercup. We're not leaving until we look perfect."

HOURS.

It's been hours and Jenny still hasn't found a dress. Neither have I, but that's not the point. I will pick any damn thing off the rack. The reason I haven't yet is that I don't want to carry it from store to store while Jenny takes her sweet time choosing, and while Mamma T isn't going to prom with us, she, for some reason, has picked out a fancy dress and shoes for herself. Why? No freaking clue, but it's her money, not mine.

"I've found it!" Jenny squeals, holding up a floor-length, navy blue dress, so dark it almost looks black. The neckline plunges low to a rhinestone waistband, and the back is a mesh material with a line of buttons going from the top down to where her ass would be. As a whole, it's a nice dress. Really nice...

"Are you gonna try it on?" I ask my eyes on a rack of dresses in front of me. I run my fingers over the hangers looking for a long dress in a color I don't hate, and something I could *maybe* wear.

Jenny holds the dress out and smirks. "Oh, this isn't for me. It's for you. I found my dress five stores ago."

My jaw drops. I look to Mamma T, who has the same devilish grin on her face as Jenny. My mind runs through the stores and dresses, and I realize that Mamma T's dress isn't for her, but for Jenny. "I thought... but you..."

Jenny shrugs, dismissing all the shade I've thrown her way today. "I know, but I wasn't about to let you show up to prom in just anything. Here." She rattles the hanger, sending a wave through the fabric. "Try it on. This should be your size, but I want to see how it falls on you. Although, with your curves, I'm sure it'll look great. Not to mention, the back will show off your killer sparrow tattoo."

How does she know I have a tattoo? My mind is fogging. This whole time I thought Jenny was being a snooty bitch, searching for the perfect dress to wear at a prom that isn't even hers, and all this time her picki-ness was for me. *What else about her was I wrong about?* "Um, okay."

I take the gown into the dressing room and slip it on. I smooth my hands over the skirt, admiring how the fabric looks black in some angles and blue in others. I was wrong; the silver rhinestones don't fall at the waist but at the bra line. The front dip isn't nearly as dramatic as I expected, but it is still reveal-ing. My boobs look great in it, and so does my ass, but I don't like seeing my panty lines. This is definitely a dress to go commando in. The more I look at myself, the more I hate to admit, but the damn thing looks amazing.

"Do we get to see?" Mamma T calls and I can hear the excitement in her voice.

My hand shakes against the doorknob. I don't know why I'm nervous. It's just Mamma T out there and Jenny. Jenny, who I clearly misjudged. I open the door slowly, but once I step out they both gasp, Mamma T's hands covering her mouth.

"Piper, honey," she says, a tear running down her cheek. "You look beautiful."

"Here." Jenny hands me a strappy silver pair of heels. "Try these on. They'll go great with this one."

I kick off my boots, slip the three-inch stilettos on and stumble my way to the mirror. The shoes are sexy but deadly. "I'm gonna break my neck in these."

"Hmmm. Okay, be right back." Jenny disappears to the shoe section of the store and returns with two other silver heels to try on. One a chunky shoe and the other a lower but still skinny heel. Both look like something I'll sprain my ankle in. I nix all heels and go with a silver pair of ballet flats. Pretty and practical.

"Well," Jenny says with an amused look on her face. "If you're not going to wear heels at the dance, you at least need to wear them at the hotel. Pack them in your overnight bag with some killer lingerie. Do you have any? If not, I saw a huge Victoria's Secret near where we parked."

Mamma T's eyes practically bulge out of her head. I'd laugh if this wasn't such an awkward situation. Jenny, however, does laugh. The girl is like a freaking bobblehead doll. Only instead of bobbling, she's giggling. "What? It's a well-known fact that everyone has sex at prom. Better to go into the night prepared than end up pregnant because you weren't ready. Speaking of..." she trails off and rummages through her purse until she finds a ribbon of condoms. "I never trust a guy to have fresh ones. Old latex can pop, and nobody has time for babies."

Mamma T's face blanches. She touches Jenny's arm and says, "Dear, Lord, child put those away!" Her eyes jump from stranger to stranger, looking for anyone who might have seen or overheard our conversation. When Jenny has the condoms safely tucked away, Mamma T says, "Let's grab a late lunch. Seems like I need to set some ground rules for tonight."

Jenny squeezes my arm, her gaze locked onto the boys who haven't noticed us yet. "Isn't he dreamy?"

I'm not sure which man she's talking about, Cooper or Rex, because they both look good. But Rex looks like he walked out of an Armani catalog. He's wearing black dress pants, a white button-down shirt with rolled sleeves, and a black tie—no jacket— and his hair is lightly gelled and styled to perfection. I smile, my insides melting, because he is beautiful. I'm going to miss him.

Jenny links her arm through mine and we cross the living room to the kitchen. Nervous needles travel up my spine from her touch. They're not as bad as they usually are, but they're still uncomfortable. I fight the urge to flinch away because I don't want to offend her.

Jenny is not at all what I thought she was. While she curled and pinned my hair into place, she told me what's been going on in her life. Like me, she's a poor kid on a scholarship, unwanted in a school full of rich bitches. The only difference is that she used to be rich, which makes her worse off. I never had friends in school, and all but one of Jenny's abandoned, ridiculed, and tormented her. I understand why she opted to go to our senior prom over hers.

Rex holds his hand out for me, the corners of his lips lifting as his eyes trail over my body. I take the offering and let him spin me once before pulling me into his chest. Both arms wrap around my waist the moment his lips meet mine, sending fireworks ablaze inside me. The kiss is quick, not even coming close to satisfying the ache burning through me, but I'm not complaining.

"Who is this model and where did my punk Piper go?" he whispers, his fingers tracing small circles on my lower back. I giggle and shrug. I dip my head, resting it against his shoulder, cheeks burning with embarrassment.

"I love your hair," he says, his thick fingers playing with one of my long barrel curls. "Especially the blue tips. It matches your dress."

"That was Jenny's idea. She has magic powers when it comes to hair."

"What was my idea?" Jenny asks, coming closer with Cooper. They make a cute couple, and Cooper looks enamored by her. I don't blame him. Jenny is gorgeous.

Her dress, a pink sequined halter with matching pink knee-length feathers, pairs perfectly with Cooper's tie. She's a little more than a head shorter than him, even with her three-inch stilettos. They stand close to each other, but not touching. Not yet at least.

I turn my cheek on Rex's soft shirt to see them better. He smells like heaven. I'll probably spend the rest of my life sniffing fragrances in department stores, searching for the cologne Rex wears. "The blue and the curls and, well, everything," I say, trying to focus on now versus what's next.

Jenny giggles, and the smile I thought was fake comes out to play. It's not. It's as real as she is and, if I'm honest, I'm envious of how she still finds light within her darkness. "Glad I finally won you over."

"You two didn't like each other?" Rex asks, a hint of concern in his tone.

Jenny shrugs and then leans into Cooper. "She thought I was a gold-digging bitch. We're good now."

"Alright, kids," Mamma T says, coming into the kitchen and tapping the screen of her phone. "I need some pictures to document this night. It's only once my babies go to senior prom."

"Mom," Cooper grumbles. "Seriously? You get one photo and that's it."

Mamma T dismisses him and starts snapping candids. After posing each of us separately, as couples, and then as a group, she's finally satisfied. She sends a group text with the best shots and disappears in the house, probably figuring out which ones to upload to her Facebook profile.

I walk to the kitchen to get a glass of water while everyone talks about the pictures as they wait for the limo to arrive. My heart is in my throat. There's so much riding on tonight—it's our last weekend together, my first school dance, the night I could lose my virginity—I think I need something stronger than water.

Logan sneaks up behind me and whispers, "You look beautiful."

I turn around and throw my arms around him because I think I'm starting to become that person—a hugger. Sure, I still get the needle pricks down my spine, but the strangling feeling of my lungs about to explode isn't there anymore. Yes, I'm a little uncomfortable, but the discomfort is manageable and almost enjoyable.

Also, I know how hard tonight is for him.

Logan freezes but soon wraps his arms around me. We both pull away after a second and stare at each other. There's a dark cloud brewing behind his eyes. Everyone thinks he won't go to prom out of rebellion, but I know the truth.

"You can still come," I tell him because it's true. Rex ordered a Hummer limousine, completely over the top for just the four of us.

Logan shakes his head, a frown pulling at his lips. "A promise is a promise."

I squeeze his shoulder and give him an I'm-sorry-smile because I don't know what else to do. Logan's misery is his own fault. I've never lost someone the way he did, so I don't even know what to say.

"You look like you're ready for a funeral," Cooper quips, clapping his hand on his brother's shoulder.

Logan forces a smile that almost looks genuine. I feel bad for him, wondering how much of his high school persona is nothing more than a tough guy act. If I hadn't just witnessed this vulnerable moment, I would never have known he was suffering.

"Maybe, but at least I'm not dressed for one," Logan adds, like our conversation never happened, then pauses to look at his brother some more. "Actually, you look like a waiter in that shit. Fetch me a drink."

I leave them to their brotherly burns because growing up this used to last for hours. Besides, maybe Cooper will see through Logan's front and offer some advice. As conceited as it sounds, he lost me. He went through a similar pain and might know what to say.

My phone dings. I grab it off of the counter and glance at the screen.

Bane: It's time.

"Time for what?" Rex asks, sneaking up behind me.

I jump, my heart racing a mile a minute. "For me to get ready. Bane was supposed to remind me hours ago. I guess he just remembered."

It's a lie, but I can't leave. Not now, besides, I'm supposed to have the weekend. I won't let Bane take the time I have left. And Jenny is right, prom is important to Rex. He deserves this night and, frankly, I want it too. I want one high school memory that's actually worth remembering.

Tomorrow, I'll think about Gerald.

Tomorrow, I'll run.

But tonight is about us, and I'm not going to let anything ruin it.

I'M PRETTY SURE MOST SCHOOLS DECORATE THEIR GYMNASIUMS FOR dances. I mean, why not? They have the space and it's a good way to save money. Not to mention, nearly every movie and TV show I can think of (which at the moment is only *Glee* and *The Vampire Diaries*) uses their school for dances.

But no, not us.

St. A's prom committee rented out the ballroom and terrace at the Horizon Hotel because they had the money and were dying to spend it.

Our limo stops under the lobby's overhang and I'm embarrassed to admit how excited I am for tonight. A valet driver opens the door for us to climb out, and my heart races. Jenny goes first, then me, followed by Cooper and Rex.

As soon as we step through the lighted archway that marks the ballroom, our picture is taken. I rub my eyes, clearing the spots from the flash, and then look around.

The room is beautiful, unlike anything I've ever seen. Sheer fabric and strings of clear lights splay from the center of the ceiling to the walls. Two dozen or so round tables covered with white tablecloths with lighted lantern centerpieces are spread throughout while a DJ plays music from a table in the corner.

Rex takes my hand and leads us deeper into the room. He claims a mostly empty table near the terrace and drapes his blazer over the back of the chair. Cooper does the same while Jenny pulls two small coin purses from the inside pocket of Rex's jacket and sets them in front of where we will sit.

"Where did the jackets come from?" I yell. The music is too loud for conversation. Then again, by looking around, most people are dancing or kissing. There isn't much talking going on.

Rex leans in so I can hear him say, "I carried them from the limo."

Right. That makes sense. Actually, it confuses me more. Limos don't come with tailored jackets. Maybe he put them in there while I was in the kitchen talking to Logan.

My heart drops a little at the thought of Logan. Danika would have loved tonight. I reach for my phone to text him and see how he's doing, but remember it's in Rex's pocket and change my mind. I'll text him later when the sting of the night isn't so fresh.

Rex's hand finds my lower back as he leans into my ear, "I'm gonna check in and make sure the limo driver got our bags to our rooms." I nod and he kisses my cheek then heads back toward the lobby.

"I'm hungry," Jenny yells. "Want to go out on the terrace and grab some snacks?"

I shake my head. I am a little hungry, but I'll wait. It's quieter outside and she and Cooper haven't had any time alone together yet. Cooper deserves a chance to be happy and Jenny might be that chance. "I'm good. I'll wait for Rex."

A few minutes after they leave, the chair beside me moves. I shift, fully expecting to see Rex, but am met with golden locks, blue eyes, and a smile laced with arsenic.

Tad.

He grabs my wrist and sets it on the table. From a distance, we look like a cute couple having an intimate conversation. We are anything but. Tad leans closer. I tug my arm to pull away, but he holds it firmly against the tablecloth. I suck and, unless I make a scene, there isn't much I can do about it.

"I'm sorry."

What? I stare at him dumbfounded. Does he really think saying sorry weeks after practically dragging me into the bathroom makes everything alright? It's a start, but I'm not about to validate his actions by saying thank you. "Okay."

"He was there," Tad yells, his eyes skirting across the room for a minute before finding my face again. "I didn't have a choice."

"Who was there?" *And where? Inside the actual bathrooms?* Tad must have been tripping hard if he was hallucinating people that day.

Tad's chair forcefully slides back, dragging me out of the seat and onto my knees. He lets go of my wrist, but not before I hit the ground. I brush myself off in time to see Rex towering over him.

I push onto my feet and grab Rex's arm before he can land a punch. He turns, fire in his eyes, ready to beat Tad's face in. They soften when they settle on me, but the anger radiating off Rex is hot. I cup his cheeks and pull him so he can hear me clearly. "I'm fine. He was saying sorry for the other day."

Rex looks at Tad again. There's a war raging behind his eyes that could lead to us being kicked out of the prom but, thankfully, he says, "Go."

Tad scampers away faster than he's moved all football season. When he's out of sight, Rex throws his arm around me and asks, "Are you sure you're alright?"

"Positive," I say and pull him to the dance floor. I may have the moves of a drunken toddler, but we need a distraction. Besides, tonight is supposed to be fun and drama-free.

Thankfully, the DJ chooses this moment to play a slow jam. I lean into Rex and let him sway us to a song I vaguely recognize. I close my eyes, imagining what it would be like if we didn't have to say goodbye. In a perfect world, we'd get married and have two beautiful kids together. He'd go pro, traveling the country playing hockey, and I'd...

I don't know what I'd do. I open my eyes and stare at the buttons on his shirt. What I'd do in that fantasy life doesn't matter because the reality is that it all ends in the morning.

THE REST OF THE NIGHT IS A BLUR OF DANCING, SNACKING, AND drinking punch, which must have been spiked because I'm feeling good. My head is spinning. Actually, my whole body is. I laugh as Rex pulls me into his chest again. What little coordination I had is gone. I trip over my own feet and fall into his arms. Tender lips find my forehead and I hug him tight, smiling into his shirt.

"Want to head up to the room?"

I look around, suddenly aware that most of the couples have disappeared. We are two of the maybe twenty people left at prom. Everyone else has taken off for the night. "What about Cooper and Jenny?"

Rex spins me again and I laugh as he pulls me back into his arms, dipping me backward when the song ends. "They snuck out a while ago."

"Oh, okay."

Rex takes my hand and leads me to the elevator. My heart pounds against my chest. I'm surprised he can't hear it. Although my ears are ringing now that the music's gone; maybe his are, too. The elevator dings and the door slides open. I step in and lean against the rail.

The moment the doors close, Rex is on me. I don't have time to think about what's coming next, his tongue dancing with mine erases all thoughts. All I can focus on are his lips, and how good they make me feel. By the time the doors open on our floor, we are a mess. My dress is wrinkled. Rex's shirt is untucked, his hair disheveled, and his tie undone. I run my hands down my sides, smoothing the fabric the best I can and step into the hallway.

Rex walks us to our room and pulls the keycard from his wallet, then slips it into the reader. He opens the door, allowing me to enter first, then closes it behind us. Our room is what I'm assuming is standard for hotels with a queen-sized bed and a TV, but I've never been in one before. I take in each feature, not wanting to miss a thing when I remember this night.

Warm lips press against my neck. I tilt my head, a sigh of pleasure escaping my own. Rex pushes my hair to one side and gently bites my neck. He's never done that before and I'm surprised at how good it feels.

I moan again and my knees buckle from the sensation. Rex spins me in his arms and pulls me at the waist. I melt into his mouth when his hands find my cheeks, then slide to my waist before finally settling on my ass.

He lifts me, one hand sliding under the slip of my dress, and I wrap my legs around him. We disconnect, smiling at each other as our bodies bounce against the mattress. When our mouths find each other again, our tongues twist together in a tango they were born to dance. Each move seemingly rehearsed to perfection. We kiss, and we kiss until my lips go numb.

Rex slides down my belly and pulls my dress open from the slit. His calloused hand rubs against my inner thigh, and I'm not sure how much more I can take. I want him.

"You're burning up."

He's right, I'm hot everywhere. His hand, ice against my flesh, doesn't help either. Before Rex, I was always cold, wearing the jacket everyone assumed was a fashion statement out of necessity rather than choice. But since being with Rex, I'm hot. My skin is on fire whenever he's near.

He dips his head between my legs and kisses a tender spot on my inner thigh. "You okay?"

I close my eyes and nod. Every nerve in my body is firing off. Rex's hand slides higher, following the edge of my bikini line to my hip, waiting for me to give the okay for him to dip beneath the lacey fabric and to take us further.

I take a deep breath and then whisper, "I'm ready."

He pushes back and sits on his heels, startled. "Are you sure? I know you want to test your limits, but we don't have to have sex."

I nod and a knot builds in my throat. My heart races as my stomach flips with anticipation, but it's now or never. I don't want to live my life with regret. I want to remember Rex and every beautiful moment he's given me. This one included.

I stand and reach for the zipper of my dress, but Rex's hands touch the pull before I can. He slides it down my back. Goosebumps pepper my skin as cold air touches me. I push the straps off my shoulder and let the dress fall before I can change my mind.

Rex's arms wrap around my waist. He pulls me backward into his chest and kisses my shoulder. "I promise, I don't mind waiting."

I spin in his arms and kiss him. I can't stop moving. If I do, my thoughts will catch up to me, and I'll chicken out. I want this.

I want him.

Rex drops onto the bed, our lips never breaking, and he pulls me down with him. I straddle him, my legs on each side of his waist, and unbutton his shirt.

"Lay on your back," Rex says, pulling away.

I unclasp my bra and slip off my panties while he steps out of his clothes. When Rex's boxers come off, I can't help but look at him. He's hard and the condom that was in a tiny package surprises me when it covers his length.

Rex leans over me and his lips find mine as he aligns himself with my center. I turn my head as he slowly pushes in and hold my breath while he kisses my jaw, neck, and shoulder, each kiss perfectly timed to distract me from the burning, stretching pain between my legs. When he's all the way in, he stills and asks, "Are you okay?"

"Yes." I kiss him again because I don't want questions or thoughts to take this from me.

Rex moves slowly. So, so slowly at first. But then his hips move faster and before I know what's happened, it's over.

"That was embarrassing." Rex chuckles as he rolls onto his side. "I promise next time it won't be that quick."

"Okay," I say and my voice cracks. My body trembles and a tear rolls down my cheek. I wipe it away, but not fast enough. Rex sees my cry and the look of horror in his eyes cuts deeper than all my scars. I feel terrible. All I wanted was a perfect night and here I am ruining it.

"Honey." Rex drops the used condom on the floor and pulls me into him. "I'm sorry. Did I hurt you?"

"Not more than expected," I say, embarrassed and ashamed. He kisses my forehead and lays us down. He holds me even as tears I can't control leak free and I tremble with too many emotions.

"I'm here for you. No matter what, Piper. I'm not going anywhere." His words are meant to be comforting, but all they do is drive a dagger into my heart. Rex is the perfect boyfriend. Patient. Kind. Considerate. So much more than I could have ever hoped for.

And I'm about to break his heart.

I wake to sunlight peeking through the window, shining on my face. I didn't expect to have sex with Piper last night. I'm not stupid. You don't go from kissing a girl with major trauma to fucking her with almost no build-up in between, but I was surprised when she let me.

What happened after, though, I wasn't prepared for. Seeing her cry was heartbreaking. The only thing keeping me together was knowing that her tears had nothing to do with me. Last night was a massive step for her. I know overcoming her trauma won't be a quick fix, but I'm not going anywhere. I'm in this for the long run.

Good, bad, or crazy, she's got me.

I roll over, expecting to find Piper in bed beside me, but there's a note on her pillow instead. I push myself up and grab it.

Dear Rex,

One moment, one seemingly insignificant moment, can change everything. Meeting you was that moment. The day you saved me from Tad changed everything. Even in that terrifying moment, I felt a shift.

Before you, every touch, whether innocent or not, was crippling, but your hands healed me. You awoke things in me I thought died long ago. So, thank you.

Thank you for teaching me how to feel again.

How to love.

I hope you'll find a way to forgive me. Believe me when I say I don't want to leave. Walking out this door is the hardest thing I've ever had to do, but I can't risk Gerald getting his hands on me. Or you. When it's safe, I'll find you again.

I don't expect you to wait for me, but I hope when that day comes, you'll want to see me. I hope some part of you will remember the good times we had together and that maybe you'll hug me again. That's what's keeping me going. I live for our memories, for your touch.

Don't try to find me. I'm already gone.

Forever yours,

Piper

My heart hurts in ways I didn't know was possible. It's been broken before, stepped on, and crumbled by those I thought cared about me. But never have I had an ache penetrate my soul. I feel empty, a hollow version of myself. How could a day so gut-wrenching follow a near-perfect night?

I slip my shorts on and grab the room card. I don't have time for a shirt. Frankly, I don't know where it is and I don't want to waste what precious moments I have to look for it.

I run down the hallway and hit the elevator button. I bounce on my toes. Impatient as it takes forever to reach me. *Screw it.*

I hightail it to the stairwell around the corner and run down three flights of stairs. My chest burns, but I don't stop. I can't stop. I yank the door open and step into the lobby. My heart just about jumps out of my body when I see her.

Piper stands, shoulders squared, talking to a burly man covered in tattoos from his neck and down beneath his jacket. *Who in their right mind wears a full jacket in May in Florida? Does he have a death wish? Fucking heat stroke is no joke.*

"Piper!" I yell.

She whirls around, her face white as a ghost. "Go back upstairs, Rex."

Like hell I'm going back to the room. Does she really think I'm not going to fight for her? I'm fucking loaded. I'm not saying that money fixes everyone's problems. Hell, it's caused more trouble in my family than it's worth, but it can damn sure keep her safe. I cross the lobby with purposeful strides. "No, we need to talk."

"You'd be wise to listen to her, son," the man growls. He turns his attention back to Piper and orders, "Let's go."

Piper takes a step closer to the man. I run the last few steps and reach out. My fingertips graze her pillow-soft skin, but the man grabs Piper by the arm. He pulls her nearly flush against him, her back to his chest. "Last chance, boy. Leave before things get messy."

"Get your hands off my girl!" I demand.

This must be him, that Gerald guy Piper has been worried about. Outside of his dark hair, this man looks nothing like Bane. The lucky fucker took after his mom.

Gerald reaches into his pocket and pulls out a small black gun. The girl behind the counter screams when she sees it. I'd forgotten she was there, but maybe she'll do something helpful like call the cops.

"Leave him alone, Gerald," Piper pleads. "He's just a kid."

I'm not a kid, but the argument is pointless. There are more important things, like freeing my girl from the near chokehold. I look around. The lobby is empty and we are in the center of it, too far to reach anything. My best bet is to tackle Gerald and push the hand with the gun away at the same time. Piper will get hurt, but he'll let her go, and she can run. Then I can beat the living shit out of this scum until the cops come.

"A stupid fucking kid," Gerald says, waving the gun in my face. "You have until the count of three to disappear before I make you disappear."

"I'm not leaving without her."

"One..."

"Rex, go. I'll be fine."

"Two..."

This dude won't shoot. My dad would have his head if he hurt me. "Let. Her. Go."

Gerald chuckles and shakes his head. "Stupid boy. Thr—"

"No!" Piper screams.

The gun goes off and the boom echoes through the lobby. I'm thrown backward, falling on my ass, but I feel ok. My ears ring and my heart races but I don't think I've been hit.

"Stupid bitch," Gerald grumbles.

And then I see her. The reason I fell. The reason I feel okay. Piper lays a foot away. A puddle of blood collecting around her, staining the shirt she stole from me a shade of red no one should see.

Sirens sound in the distance but they won't get here in time. I slide closer and pull Piper onto my lap. Blood pours out of her shoulder like a faucet. I press my hands over the hole, trying to remember my first-aid training. It needs to stop bleeding.

It has to stop.

There's more shooting outside the building, but everything sounds far away. A tremor ripples through Piper's body. It's the only sign of life I've seen since she fell, buy it's not much to go on, she's barely breathing.

Tears well in my eyes. I can't lose her. *Please, God, don't let me lose her.* "Stay with me, Piper!"

Out of nowhere, I'm surrounded by cops, firefighters, and para-medics. A set of hands lifts Piper out of my lap. Another moves me out of the way. Someone asks me questions, but I don't hear them; I can barely see them. I run my hands over my face, probably spreading Piper's blood everywhere.

"Sir," a short woman in a police uniform says. "Are you hurt?"

I shake my head. "No."

"Do you know what happened?" she asks.

"Rex!" A feminine voice calls from behind me. I turn to see Jenny beside Cooper, her face pinched with worry. She screams when she sees me, covering her mouth with her hands.

Cooper runs around the semi-hysterical Jenny toward us, probably piecing together what happened. Or, a version of what happened. "Piper!"

"Sir, you'll have to stay back," the cop says, extending her hand.

"Fuck that," Cooper pushes past her. "That's my sister."

"Sir!" the cop demands.

Two other men run interference, but it's too late. I can tell by the way Cooper stops in his tracks he saw her. He turns, backtracking towards me, and shoves me in the shoulder. "What the hell happened?"

"I don't know. I came downstairs, and that guy she was worried about, Gerald, was here."

"Gerald?" the female cop asks.

"Gerald McCarron," Cooper tells her.

"You mean the guy we shot," the cop points behind her to the door. "Was that local kingpin Gerald McCarron?"

"If it's Piper's Gerald, then yeah," Cooper says.

The cop turns her back to us. She walks towards the paramedics working on Piper, whispering into her radio. She's probably not actually whispering, but there's too much noise. I can't hear her. I look over my shoulder to check on Jenny. One of the officers ushered her to a chair and wrapped a blanket around her shoulders.

"Here," Cooper says, extending his shirt to me. "You're covered in blood. Wipe your face."

"Thanks." I clean myself up as best I can, but the blood has begun to dry, flaking off in little pieces. There's a movement to our right as Piper is loaded onto a stretcher with four different paramedics moving her out the door.

"Hey!" I yell, dropping Cooper's shirt to the floor. "Where are you taking her?"

"St. Mary's Hospital," one paramedic says. He looks from Cooper to me, then adds, "I only have room for one, and they're only going to allow immediate family back."

"Go," I tell Cooper. "I'll be right behind you."

When Jenny and I get to St. Mary's Hospital, Mamma T and Logan are already in the Intensive Care waiting room. Cooper paces the lobby, a blue scrub for a shirt since he gave me his back at the hotel. Mamma T stands and greets me with a hug, her tiny arms squeezing me as if this moment is all that's keeping her going. She pulls back, hands on my shoulders, and gives me a once-over. "You look like hell."

I force a smile and shrug. "You should see the other guy."

She forces a laugh and pulls me back into her embrace. When she finally releases me, I sit next to Logan and wait. Jenny convinces Cooper to sit and holds his hand the entire time.

Hours later, a tiny lady in blood-covered scrubs appears. "Lovelace family?"

"It's Harris, but that's us," Mamma T says and we all stand. We gravitate towards the woman and her gaze bounces from one of us to the next. We must be a sight to see—Cooper in his Batman pajama pants and scrub top, Jenny in her oversized Bruins jersey and shorts with pink fuzzy slippers, Mamma T has a dress on but no makeup and her hair's in a crazy bun, while Logan looks like a vampire in all black. And then there's me with blood-stained hands and dried flakes visible underneath my equally stained white shirt and shorts.

"I'm Dr. Roe. The bullet lodged itself into Piper's shoulder blade, but we were able to remove it and fix the artery it nicked."

There's a whoosh of air as everyone lets out the breaths they are holding. Everyone but me. My lungs ache, but I can't release it yet because there's something about Dr. Roe's expression. She's smiling, but she's holding something back too.

"But," Dr. Roe says with caution in her tone. "Piper lost a lot of blood and there were some complications. We put her in a medically induced coma so she can recover."

I take a few steps back and collapse into a chair. A coma? I have a million questions, but Mamma T is talking to her. That pain in my chest when I woke up to Piper's note, it's nothing compared to the black hole sucking me in now.

Jenny walks over and kneels before me, taking my shaking hands in hers. "Rexy-roo? You okay?"

I look into Jenny's eyes but can't find the words I am looking for. Simply put, though, no. I'm not okay.

The woman I gave my heart to tried to abandon me, only to be stolen from me. Shot. Possibly dying.

Every fear I've had about letting someone in happened in one day. The doctor may have said Piper's surgery went well, but she's not out of the woods. I've seen enough *Grey's Anatomy* to know how fast things can change.

Jenny squeezes my hands and tries to draw me from my thoughts. "Bring Gretchen down. You need her. I know she can't fix anything, but having her here will help."

Jenny is right. I dig my phone out of my pocket and text my nanny—the closest person I've ever had to a mother.

> Me: Can you come down? Something happened, and I don't want to be alone. Jenny's here but…
>
> Gretchen: Of course! Is everything okay?
>
> Me: Not really
>
> Gretchen: Are you hurt?
>
> Me: No, but my girlfriend was shot and is in the ICU
>
> Gretchen: I'll be on the next flight

"**F**or fucks sake, Rex. You look like hell," my mother says. My actual mother.

Hers is not a voice I wanted to hear, let alone expected. I've been sitting in the ICU waiting room for hours, day turning to night long ago. Cooper left about an hour ago to take Jenny to the airport and collect our things from our rooms. The staff at the Horizon Hotel were more than willing to delay checkout due to our circumstances and even comped our rooms.

Logan said he had things to do and left, too. He was worried about Piper for the first hour or so, but then he spent the rest of the time on his phone, texting. His sister is fighting for her life. And. He's. Texting.

The only person who seems as worried as me is Mamma T. She's a mess—pacing back and forth. Talking to the police—who she insists I'm not ready to speak to yet—she's right—and making various calls.

Piper doesn't have insurance and Mamma T is stressing about the money, trying to track down Monica to make her help with the bill.

Monica is a waste of life. I don't need to hear their conversation to know she's not going to contribute even a penny. Mamma T and I need to talk after I'm done dealing with *her*.

"I flew all the way here, son. You can't ignore me."

I groan, half acknowledging her existence. Why not? Isn't that what she's done to me the last eighteen years? I look up at the woman I've seen twice this year and attempt to smile. Nothing happens. I can't even fake being happy to see her. "Hello, Mother."

Mother clutches the handle of her monstrous purse against her knee-length white dress. Dark hair, similar to mine, perfectly curled under a matching white hat, falls to her shoulders—longer than the last time I saw her.

My mother is a beautiful woman. Every time I see her, I understand why my dad puts up with her antics, but I don't see her enough to let her beauty justify her actions, or lack thereof, toward me.

"What are you doing here?"

"I've been meaning to come visit for a few weeks now," she says, twisting the handle between her fingers. "Let's grab a bite to eat."

"This isn't a fucking social call, Mom!" I stand and point down the hallway. "My girlfriend is in the fucking ICU and we aren't allowed back yet. If you think I'm going to miss my chance at seeing her to go eat with you, you've lost your damn mind."

"Rex," Mamma T puts her hand on my shoulder. "Piper still has a few more hours of monitoring before they'll allow visitors. Go. I'll call you if anything changes."

"Let's run to the house. We can't go anywhere with you looking like *that*." Mother wrinkles her nose.

I know I look like shit, and probably smell like it too, but I'm not going home. Not yet. "We can eat in the cafeteria downstairs."

"Rex, I—"

I cut her off before she can insult everyone busting their asses here. Years of overpriced meals and self-entitled behavior have made my mother's filter for anyone in a different tax bracket nonexistent. I'm not about to have her piss someone off with her rude comments and risk them taking their anger out on Piper. I honestly don't think that would happen, but I'm not leaving anything to chance. "I'm not leaving the building. Take my offer of the cafeteria or leave."

"If you insist."

"Go get us a table. I'm going to the bathroom to wash my hands." My hands are as clean as they're going to get without a real shower, my face too. This is nothing more than an excuse to take some space. The thought of being trapped in an elevator with my mother, even for a few minutes, makes me want to puke.

I hate her.

I hate her for abandoning me to a stranger when I was a kid, for never showing up at a hockey game or on my birthday, but most of all, I hate her for being here now. I don't have the energy or the patience to deal with her bullshit.

"Rex…"

"Bye, Mother. See you there." I take the stairs instead of the elevator to keep her waiting. When I finally make it to the basement, the cafeteria is closed. She's sitting at a small iron table outside of an also closed gift shop with two Cokes and some chips.

"I paid the woman fifty bucks to let me buy these. She was already closing up but agreed. Here." She pushes one of the Cokes and a bag of chips to me as I sit down. "Have you eaten anything?"

Nope. I haven't even tried. My stomach's been twisted in knots, worried about Piper. "Haven't been hungry."

She nods, pretending to understand. "I'm sorry about your girlfriend. Will she live?"

"She better fucking live." If he's not dead, I'll kill that bastard myself if Piper dies.

Speaking of bastards, where the fuck is Bane? I pull out my phone and shoot Cooper a quick text to check on him. I find it hard to believe Bane wouldn't be here if he knew what had happened.

"We need to talk, son," Mother says.

I twist the cap off of my Coke and take a sip. My stomach cramps, finally realizing it hasn't had anything to eat since prom. I grab the chips and open the bag, suddenly starving. "Isn't that what we're doing? Talking?"

I crunch on the salty potatoes and almost relish how good they taste. Because of my training regimen, I don't usually eat junk food. Even in the off-season I try to eat well, only having a few beers but never getting drunk. Right now, though, I'm hungry and don't care about my diet.

"There's no easy way to say this, but your father is cutting you off." Mother doesn't even bat an eye. The sentence sounds rehearsed, like I'm one of Dad's employees she's letting go. *Do I mean that little to her that she can't even sound remorseful?*

"Excuse me?" I say, with a mouthful of chips. I swallow, then take a sip of my soda to clear the stuck bits. "You pick now of all times to tell me this shit? What the fuck, Mom! Why?"

She tucks her hair behind her ears. "Well, because Kip is not your real father. I...I don't know who your biological dad is."

Another rehearsed line with zero emotion. This is huge news. She should be crying or nervous or something, but no. As usual, my mother has no heart, whereas mine has been shattered today and now stepped on by shiny red heels. "What the literal fuck, Mom?"

"Watch your mouth! Kip may not be your dad, but I'm still your mother, and you will show me respect."

I roll my eyes. She's not my mother. My mother is back at my house doing Lord knows what because my egg donor probably wouldn't let her come to me. "Whatever. So that's it. You're here to tell me I'm fucked."

"No, Rex. Never." She reaches across the table for my hand. I let her touch it for a split second, then pull away. "We're giving you the house here and the one in New York. I figured you'd want a place to stay while visiting Gretchen. I've already given her the signed titles. They're notarized, so all you have to do is take them to a real estate agent to finish the process."

"How thoughtful," I mumble.

"You have your savings, which is more money than most people have. And, of course, if you need anything, I will always help you."

"Good. I need something."

"Anything." She sounds desperate, fearful she'll lose the fractured relationship she believes we have. At least it's better than the emotionless robot I had a minute ago.

"I need you to pay all of Piper's medical bills. She doesn't have insurance and I don't want her to wipe me clean."

Mother sits back in her chair, one eyebrow raised. "You really care for this girl, don't you?"

"I love her mom and if you love me, you'll do this for us."

"Us?"

How fucking dense is she? "Yeah, us. If Piper pulls through, I plan on marrying her."

Mother wipes a tear from her eye. She's got this proud parent look that she doesn't deserve. "I'll stop by the insurance office before I leave and put my card on file for her. Also, call me when your girlfriend is ready for rehab. I'll get her into the best facility."

I set my hand on the table, palm up—a peace offering. Mother smiles and squeezes it, then stands. "I should get going. My flight leaves in a few hours."

As pissed as I was to see my mother, we were having a moment. Our first one in I don't know how many years. I'm kind of disappointed she's leaving so fast. "You're leaving already?"

"Yeah, you don't need me. Gretchen is at the house. She'll take care of you." With a quick hug, Mother turns and leaves.

I watch her follow the signs to the payment area and then make my way back to the ICU waiting room. There's no change in Piper's condition. So, at Mamma T's insistence, I head home.

Chapter 31
REX

My house smells like spiced meat, peppers, and onions when I walk in. I drop my keys on the counter and sit at the kitchen island. I rest my head on my arms amidst the bowls of sliced peppers, tomatoes, lettuce, and cheese.

Today was a disaster of epic proportions. My girlfriend is fighting for her life and my father has disowned me because I'm not his kid. I want a drink but refrain from making myself a Jack and Coke because I need to be clear-headed. I can't drive to the hospital if I'm drunk, even if it will make the pain go away.

"Good Lord, child, you look like death has become you." Gretchen crosses the room and wraps her arms around me until the tears I've fought all day break free. She holds me until they dry and keeps holding me until I finally pull away.

"I missed you," I say, wiping my nose with the corner of my shirt sleeve.

"I missed you too, kiddo." Her tired eyes search my face. I don't know what she sees, but she pulls me in for another hug. "That big house isn't the same without you making messes."

I try to laugh, but it's choked on a sob. I did make messes, HUGE messes, with my friends and my parties. We ate everything in sight, partied like there was no tomorrow, and never cleaned up.

I knew Gretchen would take care of it but didn't realize until now how fucked that was. Gretchen is my mom, not my maid. "Sorry about all that."

She pushes me upright and walks around the counter, fixing me a plate with two hard tacos. "Don't be. Kids are supposed to make messes and have fun. When you get to my age, fun is watching a movie with a glass of wine and then going to bed early."

A memory of curling up on the couch with Piper, her falling asleep on my lap during the first movie we watched, pops into my head. I bite my lip, forcing another bout of tears to stay hidden and swallow the knot in my throat. I'd trade everything—the money, my career, hell, even my life—to do that again with her. The thought of moving on is crippling. I don't think I can do it. "That sounds like a good night to me."

Gretchen slides the plate across the island to me. "She'll be fine, Rex. Piper's doctors know what they're doing. She. Will. Be. Okay."

I nod and reach for a taco. I'm not hungry anymore. Mother's announcement was the icing on the shit cake that is today. But Gretchen has a rule: if she made the effort to make it, you're eating it.

The shell crunches in my mouth. Tacos may seem simple, but right now, they are the best damn tacos I've ever had. Hungry or not, these suckers taste amazing.

My phone dings, then dings again, and again.

> Cooper: Found Bane. His dad did a number on him, but he's alive.
>
> Cooper: Barely.
>
> Cooper: Following the ambulance to tell the nurses everything I can.
>
> Mamma T: Piper's through the worst of it. They're pulling her out of the coma soon.

I drop my taco and stand. Without saying anything, I turn, crossing the kitchen in three long strides to grab my keys.

"Where are you going?" Gretchen asks, dropping her dishtowel on the floor.

"They're pulling Piper out of her coma. I've got to go."

I shove my phone in my pocket and reach for the garage door handle, but Gretchen slips her hand on it first. I forgot the woman is a damn ninja. "No."

"No? There is no *no*. I'm going."

"Rexroth Anthony Montgomery, you are not leaving this house." Gretchen gives me that look, the one that says she means business and not to cross her. "You look like shit and smell even worse. Go upstairs and take a shower."

I groan. "I don't have time for a shower!"

"And those doctors aren't going to let you see Piper like this. Look at yourself! There are still flakes of dried blood in your hair. Not to mention, you smell worse than your hockey bag and that says something."

I sniff my pits and wince. Gretchen is right. I smell terrible. Stress sweat with no deodorant is a toxic mix. But it's not like I was thinking about personal hygiene when I left the hotel room this morning. I hang my keys back on the hook and take a step back. "Okay."

"Good boy." She pats my shoulder. "You get cleaned up. I'll pack this food in some containers. I'm sure Piper's family hasn't left her side and are hungry too."

MY SHOWER TAKES LONGER THAN ANTICIPATED, BUT THE WARM WATER feels too good to leave, melting the tension from my muscles. Almost an hour passes by the time I reach the hospital again.

The ICU waiting room is smaller than the surgery waiting room we were in earlier. Only a handful of people are hanging around at this hour, waiting on their loved ones. Cooper is one of those people.

"Hey, man." I sit in the god-awful waiting room chair beside him. The fluorescent lights change Cooper's sun-kissed skin to a sickly color. I try not to think about Piper lying unconscious and how her ivory skin is probably comparable to a vampire's—a vampire who drinks blood. *There was so much blood.* "How is she?"

Cooper shakes his head and then leans back in his seat. "They took Piper off the coma drugs but she hasn't woken up yet. Mom is back there now."

"What?" My voice bounces off the white walls around us, waking some lady across the room. She shushes us and then attempts to go back to sleep. It's late, if I weren't so stressed out I'd be tired, too. This woman has hopefully received some good news, allowing her the comfort of a good night's sleep. *I wish I was her.*

I hold up my hand as an apology, but I'm pretty sure she's ignoring me. "Why not? What happened?"

"I don't know. I'm not a doctor," Cooper snaps. He's irritated and I get it. It's been a long day for both of us but he doesn't have to be a dick. He crosses his arms and closes his eyes, trying to find the same peace the lobby woman has.

I rise and walk to the nurse's station. A tiny blonde who looks like she still belongs in high school sits behind the counter, typing away at her computer.

"Excuse me?"

She looks up, bright-eyed, with a smile. "How can I help you?"

"I was wondering if you could update me on Piper Lovelace?"

Her face twists together, almost apologetically. "Are you on the release form? I can't tell you anything if you're not."

"I..." I scratch the back of my neck. Am I? I don't remember filling out any paperwork but it's been such a long day, I might have. I hope I did. "I don't know. Can you check?"

"Sure!" This girl is too chipper for this time of night. She needs to lay off the coffee, or maybe I need some. "What's your name?"

"Rex Montgomery."

She types something, each key on the keyboard clicking. "Yup, here you are. What do you want to know?"

I let out a breath of relief. Mamma T must have added me to the form knowing I'd be asking questions. That woman is a saint. "Everything. Tell me everything."

"Okay," The nurse scrolls through Piper's file, which feels miles long by how long she's quiet. Finally, she says, "As I'm sure you're aware, Piper was shot in the shoulder."

"Yup, I was there for that," I say. The girl looks up at me, eyes wide, then quickly looks at the screen again. "What else?"

"It looks like the bullet nicked an artery and fractured her humerus. On the bright side, they were able to pull it from her subacromial space with minimal complications."

Speak fucking English! I'm not a doctor. I don't know what half that shit means, woman! "Why did they put her in a coma?"

"Hard to say. Probably because of all the blood she lost. I'm not a doctor, so that's my guess, but they did pull her out of it a little over an hour ago, which is a good sign."

"How long until she wakes up?"

The nurse shakes her head. "I don't know. Comas are tricky. Sometimes patients come around in hours, others take days, weeks even."

Weeks? Piper could be unconscious for weeks? I can't go weeks without hearing her voice. It's nowhere, not even on her voicemail. And what about graduation? Surely, Principal White won't make her repeat the whole year becasue she's missed a few days.

Oh, God... What if Piper wakes up and forgets who I am? I saw that in a movie once. The girl had significant trauma and forgot years of her life. How in the hell would I make Piper fall for me again? That can't happen. It won't happen. Piper will be fine. Everything will be fine!

The nurse reaches out, resting her hand on my arm. "Sir, are you okay?"

I'm far from okay, but I nod and tell her, "Thanks."

I find my seat next to Cooper and slump into it. Somehow, he's managed to fall asleep. I drop my head back against the wall, wishing I could do the same.

Two days.

Two days of rotating shifts with Mamma T, Cooper, and Logan, and Piper finally wakes up.

It was the longest two days of my life. At first, I was pissed—her eyes fluttered open when Logan was in the room, not me, but I quickly got over it. As much as I would have loved to have been the first person Piper saw, I'm just glad she's awake.

After running a million tests that required her to have no visitors, the doctor transferred Piper to a regular room, which is great because we can all be in there with her.

That one-person-at-a-time rule the ICU had was bullshit.

I stop in the gift shop and buy the biggest flower bouquet they have and a blue get-well bear—I know how she feels about pink.

The sweet sound of Piper's laugh carries into the hallway as I approach her room. I lean against the wall outside her door and just listen to the sound of her voice. She and Cooper are reminiscing, with Mamma T adding her own memories into the mix.

I can practically hear a smile in Piper's voice. It's melodic and beautiful and should be soothing my nerves, but it only worsens them. The last time Piper and I saw each other, she was trying to leave. What if that mess with Gerald was only an excuse? What if she doesn't want to see me?

My mom can't stand to be around me, probably because I'm a daily reminder of the mistakes she made. My Dad's actions, or lack thereof, are somewhat justified now that I know the truth. I wouldn't want a kid that's not mine. I mean, if I dated someone who had a child, I'm sure I'd love it, but raising a baby I thought was mine but wasn't would kill me.

And even though I understand why my parents are the way they are, it doesn't do anything to fill the void.

I linger outside Piper's hospital door a little longer, listening to her voice, trying to find the courage to face her, knowing that I may be rejected.

Two uniformed officers walk past me and knock on the open door. I sigh, realizing I waited too long to have the private moment we need, and follow behind them.

"Piper Lovelace?" one asks.

"That's me, officer," Piper says with a mocking grin. It's her hospital room. Were they expecting anyone else? Her gaze bounces from one uniformed man to the other before noticing me, and her smile falters, but only for a second.

"We have some questions," the other officer says. "If you're up for it."

I set the bouquet on the bedside table, along with the bear, and stand in the corner while the cops introduce themselves as Officer Shen and Officer McLean.

It may have been my imagination, but Piper didn't seem happy to see me. Or maybe she wasn't happy to see them. Lord, I hope it was them and not me.

"How do you know Gerald McCarron?" Officer Shen asks.

They're not starting with the easy ones, are they?

Piper takes a breath and lets it out slowly. I can't imagine how hard this must be for her, talking about the man who haunts her dreams. The man who tried and thankfully failed to kill her. "Gerald McCarron is a lot of things. He's my friend Bane's dad."

"The same Bane who is in Martin Memorial Hospital?" Officer McLean interrupts.

Piper looks to Cooper, concern written all over her face. I guess they didn't tell her what had happened to him. She's going to freak out, which is probably why they haven't said anything yet.

"Yes, same one," Cooper answers for her.

Officer Shen nods and writes something in his notebook. "You said he's many things. What else is Gerald McCarron to you?"

"Gerald is my birth mom's drug dealer. For lack of better words, he's her pimp and…" Piper's voice cracks. She swallows hard and looks down at her hands. "He also attacked me last year."

Officer McLean doesn't even bat an eye. Apparently, this scumbag attacking a teenager isn't surprising. "Did you file a police report?"

Piper shakes her head. "No, but I'm sure you can subpoena the hospital records."

Officer Shen writes that down while Officer McLean paces the room. He narrows his eyes, sizing Cooper and me up. "Why do you think Gerald McCarron sought you out on Saturday?"

"My birth mom, Monica, sold him my virginity to pay a debt. I never agreed to their arrangement, so I fought back when he came to claim me. I was able to get away before he could finish what he started, but Gerald made it clear that he had some not-nice plans for me."

"How did your relationship with Bane McCarron affect those plans?" Officer Shen asks.

Piper bites her cheek. I remember when Cooper made a comment about Bane, it pissed her off, but Piper isn't stupid, she won't fire off at the cops. They're just doing their jobs.

"Bane was my friend. He kept me safe and let me know what was going on in that part of town."

"So, he was involved in his father's business?" Officer McLean asks. He raises his eyebrows at Officer Shen, who scribbles in his notebook and underlines the writing.

Piper pushes on the mattress, scooting herself upright. She balls her fists, nails digging into her palms as she says, "No. Bane and his dad were estranged, but he had friends who worked for Gerald. They kept him in the loop about the important stuff."

Officer Shen nods, still writing in his notebook. "Why do you think you were shot? Was it always Gerald's plan to kill you?"

"I don't explicitly know what his plans were," she snaps. "But when I saw the gun pointed at Rex, I couldn't let Gerald hurt him."

Piper looks at me with sadness in her eyes. Her lips curl in the corners, mirroring the emotion already on her face. All this lasts less than a second before she turns back to the officers. "I'm tired. Can we finish this later?"

Officer Shen closes his notebook. "Of course. Thank you for your time."

Piper waits for the cops to leave before saying, "I love you all, but can I talk to Rex? In private."

Cooper rests his hand on my shoulder as he walks by. He's got this *I'm-sorry-man* look on his face that confirms my fears.

Piper and I are breaking up.

My stomach jumps into my throat, threatening to do something embarrassing like throw up the tacos I ate. I force my feet to move once the room is empty and carry me to the chair beside her bed. I make myself sit down.

Piper reaches out, touching my shaking hands. "Are you okay?"

No. I'm not even close to okay, but Piper has just woken up from a coma, been interrogated by the police, and found out one of her friends is in the hospital. She shouldn't be worrying about me. "I'm not the one who just got out of a coma, babe. How are you?"

Piper shrugs. "I'm okay. My head has some pressure, but nothing hurts right now." She glances at the IV drip. "I'm sure once they take this away, that won't be the case, though." She laughs, but the sound is forced. An awkward silence fills the room for a minute before she says, "Rex?"

I love the way my name rolls off of Piper's lips. I should record our breakup, simply so I can hear her voice beyond today. I don't know how I'll survive without Piper in my life. Thinking she was going to die was one thing, but knowing the girl I love will someday be with someone else...it's brutal.

What else is brutal? Realizing how much you're in love with someone right before the relationship ends. "Yeah, Piper?"

"What's wrong?"

I take a slow breath, willing the burn in my eyes to stay put, but the stupid liquid pain isn't listening. I run my hand over my face before she can see that I'm crying and clear my throat. "Just worried about you."

"Baby," she whispers. "I'm fine." She flicks her wrist, pointing between both her and me. "We are fine." But then a shadow of fear crosses her face. "Aren't we?"

I clear my throat again, masking the sound with a cough. I cover my mouth with my fist for pretend etiquette, wiping my nose on my way to shove my hands in my pockets. I crush the fabric between my fingers, feeling my nails drag against my thighs. I've avoided it like the plague because no one was worth the suffering. But with Piper, if given the option to start over, knowing she'd kill me, I'd do it all again in a heartbeat.

"I...I guess." I take a deep breath and let it out slowly, willing my voice not to break. "I'm still trying to wrap my head around the whole shooting thing." I pause for a second, needing that time to keep myself in check. "And that letter."

Piper sucks in a breath and covers her mouth with her hands. "Oh, Rex! I'm so sorry, I forgot."

She scoots to the edge of the bed and holds her hand out to me. I cave and take it, dying a little inside from her touch. Her hand is so soft, so tiny.

"Rex?" Piper's voice breaks. "Will you look at me?"

I nod and do what she says. The whites of her eyes are red and glassy. I grit my teeth, waiting to hear the words she doesn't want to say.

Again.

"So. That letter. I..." she wipes a tear from her cheek with her free hand. "Do you still want to be with me?"

"What?"

"I... um...."

I run my hand across my face again. There's no hiding them this time. A stupid tear gets halfway down my cheek before I catch it. "Of course I still want to be with you, Piper. You're the one who left me."

"Oh, thank God," she says, laughing past her own tears. "Rex, I don't want to break up. I love you. I just didn't want you to get hurt, but now that this mess is over, we can be together. Say you'll be with me again, Rex. Please."

I shake my head, not believing the words she's saying. Piper is an idiot. She never should have tried to leave. I would have taken care of her and kept her safe if only she'd let me know what was going on. "I can't be your boyfriend."

"What?"

The thought of Piper leaving me again is too painful. I'd give anything to put a ring on her finger. I've lived my life with rose-colored glasses, thinking I was invincible, that we had forever together. Nearly losing someone you love does something to you. It puts how fragile life is into perspective.

I slide out of the chair and get down on one knee. I don't care that this is selfish. I don't care that I don't have a ring. I need her to be mine. "Marry me."

"What?"

"I know it's crazy, Piper, and we haven't been together that long but I almost lost you twice in one day. My heart broke in ways I didn't know was possible. But you're here now. You're alive, and you still want to be with me. I know that should be enough, but it's not. You are so much more than just a girlfriend. You're my best friend, my soulmate, and I know I'm doing this all wrong, but will you marry me?"

Piper doesn't hesitate. "Yes!"

Yes?

She said yes? *Fuck yeah!*

I jump onto the bed to hug her and she winces from the pressure on her shoulder. I jump off and sit beside her legs. "Sorry."

"It's okay," she says with a devilish grin.

"Since we're talking crazy...."

"Oh, boy," I chuckle. I am crazy, crazy about her. This girl could ask for a unicorn and I'd do my best to make it happen. Whatever she wants, it's hers.

"Let's do it now. Today."

"Do what now?"

"Get married."

Wait, now? I barely expected a yes. My heart races as fear creeps and takes over my body again. Maybe this is a trick, Piper's way of seeing if I'm committed. I am. I'll do it here and now if she wants, but I also want it to be right. If things go the way I'm hoping, Piper will only get married once.

"Don't you want a white dress and flowers and whatever else girls want on their wedding day?"

She shakes her head. "No. I want you. They do this kind of stuff in hospitals all the time, and everyone I love is already here."

"Except for Bane." I don't know why I'm stalling. I want to marry Piper. Gretchen is the only family I care about and she's already here. So, for me, there are no hold-ups but I can't shake the feeling that most girls dream about the perfect wedding. I can't imagine this is anything close to what she thought. "We don't have a marriage license or anything fancy."

"We can do a ceremony with all of that this fall. Bane can go to that one along with whoever else you want to invite. As for the paperwork, I'm sure the hospital has a stack of blank marriage licenses. You know, for those couples where someone is terminal and it's their dying wish to get married or whatever."

My heart stops and shatters in my chest. Terminal? "Piper, is there something you're not telling me?"

Chapter 33
PIPER

I don't mean to laugh, but I can't help it. The look of sheer horror on Rex's face is priceless. Scaring him was never the goal. I just meant that hospitals are prepared for weddings. You know, just in case.

A jolt of pain breaks through the drugs, killing the moment. I suck in a breath, hoping my stilled body will end the pain. It does, thankfully. I exhale slowly and rest my palm on Rex's cheek. "No, baby. I'm healthy as a horse that has been shot."

"People don't shoot healthy horses, Piper."

"Good thing my shooter has terrible aim, then." I quip. The line between Rex's brows deepens. "Too soon?"

He shakes his head, a smile playing on his lips.

"So, are we doing this? You know, the whole marriage thing." My stomach flutters. I'm nervous and excited and kind of terrified that this is some crazy hallucination from all the drugs they've got me on. I know I should be worried about Bane and what will happen next, but I survived. I want to celebrate that my nightmare is over with the man I love.

"If you're sure about this."

I squeeze his hand. I've never been more sure about anything in my life. "I am. Send out a group text. Let's do this."

Less than two minutes after Rex sends the text message, Mamma T bursts through the door. "Are you out of your goddamn mind, Piper?"

"Mom!" Cooper's voice carries down the hallway to us. He comes into the room a second later, huffing like he just ran up a flight of stairs. "Calm down."

"I will not calm down," she yells at her son before looking at Rex and me. "Piper, you literally just got out of a coma! You can't get married. I understand that you love Rex, and I'm glad you guys have worked out whatever issues you had, but be reasonable."

Mamma T's reaction was the last thing I expected. Cooper freaking out, sure. But they seem to have switched roles during my hospital stay, and it's a little confusing. "I am being reasonable."

"No, you're not!" She paces before the bed, running a hand through her messy hair. I bet she's stressed. By the looks of the bags under her eyes, I don't think she's gotten much sleep the last few days.

"It would be nice to have your blessing, but I'm doing this either way, hopefully within the hour. If you don't support my decision, you can go home."

Rex sighs, then leans in and kisses my cheek. "I'm going to talk to the nurse about the paperwork. I'll be back soon."

I smile up at him and nod. He is so much more than I deserve. Even with the craziness that is my life and knowing that I'm dirt poor, he still wants me. It doesn't make sense but I stopped trying to figure out Life's plans for me a while ago.

"Piper," Mamma T says on an exhale, taking Rex's newly abandoned spot on my bed. "What is the rush?"

"Life is short," I say with a shrug. "I don't want to waste a minute of it wishing I had done something I didn't. If I've learned anything from this mess, it's that tomorrow isn't guaranteed."

Mamma T looks down at her nails. She's quiet, so quiet that Cooper comes up and puts his hand on her shoulder. He squeezes, pulling a small smile out of her as she reaches up to hold his hand.

"Okay," she whispers. "Let's get you ready to become Mrs. Montgomery."

It takes longer than I anticipated to get everything organized for a wedding. Mamma T insisted on me wearing a white dress because something needed to be traditional about today. Luckily, Rex's mom had one in her closet and we are pretty much the same size. Gretchen grabbed the dress along with Rex's prom jacket and brought it here so we could get ready.

My hair is up in a messy ponytail and the gift shop flowers Rex brought earlier are my bouquet, but I wouldn't change a thing. Actually, I would. I'd have Bane here with us but from what Cooper tells me he's still in the ICU with severe internal bleeding. As shitty as it sounds, there's nothing I can do for him right now. I know him though, when he gets out, he'll understand.

"Put this on." Mamma T hands me a tube of lip gloss. She gives me a once over, making sure I'm as perfect as can be for an impromptu hospital wedding. "You look beautiful. Are you nervous?"

"A little," I admit.

"You don't have to do this, Piper. You can wait until you are healed and do it right."

I love Mamma T and her persistence. I get it, she just wants what's best for me, but she doesn't understand. Rex is what's best for me.

"Why should I wait? If my bond with Rex is as strong as I think it is, what difference will it make to wait two or three years?" I pause, mostly for dramatic effect, but not long enough to allow Mamma T to respond. "It doesn't. I want to marry him now before life throws me another curveball and rips the opportunity from me."

Mamma T smiles, even though she disapproves of my decision. "I guess we'd better get going then."

ALL HOSPITALS HAVE A CHAPEL. THEY'RE TINY, DIMLY LIT, AND usually occupied with grieving loved ones praying for a miracle. Not today.

Mamma T opens the door and my breath catches. Every pew—all ten of them—has a short bouquet of white roses and three-tiered candles lining the walkway. The aisle is sprinkled with flower petals of every color: white, yellow, pink, red, and even purple. A piano rendition of Disney's *Tale as Old as Time* plays on someone's phone, and I laugh.

Rex stands at the front of the chapel, a single white rose pinned to his jacket, hands in his pockets, with the biggest grin I've ever seen. Cooper is behind him, Logan too.

Mamma T and I stop walking a foot away from Rex. She kisses my cheek, giving me away, and then sits beside an older woman in the front row.

The woman, who must be Rex's nanny, Gretchen, dabs her eyes with a tissue, a proud grin on her face. Cooper pulls his phone out of his pocket and stops the music as I take my place at the altar.

"Hi," Rex whispers.

"Hi," I whisper back, laughing. "Come here often?"

He grins. "Only with you."

"Sorry, I'm late!" An older man says, panting as he runs through a side door. "I was finishing up a last rites ceremony. It took longer than I expected." He clears his throat. "You do know the groom is supposed to be on the left side, right. Whatever, it doesn't matter. Dearly beloved, we are gathered here today to celebrate... "

"Rex and Piper," Cooper whispers.

"Yes, that's right. Rex and Piper in their union of holy matrimony." The man looks at Rex. "Do you, Rex, take Piper to be your lawfully wedded wife? To love and cherish from this day forward, in sickness and health, until death do you part?"

"I do."

"And do you, Piper..."

"Yes!" I say, cutting him off. "Hell, yes."

Logan snickers. The man marrying us—who I'm assuming is a pastor of some sort, and not some joe-schmo-notary, based on his black pants and matching black shirt—glares at me.

"And now for the rings," the pastor-man says.

"Oh, we don't..." I start, but Cooper hands Rex a box, who then hands it to the pastor-man.

"Before we commence the ring exchange, does anyone think these two should not be married?" He doesn't hesitate before adding, "No? Wonderful." He opens the box and gasps. "Sweet mother of Jesus! Uh... sorry. I don't do many weddings. Um. Here." He hands me a silver band and Rex the box with my ring.

"Piper, as you slide the ring onto Rex's finger, you are to say, 'With this ring I thee wed.'"

I take Rex's left hand and push the band over his knuckle. "With this ring, I thee wed."

Rex takes my hand and he places a matching ring, with a monster of a diamond, at the end of my left forefinger. My jaw drops looking at it. The single stone is as big as my thumbnail. It must have cost a fortune, or been his mother's. Either way, I'm kind of scared to wear it. What if the diamond falls out? What if I get mugged and they take it?

He slips the ring onto my finger, oblivious to my mini freak-out. "With this ring, I thee wed."

"By the power vested in me, you may kiss the bride."

Rex cradles my cheeks, pulling me in. Our kiss is quick and rough, like he fears it will be our last.

Cheers erupt in the room, reminding us we have an audience, and Rex pulls back. He rests his forehead against mine and looks me in the eye. "I love you."

"I love you too." We turn and face our family, which is just our not-mothers taking a million pictures with their phones.

Cooper claps Rex on the back, the way guys like to do. Today can't be easy for him, but he's smiling and putting on a good show. "You're stuck with us now, man."

"I wouldn't have it any other way," Rex says, pulling me tighter.

Logan extends his hand to Rex. "I think you guys are fucking nuts, but I'm happy for you."

His eyes are sad, but I don't say anything. Like prom, I can't imagine how hard this day's been for Logan, too. How hard the past few days were for everyone.

Rex takes Logan's moody appearance in stride, oblivious to the storm brewing, and shakes his hand. "Piper is the crazy one for marrying me."

"Hate to interrupt," pastor-man says, "but I need you two to sign some papers before I go."

Rex and I fill in the blanks and sign our names. Pastor-man takes the marriage license into the back room, makes us a copy, and then promises to put the original in the mail.

"Okay, lovebirds," Gretchen says. "Party's over. Piper needs to get back to her room to rest. She's had an eventful day."

"I couldn't agree more," Mamma T chirps. "We need to do everything we can to get her discharged before Saturday."

"What's on Saturday?" I ask, trying to figure out what day it is and how long I was unconscious. The last time I saw everyone *was* Saturday. I couldn't have been here for more than a couple of days. Could I? "What was the rush about Saturday?"

Rex groans but nods. "Graduation, babe. We're not free yet."

"It is my honor to welcome your class valedictorian, Piper Lovelace. Er... um... I mean Montgomery," Principal White announces.

I ascend the steps to the stage, white gown tickling my ankles, to a mixture of applause and whispers. I set my hands on the podium and adjust the microphone. I was discharged this morning, much to the doctor's dismay, with strict orders for physical therapy, follow-up appointments, and a slew of medications I can't pronounce. All so Mamma T could doll me up for one last high school experience. And now, as I stand before all seventy-four of my classmates and their parents, I'm glad she made this happen.

I scan the bleachers. Mamma T and Gretchen sit together in the center, whispering like a couple of Chatty-Cathys, proud looks on their faces. Mr. H sits in the back with his new wife, uncomfortable as ever. But no Montgomery's.

Rex told me what happened at the hospital, but a part of me hoped they would be here to celebrate graduation with him. Oh well, it's their loss. Rex is a fantastic man, and if they don't want to be a part of his life, then fuck them.

The stadium grows quiet, waiting for me to speak. *Show time.*

"In almost every movie, high school is portrayed as the time of your life. It's our time to live freely with minimal responsibilities before the real world hits us. A chance to make friends that last a lifetime, fall in love more times than you can count, and party until you can't see straight.

This magical experience was not mine.

It was yours.

I had the opposite experience. I was ridiculed for being accepted here on scholarship, ostracized because of where my birth mother lived, and rumored to be the school slut. I'm sorry to disappoint you all, but I never slept with anyone. I kicked every one of those jerks in the nuts and stole their cash."

Principal White jumps up from his seat. "Thank you, Piper."

He grabs my hurt arm, attempting to pull me away from the microphone without causing a scene. I gasp and wince, playing up his touch to be more than what it is. The pulling sensation is uncomfortable yet tolerable, thanks to the shot the nurses gave me.

I lean into the microphone but look directly at Principal White as I say, "Please, don't touch me. You could rip my stitches."

The crowd mumbles in hushed tones. He takes a step back, hands up in surrender. "Sorry."

I flash him a *got-you-bitch* smile and turn back to the crowd. "Oh yeah, and I was shot and almost killed the day after prom by the man who tried to rape me."

More gasps. More whispers. The look of shock and horror on my classmates' faces is what I expected. I smile, not because I'm happy about any of this, but because for the first time my classmates are seeing me.

I find Rex next to the empty seat I'll return to when my speech is done, arms crossed, a grin the size of Texas, nodding in encouragement for me to continue. He helped me write my speech on the way here. I was going to give a two-sentence congratulations, but he thought these dimwits could learn something from my story.

So, here I am.

"I don't tell you this to make you feel bad for me. I don't want your pity. I'm telling you my story because when we leave these grounds for the last time, life will get hard. College will be fun but challenging, and when we graduate we'll be thrown into the real world with bills to pay and jobs to do. Your life will never be easier than it is right now. And when you hit that moment, when the weight of the world is holding you down, I want you to think of me.

I survived.

I survived an abusive childhood and a terrible high school experience. I was nearly raped just one year ago and escaped by fighting my attacker —the same attacker who sought me out and failed to kill me.

I.

Survived.

And you will, too. No matter what life throws at you, you can't give up. If I had given up, I wouldn't be standing here today as your class valedictorian, married to the love of my life."

People turn in their seats, whispering as they look at Rex. It's our first outing as a married couple. I'm sure someone will put this on YouTube, and the paparazzi will have a field day with it, but we're ready. Rex waves, purposefully using his left hand to show off his ring.

"And so, Class of 2020," I continue. "I congratulate you. We have overcome the first of many hurdles in our path, but we did it."

The stadium erupts in cheers as I descend the platform steps and sit beside my husband. He waits palm up for me to thread my fingers with his. I happily comply, enjoying the soft circles he traces on my skin.

The rest of the graduation passes slowly, and the painkillers the doctor gave me are wearing off. My shoulder is throbbing and my head's spinning, but I say nothing. This day isn't just about me—it's about Rex and Cooper, too—and I'm not about to ruin it for my family.

I rest my cheek on Rex's shoulder, waiting for our names to be called. When Principal White calls my name, Rex stands and walks up there too.

"Uh…" Principal White stutters. "Correction, Piper and Rex Montgomery."

Rex and I take our diplomas and walk down the steps. He keeps his arm around my waist, steadying me even after we are on the ground again. "Are you okay?"

"My head hurts," I admit, because it's pounding.

"Let's go then." Rex veers us to the right, away from our seats. When we're close to the parking lot, he slips his hand under my legs, lifting me bridal style. I can walk, but knowing he's got me is like a security blanket. It's nice.

"She okay?" Cooper asks, his voice coming from behind us.

I look over my shoulder. He and Logan are a few steps behind, unzipping their graduation gowns and crossing the grassy knoll with long strides to catch up.

I smile, my head a little loopy from the pain. "I'm fine. You guys are going to miss the cap toss."

Rex stops walking and turns us to face them. Stopping is probably a good thing. Knowing Mamma T, she probably saw us leave the stadium and will be here soon.

Logan takes his cap off his head and throws it in the air. "There," he says as it falls to the ground. "Cap tossed."

I giggle and wince. Laughing hurts. Everything hurts.

"Here," Cooper says, digging in his pocket. He pulls out an orange prescription bottle and shakes two pills into his hand. "I swiped these from Mom, thinking you might need them sooner rather than later."

"And what exactly is she going to swallow them with?" Mamma T asks as she hands her open water to me. "Good plan, son, but poor execution."

"I tried, Mom." He shrugs and hands her back the bottle.

I toss the pills in my mouth and take a swig of water. They lodge themselves in my throat, requiring another sip before finally going down. Rex squeezes my hip. I love how he knows what to do to make me feel better.

Logan shoves his hands in his pockets, breaking the building tension between us and says, "This feels so final."

"What do you mean?" I ask.

"Well, you and Rex are married," Logan says. "I'm going to Florida State and Cooper is headed to Gainesville. It just feels like this is the last time we'll ever be like this."

"We're only a few hours from each other," Rex adds. "It won't be that bad."

Logan shakes his head. I see it again, the storm brewing behind his eyes. Too many major moments have happened this week. All things he probably never thought he'd face alone. "I don't know..."

Cooper puts an arm over Logan's shoulder, in true brotherly fashion, and pulls him in for a hug. "Stop being so cryptic, little brother. We're family. Worst case scenario, we have the holidays."

"You're only five minutes older than me, dick."

"And that makes me five minutes smarter."

I roll my eyes. Eighteen years old and nothing has changed. These two are still the same as when I moved in ten years ago.

"Well," Mamma T says. "I should go. Your dad is here, probably looking for you, and I don't want to see that man."

"Me too. I've got a flight to catch," Gretchen adds with a sad smile.

"I'll drive you," Mamma T offers, wanting to get as far from her ex-husband as possible.

We exchange hugs and watch our moms walk away together. I've given up calling them our *non-moms* because, let's face it, these women raised us. They deserve the title more than the ladies who pushed us out of their vaginas.

When Mamma T and Gretchen are gone, the four of us stand there, staring at each other. Logan is right, change is in the air and nothing will be the same when we walk away. Maybe that's why we're still here. Maybe no one is ready to say goodbye yet.

"I hate to do this," Rex says, linking his hand with mine, "but we've got to get you home for a nap if you want to see Bane tonight."

"How's he doing?" Cooper asks.

"They stopped the bleeding." Rex has gone to the hospital every day to check on Bane while I've been held prisoner at my own. Bane's dad, Gerald, beat him until he was unconscious and then left him to die in a puddle of blood. He's got a long recovery ahead, but I have no doubt he'll make it through. "He's a trooper."

"Alright." I walk to Logan first and wrap my arms around his waist, snuggling into his chest. I don't know if it's the painkillers kicking in or some psychological level unlocked in my mind, but I feel nothing. Just the warmth of arms around me. It's nice. Logan rests his chin on my head, both hands pulling me into him. We stay this way a moment before I say, "This isn't goodbye, Logan."

His body rocks as he nods. The movement is uncomfortable for my shoulder but not painful thanks to those magical drugs.

I pull back and look up into his eyes. "You're not leaving for three weeks. I expect everything to be the same and for you to FaceTime me at least once a week after you move into your dorm."

"You got it, Pipes." He takes a step back, making room for Cooper.

I turn to Cooper and hold my arms out. He does this half-laugh-smile thing I haven't seen him do in ages and steps into the embrace. His arms wrap around me, pulling me tight against his body. I bury my nose in his chest, enjoying our hug for the first time in years.

He dips his head, kissing my crown, and I look up at him. Something passes between us, a glimmer of what used to be and could have been. I understand why he was so upset with me dating Rex this year. We could have been great, but the cards didn't fall that way.

Cooper must notice it, too, because his smile falls and he takes a step back. "Just because you're married now doesn't mean you get to be a stranger," he says, sticking his hands in his pockets.

"Ready, babe?" Rex steps forward and holds his hand out for me. I nod and lace my fingers with his.

Cooper and Logan turn, heading to their cars while Rex and I head to ours. Walking into my new life, the reality of the past week hits me in full force. I'm married. I graduated. I was fucking shot!

Rex opens the passenger door for me and waits while I get in. I must have a look on my face because he asks, "Babe? Are you okay?"

I shake my head, and a horde of tears run down my cheeks. I don't know where they've come from, but I can't make them stop. "No, I don't know what happens next. I didn't apply for college because I thought I'd be on the run with Bane. The only job experience I have is working at the Red Onion, and I don't even know if I can work until I finish my physical therapy. The doctor said I need to go three times a week. I can't afford that!"

Rex pulls me close and holds me as I fall apart in his arms. "Piper, you're my wife. I will take care of you, always. As for therapy, Mom is paying for it. You have nothing to worry about."

I wipe my nose with the back of my hand and look up at him. "What about us? You're going to be traveling with your hockey team next year. They're not gonna want your loser wife tagging along."

"First of all, I don't care what anyone else wants. Secondly, you're not a loser." He looks down his nose at me, a worry line between his brows. "Are you regretting getting married?"

"No!" I wiggle out of his arms and look him in the eyes. "I just...I guess it hit me that we never discussed any of this. With everything that has happened, I think I'm a bit of an emotional mess."

"You are." Rex presses his lips against mine for a chaste kiss. "But you're my mess and I wouldn't have you any other way. I love you, Piper. More than you'll ever know."

The End

PAPER HEARTS-BONUS EPILOGUE

A QUICK NOTE

I know an epilogue is only supposed to be a few pages, but as I wrote what happened next, the words kept flowing, and the next thing I knew, I had a six thousand-word chapter. Essh. So, I broke it up into sections, and my little epilogue became a novella.

Enjoy.

Chapter 1

I beat my fists against the plexiglass behind the Falcons bench. Rex spent two years in the minor leagues, paying his dues until an NHL offer came. He had three, none of which were his dream team, the Bruins. We were bummed. He worked extra hard last season, hoping they would notice him, but, in the end, he chose the Falcons because they're based out of Florida, which means I can visit home that much more, which truthfully has only been twice since the season started because I travel with the team.

Mostly because I enjoy watching Rex play.

Partly because I don't trust the hockey hookers not to show up naked in the locker room or stalk Rex back to his hotel. Some of those girls are ruthless, doing anything they can to spend one night with the guys on the team.

Any guy on the team.

I pound my fists again, rage keeping me warm. Tonight's referee is a piece of shit, hitting our team with every penalty possible but only calling half of the other team's infractions.

Number twenty-two on the opposing team pushes his stick behind Rex's skates, causing him to fall backward. It is an illegal move that should have earned twenty-two a penalty for tripping, but the referee is clearly an idiot.

"What the fuck was that, ref?" I shout.

"Miss, I'm going to have to ask you to step back from the glass," a stadium employee says. The kid is young compared to the other workers

—maybe my age, maybe a little older—in a bright yellow shirt with the arena's name on it.

I look at him for half a second before finding Rex on the ice again. He's lined up with number eighty-three, waiting for the puck to drop. When it does, eighty-three raises his stick, both hands on it, and shoves Rex backward. Rex falls, and eighty-three slaps the puck toward his teammate. I wait for the whistle to blow because there is no way the other team won't get flagged for cross-checking, but the referee lets the play continue.

"Come on, ref!" I beat my fists against the plexiglass again, earning a chuckle from Tam, one of our forwards. His shoulder pads lift up and down just as the twenty-something-year-old kid grabs my wrists.

"Okay, ma'am. You're done," the kid in yellow demands, pulling me away from my seats. Yes, I said seats. I have three behind the bench at every game because Rex likes to watch me but also ensure that I have enough space.

The hairs on the back of my neck bristle. Touch is still a trigger, but not nearly as much as it used to be. Rex's unconditional love and my twice-a-week therapy sessions have helped. I was against them at first, but Rex insisted, citing that I needed someone to talk to who could help me process everything that has happened in the past few years. We went through fourteen different therapists until we found one I liked who was willing to work remotely while we traveled.

I yank my wrist down, a defense move Rex made me learn, and walk back to my spot. I get it, the kid is doing his job, but my man will have that kid's job if he touches me again.

The red light flashes above the net, signaling that we scored. Not Rex, he's too far back on the ice, but someone from the team. I didn't get to see who because of that fucking kid. I raise my arms in excitement, giving Rex and the team a thumbs up as they skate toward the bench for a line change, my hands purposefully close but not touching the glass because I don't want to get kicked out of the stadium.

Or cause the kid to lose his job.

But the fucker grabs my wrist again anyway. "I said," he states, "You're done."

"What the hell, dude? I didn't touch the glass."

He's got a tighter hold on me this time, one I can't shake. Needles prick my skin as my throat closes. I remind myself that I'm alright, that this guy has no intention of harming me, but it doesn't stop my heart from beating against my chest with Hulk-like intensity.

"You want to die, motherfucker?" Rex growls from behind me.

The kid freezes. I look over my shoulder and can't help but laugh as a collective gasp sounds on our side of the stadium. Rex has jumped the plexiglass barrier, hanging halfway over it, pointing at the kid with his stick, who instantly lets me go and holds his hands up in surrender.

A camera pans over to us, plastering what's transpiring onto the jumbotron. Rex's heavily padded ass is out on display for everyone to see as the cameraman pans from him to the employee, who has a deer-in-the-headlights look, and me.

I walk back to my seat, watching Coach Tanner grumble, "Oh, fuck," as he points to Rex's bottom half.

It's not until I'm firmly planted, smiling up at my husband, that Rex lets two of his teammates pull him back to the bench. The referee flags Rex with a misconduct penalty and escorts him to the penalty box across the ice. I hold my hands up in the air once he's seated, making a heart with my fingers, and he does the same.

Chapter 2

"I wish you'd watch the game from the damn box," Rex grumbles. He extends his arm, nodding to the bouncer while I duck under the red velvet rope separating the locker rooms from the general public. There's always a group of fans waiting. Most of the time, it's a handful of hockey hookers hoping to get a leg up on the competition—no pun intended—but there are usually a few fans seeking an autograph, too. Rex is a softie for the kids, constantly stopping and signing whatever they have and posing for a picture if they're there.

The box Rex talks about is a private viewing room the team provides the hockey wives. Every game, they have a heated room with a clear view of the ice that I refuse to sit in. For one, most of the wives are a bunch of preppy ex-cheerleader types who glare when I walk into any space they are in.

I've yet to drop what they likely call my "emo phase." Meaning black is still my favorite color and I'd rather wear jeans and one of Rex's t-shirts than heels and a dress. Also, I like being close to the ice. Sure, I freeze my ass off, but it adds to the experience. Can you really say you were at a hockey game if you don't have an overpriced beer, a jumbo soft pretzel, and aren't wearing a winter coat?

"And I wish we didn't have to fly to Vegas tonight," I grumble. "We can't all get what we want."

Rex throws a freshly showered arm over my shoulder. I love the man to death, but he stinks after a game. Like bad stinks. Like rolled around in a dumpster and bathed with a skunk stinks. I'm pretty sure his deodorant freezes off on the ice. Thankfully, I only had to say something once. He laughed it off with a "don't smell my bag then" and has made it a point to shower before coming to get me ever since.

"It's not my fault you promised Mamma T a real wedding."

I roll my eyes and groan. I did. I told Mamma T when I was in the hospital that we would have another ceremony with our friends and family when the time was right. She's hounded me almost every day since graduation, and the timing has never been right, especially with Rex's schedule.

This whole Vegas wedding idea came about as a joke a few weeks ago. I was sitting in a hotel room in Atlanta, waiting for Rex, and called Mamma T to catch up. She filled me in on how she started dating our neighbor, Dr. Winters, and how, now that everyone was out of the house, she was going to start using her first name again—Tessa.

For the record, I will only ever call her Mamma T.

Anyway, she'd brought up the wedding topic again, and I casually joked, "You know, Rex has a game in Vegas in a few weeks. We could just do it there."

I thought Mamma T would protest, like she had done every time I mentioned a courthouse ceremony. To my unpleasant surprise, she squealed in excitement. The rest of the conversation is a blur before Rex walked in. I must have had a look on my face because he rushed to my side asking, "Are you okay? What's wrong?"

I couldn't answer. Hell, I couldn't even swallow the saliva pooling in my mouth. Getting married (again) shouldn't bother me, but here's the thing: Rex and I aren't actually married. That pastor dude from the hospital forgot to submit our certificate to the state.

I found out in July when I went to legally change my name before starting college. That's not the only kicker, because we didn't wait the three days legally required for marriage in Florida, or take a marriage class, the damn thing wouldn't have been valid even if he had submitted it. Talk about a double whammy. Right?

Rex played the whole thing off like it was no big deal. I was upset but also relieved. Don't get me wrong, I don't regret fake-marrying him for one minute, but we were only together for what... maybe three months? We didn't know anything about each other, at least not anything that mattered. Like how Rex throws his clothes on the floor, even if there is a hamper right next to him. Or how he *hates* unpainted toenails. All the little things that make or break a couple.

Let me make one thing clear: I *never* want Rex to leave me. He's my rock—my soul mate—but it would have been nice to discover each other's quirks, and learn how to live with each other, without feeling like I'd trapped him.

Rex chuckles and opens the passenger door for me. "This was your idea. We can still call the whole thing off until you're ready. No one knows we aren't legally married. They'll never suspect a thing."

I shake my head and lean forward, giving Rex a quick— and hope-fully reassuring—kiss. "No. I want to do this. I'm just not looking forward to the flight to Vegas."

REX HOLDS HIS PHONE OVER THE KEYLESS ENTRY AND THE LOCK ON our door clicks open. I told him not to get us a suite but, of course, he didn't listen. He walks in first, holding the door for me and the bellboy who is pushing our luggage cart.

Walking into our hotel room, I put my bag on the monstrous dresser —a twelve-drawer cherrywood dresser that fills the wall separating the kitchenette and bathroom. We have a huge California King and a hideous bright blue couch that matches the pattern on the rug, and cream-colored curtains which are pulled back to give us their million-dollar fountain view.

A view I'm too anxious to enjoy.

I throw myself backward onto the bed while Rex tips the bellboy. I cover my face with my arm and close my eyes. I hate how nervous I am. Everyone already thinks we're married. Tonight shouldn't be a big deal, but I can't make these damn bats stop attacking my insides.

Rex playfully kicks my foot. I peek under my arm. He's smiling down at me, his gorgeous dimples out on display. Sweetness aside, I know I'm a lucky girl because Rex is fucking hot. In high school, he had a nice body —big arms, strong abs, and a butt you could balance a glass on—now, though, he puts his high school self to shame.

When we're not together, all Rex does is work out and practice. He eats, breathes, sleeps, hockey, and it shows in the best of ways. I bite my lip and push up onto my elbows, then wiggle my eyebrows and tilt my head toward the bed.

"Isn't it bad luck to have sex before the wedding?" he asks through a laugh.

"It's bad luck to see the bride."

Rex reaches for my hands and pulls me into a sitting position. "In that case, let's not give ourselves any extra bad ju-ju."

"You suck." I pout. I attempt to lay back on the mattress again with a solid plan to nap until everyone arrives in a few hours, but Rex has other ideas for me. He bends down and effortlessly shifts me onto his shoulder, then smacks my ass.

"You are barbaric!" I giggle.

"Pretty girl. Come play slots with me," he growls in a low caveman-like voice. He ducks under the doorframe so I don't hit my head and marches toward the elevator.

"Rex!" I squeal. "Put me down. I need my phone, my ID, and my wallet."

Rex pushes the elevator button and then sets me on my feet. He settles one hand on my waist and uses his thumb on the other to tilt my head upwards. "You're beautiful when you're grumpy."

The elevator dings, signaling that it's on our floor. Neither of us makes a move. Even after more than two years of being together, I still get lost in his eyes.

Rex dips his head and presses his mouth to mine. I part my lips, my eyes closing, and our tongues dance together. He pulls back, just as I feel the heat pooling at my center and I'm pretty sure I whimper.

"I have everything you need in my pocket," he says, his lips brushing against mine.

Rex stands to full height, wrapping one arm around me, enveloping me in a hug, and then uses his free hand to push the elevator button again.

"CAN WE TALK?"

I twist in my seat, my lips stretching in a wide grin at the sight of Cooper. I stand and throw my arms around his neck. Like I said, touch is still somewhat of an issue, but this hug doesn't bother me because I initiated it. I can bask in the warmth of his arms and breathe in his cologne without worry, which is great because I've missed Cooper.

"Yeah, of course." I grab my card from the slot machine and put it in the card holder on the back of my phone.

Using chips and coins at a casino, like I've seen in the movies, is a thing of the past. This place has digitized the money, which I guess is safer. We load however much we are willing to lose on a plastic debit-type card and it deposits our gains and deducts our losses.

Me: Cooper is here. We're going to the lobby for a bit.

Rex: Okay. Have fun.

Cooper and I sit at a tiny table near the hotel's cafe. From this spot in the room, I can still see Rex at the blackjack table. It's not that I worry he'll get mugged or run away with one of the feather-clad cocktail waitresses, I just like knowing he's nearby.

"What's up, Cooper?"

Cooper exhales a loud breath and then looks me dead in the eye. "I'm joining the military."

The military? Like sent overseas and possibly die, military? I rarely watch the news because it stresses me out—there's too much hate in the world —but if Cooper enlists and gets sent overseas, I already know what I'll do… watch the news obsessively and worry about his safety. "What about your schooling? You can't be a doctor if you die, Cooper."

"They'll pay my tuition for me. I just have to commit a few years to them."

"A few years?" I yell, panic rising to the surface. "Cooper, this is your life we're talking about!"

Cooper folds his arms and leans back in his chair. "It's no big deal, Piper. People enlist all the time."

"Is this because of me?" I know it's selfish to ask, but Cooper hasn't been the same since Rex and I got together. Even before the first wedding, when Rex and I were dating, Cooper began to pull away. Brick by brick, he built a wall between us, but when I got fake-married, he ghosted me. I've seen him once since graduation, and that was last Christmas.

For a day.

Cooper's brows knit together. He turns his head, unable to look me in the eye as he says, "I'd like to say no, but I've never been able to lie to you, Piper."

I reach across the table and extend my hand, palm up. Cooper takes my hand and smiles, but there's no joy behind it. My heart hurts looking at him. I broke this man. Unintentionally, but I broke him nonetheless. "I'm sorry."

"I'm not." Cooper squeezes my palm twice. "You are the happiest I've ever seen you. I'll get there too…one day."

I hope so. Between Cooper pulling away and Logan being a train wreck that you can't help but watch, I worry about my boys.

Cooper lets go of my hand and stands. "Enough about me. This is your day."

"Again," I mumble.

Cooper smiles and it reaches his eyes for the first time in forever. "Again," he mocks. "But we still need to get you a dress." A frown falls across his face, and he mumbles, "Fuck."

"What? What's wrong?"

Cooper looks at me straight-faced and says, "I'm a goddamn maid of honor. Aren't I?"

Usually, I'd be hesitant to leave Rex alone in a casino, surrounded by half-naked women, cheats, and pickpockets, not that I'd be of any use if any of them decided to make a move on him, but those bats start fluttering when we're apart.

I can't help that my thoughts like to dance in the darkness.

I'm not pretty enough for him. He could do better. The wives think I'm a gold digger, everyone else must too. I should have done my hair differently and chosen another outfit. They'd look better together than we do.

It's a never-ending stream when we're out in the world.

Right now, those thoughts are silenced. Rex is not alone. He'll be with the two people I trust most—Jenny and Bane—both of whom arrived minutes apart from each other while Cooper was failing at getting me to leave the hotel.

"There," Cooper mutters, gesturing to our friends. "He'll be fine. Can we go now?"

I chew on my lip and watch Jenny link her arm with Rex's. Her hair is shorter and a more natural shade of blonde than the platinum she rocked the last time I saw her, and her sundress hangs looser around her frame than I expected, but she's still the same beautiful, outgoing woman I remember.

We don't hear from Jenny too much anymore. She's studying pre-law in some community college in New York on a Rex-funded scholarship she has no clue comes from us. It was my idea to help. We have more than enough money to go around and real friends are hard to find.

Jenny may have grown a little distant but that's what happens in life. It's not how many phone calls you get or how many times a year you hang out that makes a friend. It's their loyalty and the ability to pick up as if your time apart never happened that counts.

Bane crosses his tattooed arms and shoots Jenny a dirty look. I sometimes forget that they don't know each other. Jenny throws her head back and laughs, then wraps her arms around Bane's neck. He freezes, silently pleading with Rex to help him. Jenny is a shade of crazy he's not used to, but she's a good kind of crazy.

I exhale a laugh and smile. Cooper clears his throat and those bats start flying again. It's not that I don't want to go dress shopping. I just...

honestly, I don't know why I'm stalling. "Shouldn't we wait for Mamma T? She'll be heartbroken she missed out."

Cooper puts his hand on my lower back and ushers me toward the automatic doors. They slide open with a woosh and my saliva sticks in my throat again.

"She found Logan passed out on the beach about an hour ago." He shakes his head in disappointment. "They are just now flying out. We'll be lucky if they make it in time for the ceremony."

No one pretends to hide how they feel about Logan's drinking problem. After his high school sweetheart left without so much as a goodbye, Logan hit rock bottom—which says something because he was a miserable bastard *before* that mess with her went down. We never understood why he was so withdrawn and moody until Danika left and the trial with Dr. Shaffer started, and then it all made sense.

Mamma T broke down in a fit of tears once everything came out, apologizing profusely. She and Dr. Shaffer had an affair for about a year, pre-divorce from Jeff Harris and during Logan's therapy years. It didn't excuse her behavior. Neither did her justification of why she had turned a blind eye to Logan's suffering all these years. I think that's why she's so ridiculously nice to him now. The guilt of everything she could have stopped eats at her conscience.

"Tell me he was alone?"

Cooper hails a cab and holds the door for me to get in first. "Logan... alone? That's comical."

I shake my head. Logan's inability to keep his dick in his pants in public places is what got him kicked out of college last semester. Apparently, the dean was less than thrilled to hear his precious daughter was passed out naked on the fifty-yard line.

I drop my head back against the seat. Logan was a royal dick to Danika—said high school sweetheart—and he deserved what she did to him, but he either needs to move on or fight for her. This I-don't-care-I'm-going-to-drink-my- problems-away mentality is either going to kill him or land him in jail. "Maybe this is a sign Rex and I shouldn't get married again."

"You're the bravest person I know, Piper. Why are you so scared to do this? You've already done it once."

Because I'm worried that Rex will wake up one day and realize he's a million

times better than me and deserves more than what I have to offer. "What if Rex
randomly decides that I'm not what he wants anymore? I'm nothing like
the other hockey wives, Coop."

"We're here," our driver says over his shoulder.

Cooper holds up one finger to the man, signaling we need a minute.
The dude grunts but turns back to look at the road. It's not like he can
kick us out of the car... not if he wants to be paid.

Cooper takes my hand and looks me dead in the eyes. "That man
loves you more than he loves hockey. I wholeheartedly believe you have
nothing to worry about, but if he does want out one day or he does
something to make you want to leave, I will be there in an instant to kick
his ass six ways from Sunday."

I nod, wiping away a stray tear before it drips down my cheek. I have
a feeling I'm going to do a lot of crying today. I'm jet lagged, and my
emotions are everywhere, and I think my hormones are still off from last
month's miscarriage. I wasn't far into the pregnancy, only eight weeks,
and we weren't trying. It just happened. When I had finally come to
terms and started getting excited about everything, it was gone.

"You're not supposed to cry on your wedding day," Cooper sighs,
pulling me in for a hug. The embrace isn't exactly enjoyable. A balloon
still inflates in my chest from his touch, but it's not unenjoyable either.
He pulls back, probably sensing that I'm struggling, and says, "Come on,
let's go get you a dress. We have four hours until your wedding and, if I
remember correctly, someone said they wanted to see Britney Spears'
show."

Chapter 5

"Stop." I wave my hand by my ear, shooing Mamma T off. She's fretted over my hair for the past thirty minutes, curling, pinning, and spraying. Between her on my hair and Jenny fussing over my makeup, I can't take any more. I'm already sitting on pins and needles, and I swear if I hear the woosh of the hair spray bottle one more time, I'll cancel the whole ceremony. "Enough."

"I'm sorry," Mamma T huffs. She runs her hands down her thighs, smoothing the wrinkles from the skirt of her dress. "I know you've never legally been mine, Piper, but how often does your baby girl get married?"

"Twice, apparently," Jenny giggles as she runs her thumb along the underside of my bottom lip, removing any extra gloss that may have strayed. "Perfect."

She smiles, leans over the vanity counter, and begins working on her own makeup. I know Jenny isn't being mean, it's just her personality to be crass. It's part of the reason I didn't like her at first. Well, that and the fact that she reminded me of the girls in high school who made my life a living hell. I will say, college has drastically toned down her personality.

The venue coordinator peeks her head into the room and makes eye contact with me through the mirror. "Five minutes." She looks at Jenny and Mamma T. "Ladies, take your seats."

As the door closes, Mamma T pulls me in for a hug. "I can't believe *this* is what you're choosing to get married in." She lets out a breathy laugh and then steps back and gives me a once-over.

"I think the pantsuit is hot," Jenny adds. She hip bumps Mamma T out of the way, then looks over her shoulder. "Mamma T, can you give us a minute alone?"

"Of course. See you girls out there."

When the door closes, Jenny sets her hands on my shoulders and exhales a heavy breath. "Before you say anything, I know the last wedding was a fluke, and I get why you guys kept that a secret."

"We—"

Jenny holds up one finger, signaling me to be quiet. I oblige because, honestly, my life is none of her business. I shouldn't have to make excuses.

"But I need to know before I walk out that door." Jenny hitches her thumb behind her. "Are you gonna run?"

I rear back, eyes wide with surprise. "What?"

Jenny crosses her arms and stands up taller. "Are. You. Going. To. Run?"

"Why would you even ask that?"

"Well, for starters, you chose a white, pin-stripe pantsuit instead of a dress for your real wedding," Jenny guffaws. "It's cute, but not at all what any bride who has had *two years* to plan would do."

I look down at my strapless, white pantsuit. It's flowy and comfy and works perfectly with my baby blue Converse. Cooper is the one who found it after an hour of searching for dresses with no avail. I tried it on, convinced he was crazy for suggesting it in the first place. As soon as I looked in the mirror, I knew this was the one.

Jenny purses her lips together and shakes her head. "Rex doesn't think you'll go through with it."

The bats in my stomach stop swarming and fall to my feet, crushing the butterflies. "He doesn't?"

Jenny pushes me backward until my legs hit a chair, and then I sit. The room spins and all of a sudden I'm hot. Jenny hands me a bottle of water. "No. Why would he? You've come up with every excuse not to marry him and, apparently, you have been a wreck ever since agreeing to today. Which is why I'm not walking out that door until I know your plan."

The venue coordinator opens the door again. "It's time." She pauses, looks from Jenny to me, and then sighs. "Cold feet?"

I shake my head and set the water bottle on the floor. "No, let's do this."

I adjust Logan's tie and smooth the wrinkles on the long sleeves of his shirt. He looks rough, like he hasn't slept in a week and drank his breakfast.

"Why am I walking you down the aisle and not Cooper?" He hands me the bouquet of white long-stem roses the venue provided.

"I already have a bunch of memories with Cooper about today. I want a special one with you, too." And I want to make sure Logan sits down in one of the seats and doesn't disappear around the corner to the nearest bar. Although, by the intense spearmint smell lingering on his breath, I'd say he's already had a drink, or two, since landing thirty minutes ago.

Logan smiles, but it doesn't reach his eyes. He holds his elbow for me to link my arm through and says, "I guess we should get this over with. Huh?"

"I couldn't have said it better myself."

The double doors to the chapel open and Elvis Presley's *Can't Help Falling In Love* sings through the room's surround sound. The chapel we chose is tiny, with four pews on each side of the room, comfortably seating sixteen. Our crowd doesn't even come close to filling the space, but everyone that matters is here—Mamma T, Cooper, Logan, Bane, Gretchen, Jenny, and, surprisingly, Rex's mom.

Rex stands at the front of the room in a full suit, hands linked together and the butterflies inside me win the war against the bats when he smiles. Heat rushes to my cheeks and I can't help but grin in return.

This moment is surreal. A living deja vu. When I walked down the hospital's aisle, I wasn't nervous. I was excited, not thinking about anything beyond that moment, but today my thoughts are on the future. On everything Rex and I have become and what we could be.

Rex and I may only be twenty, but I can't imagine spending my life with anyone but him. I never should have waited so long to tie the knot again. I was being foolish and selfish. Had I known I was causing Rex distress, I would have done this ages ago.

When Logan and I reach the end of the aisle I turn, throwing my arms over his shoulders, and whisper, "Thank you."

Logan nods and kisses my cheek. I know this is hard for him, but I'm grateful he's here. I turn toward Rex, whose gaze has probably never left me, and whisper, "Hey."

"Hey," Rex whispers back.

Our Elvis impersonator is still singing and dancing in front of the Venue's coordinator—who is recording the ceremony. I bite back a chuckle at his hip-shake, resting my cheek on Rex's arm.

Rex thought getting married in an Elvis wedding chapel was ridiculous. I fought for it, insisting there is no better way to get married in Vegas. Standing here, watching this fifty-something-year-old man in a wig, aviator glasses, and exposed V-neck glitter one-piece suit, I realize Rex was right. This man *is* rediculous, but I love it. Finally, the song ends and Elvis takes his place at the front of the room.

"Ladies and gentlemen, welcome to the best wedding chapel in Las Vegas," Elvis says. "We are here to celebrate Rex Montgomery and Piper Lovelace today. These high school sweethearts have decided to take the next step in their relationship and engage in holy matrimony."

Elvis swings his hips from side to side the way the real Elvis used to do. Logan chuckles behind us and I'm pretty sure I hear Mamma T slap his chest.

Elvis pays no mind to our audience and continues, "Marriage is a promise to treat each other with respect, to always be there, but marriage isn't just an agreement to be with each other. It's also a commitment between a husband and a wife to always listen and share. It's a commitment to be your partner's best friend for the rest of their life. But above all, most importantly, to be Elvis' best friend."

Elvis pauses, grinning as the room fills with laughter. "Rex, turn to face Piper, and say, 'I take you to be my wife and my lover for the rest of my life.'"

Everyone laughs again, but Rex and I turn to each other. He pulls me against him, wrapping his arm around my waist, and looks down at me. "I take you, Piper, to be my wife and my lover for the rest of my life."

"Hubba, hubba," Elvis purrs. "Piper, say, 'I take you, Rex, to be my husband and lover for the rest of my life.'"

I drop my bouquet by our feet and lace my fingers around the back of Rex's neck. His other arm wraps around my waist, pulling me even closer. I look up into his big blue eyes, twinkling and full of love. "I take you, Rex, to be my husband and lover for the rest of my life."

"Now, these vows..." Elvis pauses.

Rex and I don't wait to hear what he says next. We've heard the spiel before. For richer or poorer. In sickness and in health. We've already agreed to these things once. I press my mouth against Rex's, parting my lips so his tongue can find mine. I allow myself to fall into the kiss, getting swept away and forgetting where we are and the audience around us. Rex's lips will do that. They're a vortex, sucking away everything that doesn't matter and making it disappear.

"Well, alright then," Elvis says with a chuckle. "I guess I don't have to tell these two lovebirds not to leave each other at the Heartbreak Hotel."

I pull back with a laugh and rest my cheek on Rex's shoulder.

"I now pronounce you two husband and wife!" Elvis picks up his guitar and strums a few chords erratically. He then transitions into a slow progression and sings *Love Me Tender.* Elvis strolls down the aisle while I pick up my bouquet and hold it in the air as our family claps. Rex presses a quick kiss to my lips again before we follow Elvis out into the lobby.

The first person who greets us after the ceremony is Rex's mom. I've never met the woman and honestly didn't expect her to say yes when we texted her the invitation last week, but here she is. Sandy Montgomery, or should I say Sandy Simmons? The tabloids went crazy last month when Rex's parents announced the news of their split.

Rex and I figured it was coming. Honestly, we thought the divorce would come sooner.

"Piper," Sandy says, pulling me into a hug. "It's so nice to finally meet you."

Needles dance under my skin. I knew people would be touching me today, and as much as I've mentally prepared, I'm not ready. I squeeze her tightly for half of a second, then pull back. "It's so nice to meet you, too, Mrs. Montgomery."

"Call me Sandy." She turns, holding her arms out again. "Rexy!"

Rex stiffens under her touch but forces a smile. "Hi, Mom."

Sandy pulls back and swipes her knuckle under each eye. "Look at me. I'm a blubbering mess." She exhales a breathy laugh, then backs away. "I won't keep you. I just wanted to say thank you for inviting me and pass along my congratulations."

"You should come to tomorrow night's game," I say before she walks away.

Rex shoots me a pointed look, but I ignore him. He may not like his mother, but I want to know the woman who made him. I say made and not raised because Gretchen raised Rex, and we make it a point to visit her every couple of months. Rex's birth mom, Sandy, is a mystery to me.

"I would love that." Sandy pats Rex's arm and then heads toward the venue coordinator's room, probably to look at the photos the coordinator snapped.

After a bunch of hugs and words of congratulations, Rex pays the venue, and we collect a SIM card with all of our pictures and the video. Outside, everyone is snapping pictures in front of the chapel's sign. Logan even looks like he's having fun, laughing lightheartedly.

"Well, Mrs. Montgomery." Rex throws his arm over my shoulder and we walk together to our family. "What do you want to do next?"

"Let's find some strippers!" Logan shouts. Mamma T, apparently not finding his comment funny, backhands him across the chest.

"I'm starving," Jenny adds. "Dinner and a show?"

"And then the casino. I'm gonna *Rain Man* this bitch," Cooper says, pushing invisible cards, or maybe money, out of his palm and into the air.

I shake my head. Only Cooper would try to count cards. He saw that movie once and now thinks he can do it. I would personally like to head back to our room and get to the baby-making—or at least practice—but we have all the time in the world for sex. Rex and I only have one night with our family, and I'm not going to waste it. Tonight, we'll spend money like it's nobody's business, drink with Logan's fake ID, and party. Everything else can wait.

The End.

LOOKING FOR SOMETHING
ELSE TO READ?

Sign up for my newsletter to access an exclusive, subscriber-only section of my website. There are freebies, bonus chapters, and more!

JOIN MY NEWSLETTER

FOR WEEKLY UPDATES ON ALL THINGS BOOKS AND
BAILEY PLUS RECEIVE AN EXCLUSIVE SHOP DISCOUNT

And turn the page to learn about some other great books Bailey has to offer.

BOOK 2 IN THE BROKEN LOVE SERIES

She's beautiful. Fierce. Nothing at all like the girl I used to know, which is absolutely terrifying because Danika Winters is the only person outside of that room who knows the truth. She could ruin me, and I'm not talking about my reputation. I couldn't give two shits about what the kids at St. A's think. I'm talking major, life-altering, jail time ruined. I'll do whatever it takes to keep her quiet. Even if it means destroying the only person I've ever cared about.

Asher Anderson is a dick.

We aren't friends, so when he seeks me out in the cafeteria on the worst day of my life, I'm suspicious. When he tells Liam Heiter that we're dating, which couldn't be farther from the truth, I want to kill him...Until I see Liam's reaction.

Liam—my best friend, the guy who crushed every hope of us *officially* being together—is jealous. He has never looked at me this way and I love it.

So, I play along. Maybe watching me with someone else will make Liam suffer like I have the past four years. And maybe, just maybe, he'll come to his senses and realize we belong together. It's not like I actually *like* Asher. At best, I tolerate him. What's the worst that can happen?

Small town, Opposites attract, Cowboy, New girl in town, Unexpected parenthood (+denial)

Josh

I met the girl of my dreams in a church parking lot while my best friend was having sex in my truck. Her name was Layla and she was trying her hardest to ignore me and them from two parking spaces over. I swear, I've never seen someone so beautiful in my life. I've also never struggled to get the girl but, for some reason, my foot and my mouth became friends that night in the worst of ways.

Cheesy pickup line, that failed? Check.
Inability to form coherent sentences? Check.
Ego crushing letdown? Yup. That happened, too.

I can't put my finger on it, but there's something about Layla that sucks me in. I need to get to know her. Spend time with her. Make her mine. Who knows, maybe she will be the one to finally settle me down. That is, if I can convince her to give me the time of day.

Layla

Everything about Joshua Thomas screams, run away. His sharp jaw.

Those vibrant eyes. Lush lips that have probably tasted every girl in this tiny town. I know better than to give him a chance, but knowing what I should do and listening are two different things. He makes my heart flutter in ways I thought only possible in Hallmark movies. He makes my legs shake from one look. I resisted him once. I don't know if I can do it again.

Second chance, The dare/bet, Insta chemistry, Learning to love, Shared Pasts

I've sworn off men forever! Okay, not forever, but for a few months. After my last hook-up, my vag needs a reset because the last man to touch me broke it in the worst of ways. Not a problem until my new dance partner comes into the picture. He's turning into my forbidden fruit, tempting me in ways I didn't know possible.

I have three months of celibacy ahead of me and eight weeks to whip my new dance partner into shape.

Someone save me.

Fake dating, Second chance, Friends to lovers, Everybody can see it, Short and Spicy novella

A wedding. A lie. And regret.

I'm in over my head with not one but two ex-boyfriends at the same wedding. Both of which I haven't seen in over a year. When the one who ripped my heart into pieces backs me into a corner, I grab the other and kiss him.

Yup. This is how I ended up fake dating Noah Ruckers, and let me tell you, it's an emotional roller coaster. I thought I'd put my feelings for him behind me. We spent years as friends after our break up, nothing more. But no matter how hard I try I can't forget what his lips feel like. Or the way his arms wrap around me.

In two days, I'm walking away. There is no future for us. But that doesn't mean I can't pretend.

How About a Fantasy Adventure?

A witch in a world where magic is illegal, A revenge mission, A rescue mission, Death. People die. Sorry, not sorry, 2 love interests (not a RH and not a triangle), A touch of enemies to lovers. He falls first she falls harder

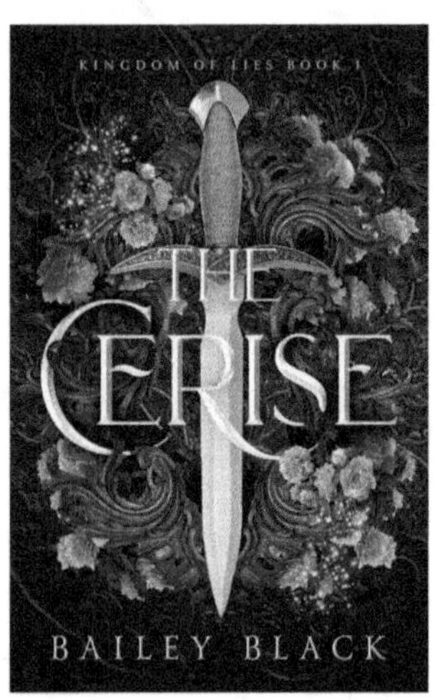

I had a plan. Find the soldier who killed my family and make him pay. It should have been an easy feat. I'd done it over a dozen times, taking out each member of that regiment one by one, but the mission went sideways. It all started with the man in the woods. The one my webs of magic couldn't sense even when he stood before me. Then my partner made a mistake, and now he's lying in one of the Crown's dungeons, fighting for his life. I couldn't leave him to die, but I couldn't just walk into the castle either.

Or maybe I could.

With the help of some unexpected allies, I entered the Culling—a one-in-a-lifetime chance to become queen. I have no interest in winning the prince's heart, or the crown. My only goal is to get into the castle, find my friend, and get out before someone realizes I'm a Cerise.

But when the welcome ball turns from a grand event into a nightmarish dance of death, all eyes are on me. As if that's not bad enough, the soldier, the one who took my family, he's here.

If you loved "The Selection" by Kiera Cass and "From Blood and Ash" by
Jennifer L. Armentrout, get ready to fall in love with this enchanting
fantasy romance!

Or you can dive into the completed Neverland Novels. Characters have been aged up for this darker, grittier version. If you like your fairytale retellings with hot, ruthless, morally gray love interests, you'll enjoy this series. The Lost Darling is the first book in the main storyline. Please read this series in order.

Twisted Fairy Tale, Peter Pan Retelling, Multiple Love Interests, Morally Gray Males, She's Mine, Scorching hot lost boys, Spice, and more!

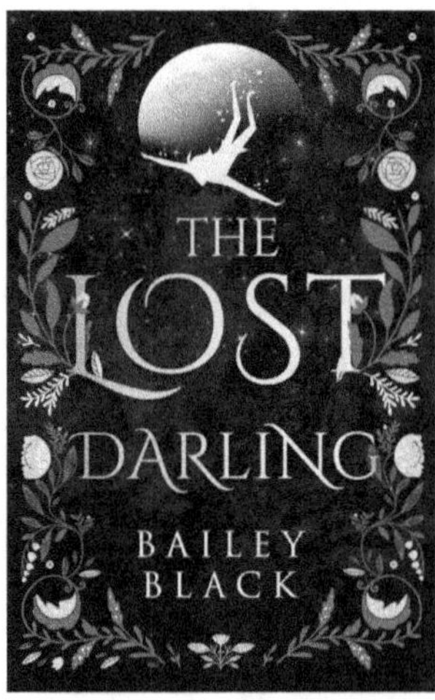

Second star to the left and continue until morning.

I got that line tattooed on my wrist the day I turned twenty-one. So much symbolism in such a simple sentence. At the time, it was a nod to the future and the infinite possibilities to come, while reminding me to remember the past and to look for magic in the world.

Growing up, nothing was ever what it seemed. The shift of leaves on a tree was a faery skipping by. Shooting stars were a chance to make wishes. Shadows were souls stuck between this world and the next, mirroring a life they once had.

My imagination was limitless, the world a wonderful adventure waiting to unfold.

It's easy to lose that sense of wonder with the weight of life on your shoulders and I wanted a reminder to get me through the hard days.

Most importantly, it was an ode to the boy who earned the title of my first crush, even if he was animated. Peter Pan wasn't a *save the damsel* kind of prince. He was daring, and selfless, and took care of the ones he loved. He was a friend to all but never afraid to fight the Pirates when their moral compass broke. Wendy was an idiot for leaving him. She rushed home to a heartless world full of men willing to lie through their teeth to get down her pants.

But that's the beauty of a book, the characters are perfectly flawed. Damaged just enough that we still love them. Whereas reality is nothing but empty promises and baggage the size of mountains.

The day I got my tattoo, I would have given anything to be whisked away into a fairytale. My world was crumbling, and all I wanted was to go back to when life was simpler. I didn't realize I had sealed my fate in ink.

Branded myself as one of the Lost.

Neverland was everything the stories made it out to be. Beautiful. Full of magic. Filled with handsome men and debonair pirates. But the author of my favorite tale left out one crucial detail.

In order to get there, you have to die.

First and foremost, I want to thank Jessica Richards, for telling me to keep going on this book. I wanted to give up so many times because Piper was a complicated character for me to write. I put so much of myself into this character; at times, it was like looking in a mirror. I should add that I did not go through the same struggles as Piper. The events of this story are fictional, as are the characters. But as an author, I see bits of all my friends in everyone.

My editor, Shantel Eddy at Poisonous Promotions, you rock.

A huge thank you to my Mom for reading everything I write, even if it makes me cringe when she gets to the dirty bits.

Shout out to Maryanne at Goddess Fish Promotions, who not only edited this book but also arranged a kick-ass blog tour. Which leads me to...

The fantastic bloggers and bookstagrammers who bring my stories to the world. I cannot begin to express how grateful I am to you.

To my kick-ass PA, Becky... you make it possible for me to focus on writing. Without you, I'd be a squirrel with half-thoughts, open give-aways, and a dead Facebook group.

To everyone, I'm sure to have forgotten because I'm Dory's second cousin twice removed, and I feel like I'd forget my head if it weren't attached.

Finally, I'd like to thank my readers. Whenever you open one of my books, you make my dream come true.

Thank you.
Xoxo
Bailey B.

ABOUT THE AUTHOR

I've always wanted to be a writer. I remember my first time really trying to write. It was after I saw Practical Magic and I knew there was more to those characters. Being the creative ten-year-old I was, I managed to write a solid two paragraphs on my mother's dinosaur of a laptop. Fast forward fifteen years, when I was a new stay-at-home mom with no time for friends, let alone a life. I rediscovered my love for reading, which turned into a love of writing. There were A LOT of bad stories in the beginning (those aren't published) but I eventually honed my craft and grew brave enough to publish them in the world.

I'm not a full-time author as of yet. I'm still a mom and a wife and somehow balancing a job along with all the responsibilities tied to adulthood. My writing hours are slim, but man when I dive into a world it's hard to get me out of it.

So far, I've been lucky enough to have readers just as enamored with my characters as I am. It still humbles me that there are readers and bloggers out there willing to take a chance on my stories. So while this is a little bit about me, it's also about you because without your support I wouldn't have a career.

Thank you, from the bottom of my heart, for always believing on me.

@baileysbookbesties

@baileysbookbesties

@baileysbookbesties